OPERATION
SERPENT

DAVID E BRODHAGEN

 FriesenPress

One Printers Way
Altona, MB R0G 0B0
Canada

www.friesenpress.com

ISBN
978-1-03-914082-0 (Hardcover)
978-1-03-914081-3 (Paperback)
978-1-03-914083-7 (eBook)

1. FICTION, THRILLERS, TERRORISM

Distributed to the trade by The Ingram Book Company

CAST OF CHARACTERS

Canadians

C.S.I.S Canada
>Robert Rolfen -- Senior Director

Canadian Military
>Spencer Cook –Soldier, team leader
>Wil Wright- Childhood Friend and soldier
>Richie Miller- Childhood Friend and soldier (Spotter)
>Michael Parker- Childhood Friend and soldier
>Andrew James- Childhood Friend and soldier
>David Dunsmoore- Childhood Friend and soldier
>Robert Jones- Childhood Friend and soldier (Sniper)
>Sally Cowalski- Medic

Canadian civilians
>Mrs. Mary Cook -- Mother of Spencer Cook
>Mr. William Spencer Cook- Father of Spencer Cook

Muslims
>Mohammad Hassan- Terrorist.
>Abid Hassan- Terrorist
>Desmond Atutu (informant)
>Saabira Hassan- Wife of Mohammad Hassan

Irish agent
>Jimmy O'Brien- Irish Agent
>Ralph - Irish Chemist

PART ONE

To Judy

David B

BASIC TRAINING

What the heck was that? Booms echoed down the valley, thundering southward until they could no longer be heard. I had just finished re-reading the Canadian Armed Forces recruitment flyer when our family vehicle crested the long rolling hill. The road slowly disappeared behind a large wooden sign, "CFB Meaford—4th Division, Canadian Training Centre." To the right of the roadway, two large flags flipped about in the gusting wind. On top, the bright red and white Canadian flag stood proud above the base flag. Blue choppy waves of Nottawasaga Bay could be seen bouncing about on the windswept lake, disappearing as they neared the distant horizon.

"That, young man, is the Eleventh Field Regiment from Guelph finishing their artillery weekend training." Uncle Bob recognized that sound all too well, for he, too, had served.

Although I could not see the action, I envisioned the scene. Closing my eyes, I could hear the blast from the exploding shell—smoke and flames spewing from the long muzzle as the shell flew toward the target, huge clouds of debris exploding up into the air, then the rumble. The pungent smell of gunpowder drifted through our open windows as the truck crested the hill toward the distant sounds.

Registration today would be the start of my basic training. It was a day I had been looking forward to—yet fearing. I stared blindly out the window recalling my childhood and the countless times my father had left on assignments to unknown places. I always missed him—the lonely time apart and the thing I hated most: the not knowing. Painful memories, of each time I watched him drive away, never sure of how, when, or if my father would return. Each evening, pictures of dead and wounded soldiers flashed across the news, constant reminders of what could be. Would I, myself, be able to walk home, or would I be one of the unfortunate souls unable to walk, or, worse yet, be carried home in a casket?

I knew all too well the torments of being a soldier's child. My dad had been a strong, powerful man, always pushing us boys to be our best in everything. His voice echoed in my head with his favourite saying. *"You do not have to be perfect, Son, you only have to give a perfect effort, to push yourself and always do your best."*

My mind drifted back to that devastating day when I saw my father roll through the doors at the arrival gate, sitting helplessly in that God-awful wheelchair. Old enough to understand what had happened, but not why—I knew I could not just sit by and watch. My Christian upbringing had taught me to forgive and forget. This I could not do.

Normally, I would have to take my officer basic training at Saint-Jean, Quebec, but since I still had one last semester to complete at the University of Waterloo, I was permitted to start my training at Meaford.

Hours of dwelling on my own misery had only increased my anger and my desire to get started, In my youth, hatred was a feeling that I had seldom experienced, but now it seemed to pop up daily. Every experience somehow frustrated me. Wrapped up in my circular thinking only made things worse, always bringing me back to that same awful point. My decision had been made. I would join the Armed Forces. Soon I would show them.

Two seven-week sessions would be all I needed to complete the training. Then I could go somewhere, anywhere I could be effective. Eager to get into the action I decided to take both sessions, all fourteen weeks, back-to-back—easy enough. I would not see my family for weeks. Living in a university dorm for the last three years could not be vastly different from life in a military barracks. Or so I thought.

I leafed through the literature, pages describing how the training would prepare me as an officer. How I would lead teams of men, first in simple operations at the garrison, then in more serious field manoeuvres. Leadership roles in scouting and student council had led the way for what I assumed was to be my pre-ordained destiny.

Like a sponge, I soaked it up. Again, the aroma of gunpowder drifted through my open window, intensifying the excitement. Today I would embark on my newest adventure; more determined than I had ever been.

Flashbacks of my youth—my very first day at summer camp, the countless days at our cottage. Today, the new sights and sounds filled my consciousness.

As our Ram 1500 pulled up to the entry gate, a uniformed soldier stepped out. Rain dripped down the brow of his hat as he uttered, "How can I help you?"

From top to bottom, the rain-drenched soldier exuded order and discipline, right down to the shine on his boots.

My uncle smiled as he replied. "Spencer is here for the basic training registration." Uncle Bob gleamed from ear to ear as he spoke those words; obviously proud.

My mom's family was big on tradition. Like a father, Uncle Bob always managed to be present for family events, always filling in for Dad when needed. For a moment, I wished dad could be here.

Small droplets of rain dripped off the clipboard as the officer extended his arm through the half-open window. "Please sign the log and jot down your licence plate number. Sir, normally the ceremony would be held on the parade field, but, since it is raining, it will be in the auditorium. The auditorium is just over the hill on your left."

His deep raspy voice seemed stern and hollow, as if coming from his toes.

A solitary security camera blinked red as their vehicle inspection continued. Sheepishly, I retorted, "Smile everyone. We're on *Candid Camera.*"

As the traffic arm began to lift, the officer gestured. "You may proceed ahead to the auditorium."

The indoor location had to be for the benefit of the families; I had listened to countless army stories and knew that even if it was raining, the enlistees would assemble and practise outdoors.

Momentary doubts crept in as the truck crested the hill. *I can do this. I will do this.* I squeezed my hands together, reaffirming my commitment. *I'm twenty-three, an engineer, and I am ready.* I waited anxiously for the others to arrive. All my best friends were to meet me here today. Seven individuals, no, the Seven Musketeers. Friends with whom I had spent most of my youth—countless days and weekends afield.

Years of Scouts, then Rovers, had taught us to think as one—to understand the bush. Each capable of surviving in the wild. What Scouts and Rovers did not teach us, survival trips into the wilderness did. I recalled the numerous weekend trips to the remote north of Ontario. Making fire without matches, collecting edible plants, and constructing temporary shelter. Oh, how I missed that time in my life.

Robert Jones and Wil Wright would plan the meals, while Michael Parker would be responsible for securing the food. Richie Miller had the onerous task of plotting the route. Andrew James and David Dunsmoore enjoyed making the lists and organizing the equipment. We all loved the wilderness and had become a very proficient group.

The auditorium seemed small; not at all what I had envisioned. I turned back toward the entrance and smiled, recognizing familiar voices. The remainder of our group had just entered the building, and rather loudly advanced into the corridor.

At the opposite end of the hallway, adjacent to the second set of large double doors sat a solitary, rather sober-looking soldier. The jovial mood disappeared as each noticed the stern look directed our way. Centred on a small, nearly barren table lay a clipboard and solitary black pen.

"Recruits, please sign in and take an information package. You are to fill in all the requested information.

"The completed package is to be left in the wire basket outside your dorm room by twenty-one-hundred hours today.

"Please take a seat on the bleachers. The welcoming ceremony will start shortly."

"At the end of the ceremony your name will be called, you will stand and identify yourself.

The odour of fresh paint saturated the air as we plopped ourselves down onto the squeaky bleachers. Evidence was everywhere; the auditorium had just recently been constructed. The people in uniform all saluted, holding their salute for the commanding officer as he entered the room; he approached the microphone.

A hush came over the room as we all rose for the national anthem.

Scanning the bleachers, he called out, "*Vigilamus pro te*. We stand on guard for thee." He shouted, "You will learn this phrase."

His voice echoed across the floor, demanding yet inspiring as he welcomed the recruits with words of appreciation and encouragement. Flickers of light bounced off his service ribbons, proudly displayed on his chest. I could see he had served his country, no doubt experienced what he was about to preach.

Did this man know my dad? Had he served with him? One day I would have to ask him. With anticipation, I listened to him describe the weeks to come. The rigour and enthusiasm with which he described the details showed his love for the military and the position he held. He talked of pride and love for his country. Eloquently, he described the various aspects of the upcoming weeks.

"You will march until you are ready to drop, you will be tested to your limits both physically in the field, and academically in the classroom.

"To become good soldiers, and officers, you will need to know and understand your own and your men's limitations.

"From here on, you will need to have total trust in your brother soldiers, and they in you. When the fighting starts, you will need each other. Each other will be all you will have."

Stepping back from the microphone and without instruction, a marching drill team entered the auditorium to perform a weapons exercise. I watched in awe as they marched and flipped their rifles in unison. I knew I would soon be able to do that and confidently smiled as they marched past the bleachers and stepped off the drill floor.

"Recruits stay seated, your families are asked to leave and encouraged to look around the base until you are released.

As if timed perfectly, the sky cleared, allowing the families to exit.

Bright blue skies peeked through as the menacing grey clouds blew eastward across the bay, leaving only intermittent sprinkles of rain. With the parents gone I looked shyly around the room, assessing the others. I could not help myself; I too tried to determine who had the potential to be my friend. Someone with whom I could entrust my life. I would have plenty of time over the first seven weeks to resolve that question.

The recruits spent the next hour receiving the balance of their orientation then dismissed to explore the base, to learn the lay of the land, and ultimately to say goodbye to their families. Bubbling with enthusiasm, I approached my mother's side, eager to start our tour. Off to the east, the new three-storey red-brick barracks stood in contrast to older, cottage-sized wood structures on the opposite side of the parade field. The faded grey structures had clearly been there for a lot of years. In many ways they reminded me of my public-school days.

The rectory and the first aid building were first on the tour. Off to the northwest, I could see the sewage treatment plant. As a cool wind drifted in from the north, I became aware of the plant well before I saw it. Beyond the source of foul odours stretched numerous target and practice ranges. The vehicles were still noisily moving about the range: stopping, turning, firing, then moving on.

Families could be heard laughing and discussing the activities. In a slightly louder than normal voice, we all attempted to compete with the rumble of vehicles and the continuous popping of rifle fire. I watched intently as two soldiers ran crouched across the open field, one with a machine gun: the other a box of ammo. Dropping face-first onto the muddy ground the belt of shells slid easily into the weapon. *Pop, pop* rang out and then, nothing—the gun had seized. Anxiously, they extracted the belt of shells and reinserted it. Closing the breech, they started the routine again. But again, the gun seized.

"I hope I don't get that gun. Hey Mom, this reminds me of a video game, looks like fun!"

She frowned, not seeing the humour.

"Those vehicles sure do make a lot of noise. Kind of hard to sneak up on the enemy with them."

My enthusiasm grew with each new sound. I could hardly wait to get started. Everywhere soldiers marched with arms swinging, breast-pocket high. We were all advised that the enlisted personnel must be dressed in camouflage fatigues, and march whenever moving about the base.

I hustled our family about, allowing only a few minutes to observe each building. I wanted to see the whole array of displays and demonstrations. As we approached the rifle range, a burst of machine-gun fire startled me.

Without even thinking, "I had better get used to that sound!" flew from my lips as I gave a nod and a grin in Mom's direction.

Raised in a strict religious family, I was pleased to find the chapel and know that I had a place to pray and receive spiritual guidance. In the largest room I noticed two life-size coyote taxidermy mounts. The animals were standing on all four legs and howling toward the sky. When approached by the pastor, I just had to ask. "Why are you displaying this type of art in a military facility?"

"Well, son, that particular animal was chosen as our emblem for two reasons. Like soldiers, these animals hunt not only in packs, but they also hunt alone."

I then remembered the camp flag flying high above the guard station, and also above the administration building. It was a solid white flag portraying a graphic representation of a howling coyote. Now it made sense.

The water-soaked pathways marked with small wooden signs guided us through the maze of buildings, eventually leading us back to the main parking lot. A glance at my watch indicated 3:00 p.m. We were nearing that time when I would have to say goodbye. With hastened footsteps, we retraced our route past the parade field, then down the damp puddle-ridden roadway, back to Uncle Bob's waiting vehicle.

In bold letters the schedule of events indicated sixteen-hundred hours (4:00 p.m.), we would be shown our dorm room and then introduced to our roommates.

Slowly, we walked the final few steps to the parking lot, and teary-eyed Mom wrapped her arms tightly around me. I remembered all the scraped knees, the big hugs, and then her typical, I love you.

"You take care of yourself. I want you back in one piece. Your father and I are very proud of you."

"Oh, how I wish Dad could have been here," escaped my now quivering lips.

Holding on tight for what seemed an eternity, I briefly had second thoughts. I contemplated leaving, then uttered to myself, "*Suck it up, Spencer.*" Briefly, I recalled Dad's parting words each time he would leave. "You're a man now; nobody here wants to see you cry."

With a prolonged wave, I watched the truck inch down the road and out of sight. They were gone. I had felt this kind of loneliness before. It too would pass.

Immediately after the families departed, the recruits were ushered to the base barber. I frowned as I watched my long blonde curls drop to the floor. Those same blonde curls that had charmed the girls in school lay scattered about me on the floor. My first buzz cut—not what I would have ordered, but I knew it would be the norm from this day forward.

AT THE BARRACKS

Back at the barracks, Sergeant Black introduced himself. "In case you are not aware, I am a lifer—I eat, sleep, and bleed military."

"As of tonight, you are to leave your civvies behind. Stow them in your lockers."

We listened intently as the sergeant proceeded to outline what would be our daily routine for the days and weeks that followed. Loud, deep, raspy words echoed around the room as he described our future with detail.

"I will be your company commander for the next seven weeks. I eat, sleep, and bleed green. If you do not like me, I really don't give a rat's ass. I will not pick up after you, I will not coddle you, and I sure as hell will not be your mommy.

"Your uniform will be pressed and folded. Your black Cadillacs, spit-shined until you can see your ugly faces in them.

"What you may think is a meaningless routine is what will save your life when the going gets tough.

"The following will be your schedule, and unless you are dead, you WILL be there, and you WILL be on time.

"Today we have thirty-six recruits. How many will remain after the next seven weeks is up to you. You, six females, step over there, the rest of you stay where you are.

"Stand in single file, and sound off."

I promptly stepped to the front. I always liked to be at the front, even in church. Sharply yelling out, "ONE!" I then heard two, three—then a pause caused everyone to look down the row.

Sergeant Black walked over, yelling at the next man in line, "What is your name?"

Rather meekly, Wil replied, "William Wright."

"I will be addressed as 'Sergeant.' If you wish to speak to me, you will need to get my attention. To do that, the first word out of your mouth will be 'Sergeant,' as will the last word out of your mouth."

The sergeant then barked back at William, "And DO NOT call me SIR. Now, what the hell is your number?"

"Sergeant, number four, Sergeant."

"Great, now if the rest of you Chuggernuts can finish the sound off, we will proceed."

Sergeant Black looking harshly at the haphazard line and roared, "Now, if you also know your left from your right, evens on the right, odds on the left."

A glance in William's direction assured us all that he was serious. At that instant we all knew that something was wrong: one line was longer than the other. Oh no, Wil was number four. He had stepped into the line on the left.

Our hearts went out to Wil. I always knew that Wil was a little slower than most. I had grown up with Wil, spent most summers with him. I had learned at a very early age that Wil did not function well under pressure. Although William was not my roommate, I knew I would have to watch over him, aiding him in whatever way I could.

Sergeant Black looked over at William, and with disgust announced, "I expect that not all of you will graduate."

William quickly switched lines, all the time staring straight ahead so as not to catch the glare of the sergeant.

"Now that you all can count, you also know your right from your left, so let's get started.

"Each of you will be bunked with the man directly across from you. Should you decide that you do not like the look of the man across from you, or if you think you are better than him, too damn bad. He is your partner; you will remain inseparable for the next seven weeks. If he falls you will help him up. If he needs to bake a brownie, you will be there to hand him the toilet paper.

"At zero-five-hundred hours your alarm will sound. Yes, I said 5:00 a.m., ladies.

"Zero-five-five hours you will be out of bed and dressed.

"By zero-five-ten hours you will be dressed in your exercise fatigues.

"Exercises take place in the lower half of your dorms. At zero-six-hundred you will shower, be cleaned up, and be ready for breakfast at zero-six-thirty. This is not the Hilton, you are not on vacation, so do not be late."

"Zero-seven-hundred is an inspection of your bed, footlocker, and personal attire. They must be neat and orderly. You will be instructed on how they are to be folded.

"Zero-eight-hundred is morning instructions. Your morning outline will be provided. No notes will be given as we will expect you to remember them. From zero-eight-hundred to eleven-twenty-nine, you will take whatever classes or training you are assigned, and you will follow whatever direction you are given.

"From eleven-thirty hours to twelve-thirty hours is your lunch. You will eat whatever is served or you will go hungry.

"Seventeen-hundred hours to seventeen-fifty-nine hours is dinner.

"Eighteen-hundred hours will be maintenance of your quarters and military kit. You will keep your quarters clean and orderly at all times. Your bed will be made with military corners, plus your boots will have a shine at all times. Remember, in the bush your gun is your best friend. Keep it clean; a well-oiled gun is essential.

"Twenty-three-hundred hours is lights out—no exceptions.

"Your entire schedule is in your course book on page four. You have no excuse for being late.

"Tomorrow you will start your official training—training that will include classroom instruction, field exercises, physical fitness, and yes, you will be tested.

"Those of you who think this will be like playing Call of Duty, you are mistaken. If you are soft and cannot handle the physical rigours, you will be weeded out.

"Now let's get you assigned to your partners, then up to your quarters.

"Fall in."

Silently, two by two we followed the sergeant throughout the corridors, dropping off individuals as we moved.

Entering first into our room, I stuck out my hand, firmly introducing myself. "Spencer Cook."

Without hesitation, my roommate extended his right hand while announcing, "Robert Jones. You can just call me Jones."

"Jones it is. You can call me Spencer." I smiled at Robert. We already knew each other but the snappy salute with a click of his heels seemed humorous, breaking the tension.

Looking about the sparsely decorated room, I spoke up first. "I can take the bed on the right."

"Great!" replied Jones. "Let's unload our belongings." The only items on either side of the room were the beds, neatly folded sheeting with pillowcases on each bunk, a stand-up closet, and a footlocker.

Jones glanced over in my direction. "Boy, the next five weeks on the base without TV or visitors is going to be tough."

Raised in a lavish household, Jones was always pampered. I was confident that this would be harder for him. I would miss video games the most. I and my brother Randy had spent many hours deeply absorbed in war games. Many a time I had to wonder if I was the handicapped one as Randy usually managed to whip my ass. He would also not tell me secrets like how to short-cut the games. As a result, victory was usually his.

Once we had our beds made and all our gear stowed, we sat, talking about our lives, families, even girlfriends. Eleven-hundred hours came quickly; it was lights out. It may have been lights out, but my mind was going a mile a minute. My thoughts kept drifting back to my childhood. Again, I found myself focused on Dad; no matter how hard I tried, I always ended up at the same point.

Tonight, seemed different; I already missed my family.

I had been raised in a happy home. A place where responsibility and discipline ranked high. Dad was a career military man, which meant he moved around frequently. He was deployed to wherever he was needed, often leaving us for months, occasionally for as long as a year. Constantly meeting new people and experiencing new places had become my norm.

Dad had insisted I see as much of the world as possible. Every summer, Mom would pack up our luggage and we would travel off to meet Dad for a vacation in some faraway place. Luckily, Mom had been able to keep grandpa's family estate, thus we had been spared the nomadic life of a soldier's family. I enjoyed the fact that we had been able to establish a few good long-term friendships.

For the last five years, Dad had been stationed in Johannesburg, South Africa. As a military advisor, he had access to many influential individuals. Many a night I had lain awake listening to them talk of events in faraway places. Dad knew many secrets, secrets that he could not divulge, as well as other gruesome events that he would rather not discuss.

A quiet nurturing individual, Mom always seemed to be puttering around the house—a trait that was required for the many years spent helping Randy achieve his limited potential. I resented the fact that Randy would never be able to achieve the things that so many others took for granted. I promised myself that as soon as this five-week lockdown finished, I would call them all to tell them how much I loved and missed them. Slowly, without even knowing, I slipped off into a peaceful, uninterrupted sleep.

Abruptly, without warning, I came fully awake as the zero-five-hundred alarm sounded—an alarm that could not have at a more inappropriate time. I had been wrapped in the arms of my sweetheart Jenny—Jenny, with her long, sandy-coloured hair, and a body that could stop a freight train. Springing out of bed, the dream drifted away as my eyes sprang open.

"OK, Jones, let's hurry, ten minutes to get dressed before we have to be downstairs. I have no desire to be late."

I always looked at myself as athletic, a member of the high school wrestling and football teams, with some junior basketball. Two inches shy of six feet, most of the basketball team looked down at me. For obvious reasons, I tried out for junior football, then decided that it was not for me. I had made the team; paid my dues but sitting on the bench all season and watching the others play held no interest for me.

Sergeant Black stood in front of the class in his tight-fitting exercise fatigues, muscles bulging from places where I was not even sure I had muscles.

His instructions were brief. "Today we will give you a taste of the exercise program that you will be required to pass to complete your basic training. Physical fitness is not only exercise, but a complete mindset, a way of life.

"The phrase 'you are what you eat' holds true. By the end of the next seven weeks, you will not only become strong and toned, but you will also understand what is required to maintain that healthy physique. If for any reason you are not able to complete the physical fitness standard required, you will be dropped from the program.

"OK, that being said, everyone drop. Give me twenty-five push-ups. NOW!" With a discerning eye, he watched as the recruits tried to fulfill his request.

William was already done and waiting for the others as I bounced upward to attention. Wil Wright may well need help with the academic part of the training, but he would definitely surpass all the others in the physical requirements.

Sergeant Black waited until all, including the females, were finished. Then, looking toward Wil, he commanded, "Candidate Wright, show them how a real push-up is done."

Sharply, without hesitation, he dropped to the floor, performed another ten—perfect push-ups, from the floor to fully extended. It was at that moment, when I saw a tiny glint of a smile in the sergeant's eyes, that I knew William Wright was no longer at risk of being the troop whipping boy. He had just gained the sergeant's respect. Wil could also see that strength mixed with physical fitness was something that the sergeant respected.

Sergeant Black reminded us all. "This mental and physical toughness I am driving at you may save lives—one being your own."

Sergeant Black would no doubt find the next weak link in the chain and browbeat on him or her until they improved or quit. I realized it was no different here and this was the way of the world: the weak always get abused or exploited by the strong. In the military world, I had no choice but to be on the top of my game.

The exercise session continued with up-downs, running, ab crunches, leg lifts, and sit-ups. The days quickly ran one into another with repeated monotony. Day after day was exercise, exercise, then more exercise. I understood and accepted the logic behind the routine, soon falling into a rhythm. Then I found myself craving the euphoria created from extreme exhaustion—that moment during a long run when I seemed to glide on air, and I no longer gasped for breath.

OUT ON THE TOWN

Once the recruits were allowed to leave the base, it was common practice to visit a pub in the nearby town. No longer the shy introvert of my school days and feeling a little more relaxed than usual, I decided to ask one of the ladies to dance. Confidence oozed from my every move as I sauntered over to the pretty redhead leaning against the bar.

Without delay in my introduction, I commented, "Hi, I'm Spencer. Would you like to dance?"

It was obvious from the start that she was also attracted to what she saw. Her eyes rolled slowly down to the floor then back up across my snug-fitting, baby-blue shirt. Stopping only once, she stood staring directly into my deep blue eyes. Without hesitation, she grabbed onto my already waiting hand.

"Yes, I would like that very much, Spencer. I'm Bonnie."

Across the room, tension grew. "Hey boys, that girl is not one of your base bunnies." It was apparent the local boys did not approve of their ladies being courted by outsiders, especially jugheads.

One second, I was dancing and having fun; the next, I was under attack. After the crunch of knuckles striking my jaw, I could feel the puffiness in my lips almost instantly. Bonnie gasped as the second set of knuckles approached my head. Ducking, I could see the closed fist skimming past my head. Like a football lineman, I thrust upward, lifting the attacker and propelling him toward a nearby table.

Stopping in mid-flight, I was now in a position to return the favour. With hands open, I drew back both arms, thrusting both palms squarely into the chest of the now off-balance opponent. Although I had practised this particular move hundreds of times at the base, I could not believe how much force I was able to apply. Both arms now fully extended, I watched as my quarry rose upward off his feet, flying backward over a nearby chair.

The sound of the chair crashing, then the sickening thud of a skull hitting concrete confirmed I would no longer have to worry about that individual. Laid out cold on the floor, he no longer moved—the whole room watched in disbelief.

The silence was broken by the sound of glass breaking. I prepared myself for another assault as a second attacker charged in my direction. I moved swiftly sideways, swept his arm away, sending the shattered glass across the concrete floor. A quick sweeping motion, then a pull on his arm sent him headlong into the bar.

From the darkness of a corner table, two more attackers lunged forward toward me, shouting, "We do not like you soldier boys coming in here, hitting on our ladies. We're going to show you what happens when you are not welcome!"

Very calmly I replied, "We are not looking for any more trouble."

However, experience told me the comment had landed on deaf ears; they were not going to be calmed down. It was apparent that this one was not into the moment as he swung wildly in the direction of my head. It took little effort to redirect his extended arm to the side, and with a foot sweep I picked him up off his feet. From three feet off the ground, he fell helplessly onto his back. As I stared across the dance floor, I could see that the trouble was not over. Another wave of assailants jumped to their feet and headed my way. Enough was enough. As the last two drunks started throwing punches, Andrew stepped in and locked an arm thrust. With an open-hand thrust, his palm slammed into the back of the elbow. Instantly, the sound of breaking bone echoed across the now silent room. Wil tossed the other drunk to the floor, and from a quick blow to the temple, he too posed no further threat.

"Balls to the wall, boys," I ordered. Without a word, the team circled me, ready for more.

The room was silent, the music had ceased, and all the patrons were just staring. The only movement came as the bartender lifted the phone receiver to his face.

I knew at that moment it had happened; we had finally become a team. This little escapade would cost us dearly; we would have much explaining to do. Along with the others, I would probably spend some time in the brig; at the very least, I would be confined to base.

Inwardly I smiled; the sergeant was right. All that repetition had paid off. Without even thinking we had reacted to the danger, adapted, and overcome the problem. Even so, maybe next time I could find a way to avoid the violence, but, if not, I knew I would be ready.

As the local police rushed through the door, we all knew, we had more pressing things to worry about. Two people out cold and one broken arm—Sergeant Black was not going to be happy.

Just as I had suspected, Sergeant Black was not the least bit impressed. The following morning, we all stood in full combat gear as the rain poured down upon us. In unison, we marched onto the base football field. Flocks of Canada geese squawked as they departed their water-soaked feeding grounds. For weeks, the geese had made this their home. In their usual manner, whatever went in one end came out the other. The whole field was covered with their soggy sewage.

"All right, boys, down on your bellies. Start crawling to the other end and back. I will tell you when to stop."

By the time we had crawled the length of the field three times, we wished we had never gone into town. Covered in mud, soaking wet, and smelling of goose shit, we headed back to the barracks. We did not get much sleep that night; all our gear had to cleaned, washed, and polished by zero-eight-hundred.

Time flew by, before we realized it our team had passed the four basic training force evaluations; we were ready, eager to continue. Each would now be funnelled into their specialty field. All of our team had decided to take the training sessions back-to-back, enabling us to graduate together. By doing so, we would also increase our chances that we could be stationed together, wherever that may be. Most of the other recruit teams were already split up, deployed to various bases and abroad. My team, due to our exceptional performance, stayed together. We had become so good at camouflage that even the training staff took notice. We evaded and hid so well that on more than one occasion, we were actually stepped on by trainers. Subduing the trainers became a game for us.

No sooner had I flip the page on the calendar, and I was flipping it again. Theory became practical situations. With each exercise came a new engineering challenge. Building bridges and constructing artillery-proof structures were by far the most intriguing. I soon learned to adapt the simplest of materials into sturdy structures. Where my university education had taught me most of the basics, my army training expanded on and opened up a whole new way of looking at both permanent and temporary structures.

I had completed basic training with relative ease. Except for Wil, our grades and field experience had surpassed all other recruits. Six months had passed since we first enlisted, and I grew restless. Not only did my leadership skills surpass all other recruits, but the base commander had also advanced me two pay grades and offered to recommend me for early officer training.

Relocation to Saint-Jean, Quebec, or Victoria, British Columbia, for the start of my officer developmental periods meant I would need to leave all my friends. This would be a big change. Not only had I spent my whole life close to home, but I had also never left my friends behind. One year as an officer cadet, one year as a second lieutenant, and another two as a lieutenant meant at least four more years. Would my dad hold out that long? I needed to be able to tell him that I had fulfilled my promise, but time was running out. Acceptance of the transfer application soon followed, and I settled in, hoping that I had made the right decision.

Arrival at the Saint-Jean academy did not have the same impact as Meaford. I had fallen into the routine of military life very quickly at Meaford; Saint-Jean academy was no different. Even the mandatory short haircut on enrolment day seemed normal. The five-week orientation was the toughest. With none of my buddies around, I was forced to introduce myself to all new people and develop new friendships.

The philosophy and second language courses ranked number two and three, while the physical education still stood out as my number one mandatory activity. Leadership and philosophy had never been taught in my university courses and I found myself engrossed. Learning what things motivated each personality type and how to get people to willingly buy into my ideas became not only a course subject but an everyday game.

Tormented, I would have to spend more time in training. I dove headlong into this new objective. If nothing else, the refocus provided additional vigour and the months flew by. Four years to the day, I strolled back into CFB Meaford. Now a lieutenant, my duties would change, hopefully, I would be able to reunite with my friends.

Robert Jones now held the rank of corporal, Michael Parker was promoted to sergeant, while David Dunsmoore, William Wright, and Andrew James were happy to remain as privates. The excitement of once again collaborating with my old friends soon became evident. Renewed vigour, and enthusiasm soon took hold. My new responsibilities included supervision of a training cell. I was now able to appoint the teams, it was not long before my friends and I were once again wading through the mud and muck together. To the delight of the course directing staff, we excelled beyond everyone's expectations.

Both in the classroom and the field, my team once again shone above all others. Running the obstacle courses and completing our missions in record time became an expected outcome. Daytime exercises and skirmishes, although fun, were not as challenging as the nighttime exercises. Under the cover of darkness, we infiltrated the outer lines of the opposing teams by whatever means possible. Crawling on our bellies through puddles of water while black flies and mosquitoes chewed away at our bare flesh became a daily routine.

Training had taught me to understand the environment that we would be working in, predicting the potential dangers—disease, hazardous bugs, snakes, or even aggressive animals. For each exercise, my team was given a country and location, after which we were expected to prepare an infiltration plan. Once the plan was reviewed and discussed, the individual team members would present their supplies and armament list.

Planning requirements increased, as the new team leader, I needed to make sure that every possible scenario was considered. Once we were dropped off, there would be no going to stores to grab the missed items.

Our first self-directed infiltration became next on the list, before handing out the mission details I must first assign each person their role:

Spencer Cook, Team Leader, Lieutenant

Michael Parker, Sergeant

David Dunsmoore, Communications, Private

Richie Miller, Spotter, Private

Robert Jones, Sniper, Corporal

William Wright, Supplies, Private

Andrew James, Armaments, Private

Sergeant Parker managed overall quality, he would assure that all possibilities were considered. He addressed each team member individually and reviewed their list, right down to food, until he was satisfied. Then, and only then, he would present it to me.

"Private Dunsmoore, what is on your list?"

"Sir, we will be taking two Clansman RT-320/PRC-320 radios."

The sergeant acknowledged with a nod then replied, "Make sure they are charged and in tip-top condition, with a full charge…"

"Yes, sir."

"Corporal Jones, are you and Private Miller prepared?"

"Yes, sir. We have our C7 exercise rifles, two ghillie suits, one hundred rounds of practice ammo each, and our miscellaneous supplies as issued by Private Wright.

"Sir, we have distributed three days' rations to the men, a canteen full of water, rain poncho, helmet, backpack, flashlights, night vision goggles, bayonets, tactical knives, and a first aid kit. Sir."

Noting that climbing or rappelling may be required, Sergeant Parker requested that they add two one-hundred-foot lengths of three-quarter-inch rope.

"Good," replied Sergeant Parker. "Include the rope, then requisition the supplies."

"Private James, what is our armament status? Weapons, Private?"

"Sir, each man has his C7 practice rifle, semi-automatic pistols complete with fifty rounds each of 9×19-mm ammo, six practice grenades, and one hundred rounds each of 5.56×45-mm C7 ammo.

"Sir, we do not expect that any heavy arms resistance will be experienced, so the C7 rifle and personal sidearms are what has been requested."

Sergeant Parker thought for a second. "I concur with your analysis. Get ready."

PART TWO

OPERATION LION'S HEAD

Team training for special missions soon became our primary focus. I expected my team to be number one and I would accept nothing less. The sun was rising high into the sky when our team received orders. When darkness fell, we would be flying out. Already tired from the daily exercises, I wondered where or when we would get to sleep again. Walking slowly toward the chopper, I ordered another equipment check before we boarded. Today's mission was to drop into hostile territory without being detected, snatch a kidnap victim, eliminate the captors, then return to base.

From the helipad, the chopper rose into the dark of the night. As we ascended, glimpses of the neighbouring towns appeared like sparks of light on the land below. First a haze, they turned into sparkling spots of yellowish-white light as the chopper drew closer to the source. I envisioned the small moving vehicles as enemy troops moving about like ants on a sandy mound.

The flight would take us westward, high above the bay, then out across the open water. The night was overcast with low clouds; in the distance, I could just barely see the long peninsula. According to the mission plan, the landing zone would be central, about fifteen kilometres up the length of the peninsula.

The destination was a small building, probably an old cottage. Here we were expected to find a kidnap victim being held by an unknown number of assailants. The objective was to approach the area from the north, encircle the cabin, then extract the prisoner.

Approaching low, just above the water, we quickly stopped, hovering close to the shore. A large rock outcropping with thick bush concealed our approach. One at a time, we jumped from the chopper. Once all personnel were on the ground, the chopper retreated to base.

"Sergeant, we should be near the five-kilometre mark. Take a quick check of the radios before we leave."

One by one, the earpieces verified reception.

"I will follow second in line."

"OK, let's head out. Corporal Jones, you take point. Be careful; these wet rocks can be treacherous."

Gazing down the moonlit shore, I saw nothing but cliffs and steep rock faces, as far as my eyes could see. I feared we would have to go past the coordinates. "Halt here." I called out. With a wave, Sergeant Parker moved forward, stopping beside me.

"It looks like we will have to climb this rock face. Take Private James, see what you can do to get us up there. The rest of you, take five."

Smiling, Sergeant Parker handed James the rope. Private James had proven his prowess at climbing and was by far the stronger of the two. "Find us the easiest route to the top."

With the rope draped around his shoulders, private James slowly ascended the rock face.

"Sarge, I will need to tie off here. I cannot make it any further without falling."

Steadying himself, the Private tied the loose end around his waist, leaving only enough length to prevent himself from falling. Cautiously, he secured the rope to the cliff face.

Hand over hand, he slowly moved upward across the rock face. Each shift of position meant he had to find a new hand hold to support himself. The rope had to be secured to the next available rock or root; he reached up. Caution was the word; a fall from that height would surely be fatal. The lack of moonlight and darkness made it even more treacherous. The occasional look downward sent butterflies tingling up his spine; stopping to re-focus helped. Staring skyward became the only way to make the butterflies cease.

Fear of heights had never been a problem, but tonight for some weird reason things seemed different. Nearing the top of the climb with only three more feet to go, he reached out, grabbing onto what he thought was a rock; a rapid hissing soon alerted him to the fact that he had invaded the peaceful slumber of a rattlesnake. Unable to retract his hand fast enough, he felt the pressure of the small, sharp fangs biting into his Nomex gloves. Instantly, the snake let go as Jones flung his arm outward away from the cliff. The soft flesh of his palm stung where the venom touched his broken skin. Without warning, his whole body jerked, and the rope became tight. Suddenly, he found himself swinging uncontrollably across the rock face. *This fall is going to hurt,* flashed through his mind.

Instantly, his trouble increased as the left side of his face smashed against the edge of a protruding rock. Dangling with an injured jaw, he tried calling out. Straining, still conscious, with a tingling pain in his left hand, he managed to call.

"Help."

Dangling from the rope above, he waited while waves of pain shot up his arm. Sergeant Parker scrambled upward toward the now dangling private. Using a second rope, he looped through the last tie-off and formed a bosun's chair.

"Pull up the slack." He yelled to the men below. "OK, you have his weight."

A quick swipe with Sergeant Parker's tactical knife cut the tether rope, transferring the weight.

Inch by inch, they lowered Private James to the rocky shore below.

In a single motion, Corporal Jones swung his pack to the ground, pulling out his first aid kit.

"Sir, we anticipated nicks and cuts; but not snake bites."

"Lieutenant, we don't have any anti-venom. What should we do?"

"Private Dunsmoore, get onto the radio and request a chopper for medical extraction. Inform them of the situation and our location. Make sure they have the anti-venom ready on arrival."

How had we completely overlooked this possibility. The kit had been stocked with ample antiseptic and bandages. Although Private James was bleeding profusely from his face, the snake bite became my primary concern.

How did we forget this? We all knew this peninsula was home to the Massasauga Rattlesnake. This nasty little reptile with an unforgiving bite. We should have been prepared for this.

Fearing the worst, I remembered the horrible pictures and descriptions of victims who had inadvertently pissed off one of these little creatures.

"Time is of the essence, Private, let me know their ETA as soon as you know." I ordered.

Stepping in close, I removed the Nomex glove. I could see that the snake's fangs had only scratched the side of his palm, but even a small amount of venom in an open wound concerned me.

Staring him in the eyes I asked. "Private, what are your symptoms?"

I had to make every attempt to keep him calm and awake. Any accelerated heart rate would only push the venom farther into his circulatory system and closer to his heart.

My wilderness training had taught me that rattlesnake bites contain hemotoxic elements that, over time, damage tissue and affect the circulatory system. Eventually, the venom destroys blood cells and skin tissues, then causes internal hemorrhaging. The neurotoxic components will then immobilize the nervous system, sometimes stopping the victim's breathing. To say the least, it was a nasty substance.

Opening his canteen, I poured water over the scratches, washing away any remaining venom, then I applied liquid antiseptic. I could see the private's hand rapidly starting to swell. I removed his wristwatch and stuck it in his breast pocket.

Things could still get worse. I had no way of knowing if the snake was an immature specimen or not. I could only hope that it was not. A juvenile rattler's venom is reportedly much nastier.

Unable to do more about the venom, I dressed his facial wounds. All we could do now was wait for the chopper and pray for the best. With at least a thirty-minute wait, we could only watch, hoping shock would not set in, or that his heart or breathing would be compromised.

"Keep him elevated, his arm lowered. Private Wright, prepare a tourniquet, we will need to slow down the movement of the venom. I want you to keep the pressure on; release it every minute or so to allow blood flow into the arm."

The private grabbed a small stick and the primitive tool took form. Twisting a short piece of parachute rope around the upper arm, he applied pressure.

The wait seemed endless; *we needed that chopper ASAP.* Hopefully, enough medical gear would be on board to keep the private stable and alive.

"Swelling seems to be localized, only the side of his hand has puffed up, sir."

"Corporal, what is your assessment on the facial wounds?"

"Well, Sir, the cheekbones do not appear to be broken, so we should be able to cleanse and bandage it for now."

"Good, Corporal, make it so." In the distance the flashing lights on the chopper glided across the water's surface. Only feet above the rolling waves it stopped, hovering above the rocky shore, we waved them down. Strapped in, James lay grimacing in pain.

Whoop, whoop, whoop of the chopper blades disappeared into the distance. Shaken, the team hurried to gather their gear and return to the mission. The team was now three hours behind and one man short.

Sergeant Parker completed the climb to the top of the cliff. Tying the rope securely to a sturdy tree, he waited as the remainder of the team scaled the rock face.

I glanced at my watch; we were now into the wee hours of the morning. We had lost too much time; even with a steady, uninterrupted pace, I knew that we would not make our destination before sunrise. Extraction under darkness had been essential. Our mission was to remove the hostage while remaining undetected. Under the cover of darkness, we were then to return to base. Upon completion, we would need the remaining darkness to return to the extraction landing zone. With such a narrow peninsula, the helicopter would be easily seen, and the mission foiled during any daylight activity.

I called Sergeant Parker over. "Have the men settle in. We will have to wait out the daylight hours here; we will resume tomorrow night.?

Our intel had no indication if the hostage may be moved. We hoped not; we had to complete the mission. With the loss of almost a day, I feared we may have failed; only time would tell.

Back at the base, the emergency helicopter flew in low over the trees, settling quickly onto the pad. Private James lay motionless on the gurney as medical staff scurried around in preparation to receive their new patient.

During the thirty-minute flight, the medics had inserted an IV and tracked his vitals. Although conscious, his eyes were closed, and his face grimaced from the pulsing pain in his head. Both eyes were starting to blacken as the eyelids swelled closed. He looked quite the mess.

Vomit sprayed from his open mouth as they pulled Private James off the chopper. His breathing had become more irregular, and his heart raced. Although his hand had not swollen any larger, it was obvious the toxins were eating away at the rest of his body, playing havoc on his vital organs. Quickly, the gurney rolled into the emergency room toward the waiting surgeons.

THE WAIT

Settled in, the men spent the next fourteen hours leisurely talking while observing the wildlife. I had decided to break up into three two-man sentry teams. One team on the north, south, and west sides of our location. The east side faced the water, making it easily covered by both the north and south teams.

"Men, we must avoid being detected. Keep your movement to a minimum and your voices low. We are going to hold up here until dark tonight."

Boredom led to lethargy. Eventually, the warmth of the midday sun drew the exhausted men toward sleep. The midday silence was occasionally broken by the heavy breathing or a snore as individuals drifted in and out of their slumber. Darkness slowly settled in as the sun whispered good night to the rising moon.

"Sergeant, ready the men. We are now twenty-four hours late, twenty-four hours we cannot get back." Crouched beside a deadfall, we reviewed the aerial photographs. Our approach plan had not changed; each man knew what was expected. Without any questions or further comment, the men grabbed their packs and guns, ready to proceed. Corporal Jones established the new GPS coordinates. He folded the map and readied to proceeded.

"Jones, you take point." His eyesight and powers of observation surpassed all the others; he was the obvious choice to take the lead.

"Sergeant, take up the rear. Stay back about twenty metres; watch for any ambush parties. Although this is a training exercise, we never know what little surprises might be in store. I want you at the rear for just that reason. Stay sharp."

The aerial photographs showed four small buildings and a barn near a single cabin. I suspected the captive may be concealed in one of the smaller buildings. A single man was assigned to each building, leaving me free to survey the area. I would be able to radio them should I detect any suspicious activity. Perched atop an adjacent rock ledge, I lowered my night-vision glasses, watching.

Private Miller crawled in toward the barn. Slowly, he lifted himself, peering into a small window. My infrared glasses detected no heat signatures. The ground floor appeared to be empty. Gradually, Miller moved around, inspecting the remainder of the building.

"Miller here, Station One, all clear, ground floor empty. I will need to get inside to check the second floor. I suspect rusty hinges; not going to open the door, sir."

Slowly, Miller worked his way around the barn until he found a couple of boards missing. Stripping off his pack, he squeezed through the narrow opening. Standing motionless for a couple of minutes, he surveyed the hay-covered loft.

"Miller here. Checking the upstairs."

"Jones here. Station Two all clear."

"Wright here, one lone male observed. Permission to immobilize?"

"Roger that," I replied.

Private Wright quickly opened the door so he could step into the small room. To the surprise of the soldier inside, he was standing with his C7 practice rifle pointed directly at his chest. Pulling the trigger, he watched as the light and beeper signalled a kill.

"Wright here. Target immobilized, awaiting further orders."

"Corporal, proceed toward the latrine."

I watched intently as Private Wright approached the outside latrine. Without warning, a tall, heavy-set male opened the door and stepped out. No time to think! Wright grabbed the man, with a roll, flipped him to the ground. Instinctively he pulled out his knife and held it to the man's neck.

"Wright here, Station Three, target immobilized."

I was becoming increasingly alarmed; Station One had not checked in since he had entered the barn.

"Station Two, have a look, see what's up with Station One."

Jones turned, retreating backward toward the barn. The silence was broken as Miller checked in.

"Miller here. Station One is clear. Sorry sir, I had a standoff with a skunk."

We now had only one building not cleared.

"Station Four, where are you? I asked. "All men proceed to Station Four, then report in."

Cautiously, all three soldiers approached the small, dilapidated building. Private Miller was the first to arrive. Peering inside, all he could see was the head of Private Dunsmoore. He chuckled. Private Dunsmoore had fallen through the rotten floorboards into some kind of pit. Using his C7, he had managed to support himself, but he was unable to move for fear of falling further into the hole. Afraid he would give their position away, he remained silent.

Pulling Dunsmoore upward, Miller reported in, "Miller here. Station Four secure. I will give details later."

THE EXTRACTION

I stood overlooking the remaining building. If the hostage was indeed still in the building, I could not assume there was only one captor. A plan to approach the structure had to be devised. The building, a small wartime cottage, housed a mudroom on the back with an old screened-in porch. There appeared to be no way of determining how many assailants were inside. We would have to make entry by rushing both entrances. The latrine was to the rear of the cabin—the back door seemed a logical entry point. The man in the outhouse would have had to leave the rear door open. The front door would be the other point of entry. I decided I would play the odds.

"Station One. Meet up with Station Two, then proceed to the rear door.

"Station Three. Cover the side window. Station Four, guard the front door and prepare for entry.

"Station Four. Enter only on my command.

"Station One. you have the lead; I will cover the rear windows from here."

Private Miller cautiously eased his way across the rocky driveway. Crunch after crunch from the shifting stones awakened every one of his senses. In the silence of the night, every sound seemed to be an explosion.

"Sir, they would probably not be expecting anyone but their accomplice to enter the rear door. I think that will be our best breach point." Private Miller quietly commented.

"Logical, breach the back door," I replied

With a steady but unhurried approach, Miller turned the doorknob. No one was in the kitchen. Miller could see down the hall to the front door; no one there either. There were two bedrooms, one on each side of the corridor with the main living room beyond that. Cautiously, he extended his neck, listening to the left—nothing. Then to the right: a faint sound of snoring emanated from behind the door. Miller waved Jones forward and they stood side by side; he would take the snorer while Jones would rush the quiet room. Slowly both doorknobs turned, only one room was locked. Miller pointed toward the unlocked room, could it house another assailant. Slowly Miller signalled Jones, stop. Finger extended he pointed toward the living room, cautiously he peered around the room. Another individual lay sleeping on the couch. Without hesitation he stepped forward. In one smooth motion he covered the sleeping face, while pressing his knife against the throat.

Jones rushed into the unlocked room. His infrared glasses verified, no one was in the room. Miller immediately broke down the locked door. By this time, the heavy breathing had stopped, replaced by a rather feminine scream. Huddled in the corner a young female jumped to her feet.

"Hands up," Miller shouted.

"Miller here. Parcel retrieved." Grabbing her coat, Miller hustled her through the kitchen, exiting the back door.

Perpetrator one was dragged from the cabin and lashed to his accomplice.

"Site secured, Sir." Miller announced.

"Good lets head back to the Landing Zone." I whispered into my radio.

"Sergeant, as soon as we lift off, radio the base to have them visit the cabin and release the two prisoners."

Descending the rock face to the shoreline below, the team prepared for extraction.

"Private, call for the chopper. We will advance to the LZ and wait there."

"If we double time it, we should be able to reach the LZ before the chopper touches down."

Winded and sweaty we rested on the rocky shore.

"Gather round, just a few comments on our field exercise. Except for the delay caused by the medical mishap, the team's calculated timing to execute the retrieval of the hostage had been correct. The overall situation had been assessed correctly. In my evaluation, the assault and subsequent extraction was a success. I will issue my report to the base commander tomorrow. Well done."

Back at base, the hostage was handed over and a brief check made to confirm the prisoners left behind had indeed been released. The following morning, I filed my operational report; the base commander would respond shortly.

"Sir, the mission was a success. Except for Private Jones's medical mishap, all went as planned."

The commander stood. Walking from behind the desk, he approached me.

"I cannot accept even a near miss. Had this been a real mission, it could have been a fatality.

"Your team would be escorting a comrade back in a body bag. However, tell your men they did good. But in the future, they must plan for all contingencies.

"Just so you know, Private James did not lose his hand. The medics did a great job. The private should be back with your team within a couple of days.

"Lieutenant, I expect a full written report on my desk by zero-eight-hundred tomorrow."

"Yes, sir," was my reply. Saluting, I dismissed myself.

James lay on the bed, his left hand bandaged up past the wrist.

"How is your hand, Private?"

"Thanks to the painkillers, it is only throbbing, although I still have a stabbing pain bouncing around inside my skull." He replied.

As the remainder of the team entered his room, the Private managed a smile. Gradually, he stuck out his right hand, greeting them all. Each of the men acknowledged his gesture with a handshake and a smile.

"Looks like I will only be out of commission for a couple of days." Private James then asked, "how did the exercise go?" Eagerly he awaited a reply.

Addressing the team, I announced, "Gentlemen, all went well. Soon we will be able to undergo the next and final test—the single man infiltration exercise.

"Unfortunately, since Private James was unable to complete the exercise. In order to graduate he will be required to undergo and complete another mission."

Peering at the private, I assured him, "I will hold open your spot on the team as long as I can."

Individually I congratulated the team. Private James would be out of the infirmary shortly. Losing only two days to sick leave, he had not lost his position with the team. All in all, excellent news. Even with his limited ability, he would still be expected to prepare his lists and attend the planning meetings for the upcoming individual field test.

"I will carry my share of the workload." The private wholeheartedly assured us.

The final weeks raced by Private James had been released from the hospital, and, though experiencing localized tenderness, he recovered fully.

Preparation for the one-man field exercise was progressing well. Four hours a day, the men prepared their lists, then sat as a group to fine-tune the details. Private James awaited his orders to redo his extraction training— hopefully soon, so he could be ready to rejoin the team for the single man infiltration exercise.

PART THREE

QUALIFYING

As I hopped onto the CH-148 Cyclone chopper, memories of my first flight flashed through my mind: the rush of the wind passing my face and the enormity of the "butterfly churn" as we lifted off. It was a training mission that would be the first of many. Today's flight would be different—it was the required qualifying exercise, the field exercise we must complete successfully for consideration into the Elite Task Force Training Program.

The world had changed drastically since 9/11—terrorism was being fought at all levels. Soon our team would be pitted against the world's cruellest and most sadistic people. I knew I was ready for the task. As I jumped off the heli, both feet landed solidly. Dropping to one knee, I strained to maintain my balance.

Alone with no one to talk to, my mind hashed over the mission plan again and again—reviewing the copious details, all the cautions and concerns. Navigating through the thick undergrowth loaded down with a one-hundred-pound pack and my trusted C7 would be a test of my endurance. The C7, a modified M16 assault rifle in 5.56×45-mm calibre, proved over the years to be an exceptionally reliable weapon. Slipping the sling higher on my shoulder, I glanced sideways at the weapon, flashbacks darting to my favourite rifle—not a military-issued weapon, but my trusted Ruger 30-06 hunting rifle that was sitting locked away in my hunting safe.

My fondness for the Ruger—the stainless-steel barrel, the camouflaged composite stock—would last a lifetime, or at least my lifetime. That trusted rifle had harvested many an animal. With the Leupold red dot scope, it was a deadly combination. Season after season, Dad had awakened me long before dawn to head out into the northern bush. Hours later, we would return to our cabin with the quarry in tow. How I loved shooting that rifle, but for now I had my C7.

There were no vehicles on this mission; all my provisions had to be carried in. As long as I could sneak within range, I knew I had everything needed to complete this mission. Most military firefights are conducted at short range—this exercise was expected to be under a hundred yards. Although the C7 was not the flattest shooting rifle, it was light, a good bush gun with plenty of punch. For this exercise, my C7 would do the job nicely.

Today the sun was shining from a cloudless sky, and the humidity was stifling. How I detested the sweltering heat. With my fully loaded pack and rifle, the day would only get hotter—oh, how I looked forward to the coolness of the coming evening.

Opening the mission envelope, I located my final destination. The helicopter lifted from the landing pad. Upon departure, the commander had handed me a compass, a map, an electronic GPS, along with a set of coordinates. I programmed the coordinates into the GPS. Moments later I had an X on the topo map. I was headed north-west.

I was now on my own. Judging by the topo map, I could see that the path to the finish line would be through some nasty country.

Resting briefly on a large deadfall, I reached into the side pocket of my pack, pulling out a camouflaged scarf. I tied it around my forehead. Wiping sweat from my forehead, I realized how much movement this simple task created. Movement in the bush, even this simple act, could lead to detection—another of the constant reminders of all the little things that could go wrong, potentially spoiling my possibility of success. Dad always said, "watch the details, that is where you will find the devil."

The constant drone of mosquitoes buzzing around made it near impossible to hear any potential enemy sounds. In this case, the enemy were silent spotters, placed in the wilderness as sentries. These individuals could at any moment spoil my attempt to reach the destination or complete the mission.

Travelling through the mosquito-infested bush showed me what it must have been like in prison camps—soldiers could go mad when subjected to the constant buzzing of these little pests. Mosquito repellents were not an option since even the slightest odour may lead to detection. In a real-life situation, that could mean death. Rubbing mud onto any exposed parts of my body helped with the bugs, but the buzzing was still a big annoyance.

"Ignore the buzzing, it is not there. Ignore the buzzing, it is not there," I silently repeated over and over, until finally, the drone of the mosquitoes disappeared, replaced by less annoying sounds.

The northern wilderness provides the ideal conditions to practise guerrilla warfare—sneak, evade, surprise. From my drop point, I would have to hike across sixty miles of rocky, wooded terrain, through some of the thickest, dirtiest bush any soldier could experience. All the survival training weekends with Dad had made me aware of what to expect, prepared me for this very moment. I was determined not to fail; I would overcome whatever lay ahead.

The other candidates were equally determined to achieve a spot in the CANSOFCOM (Canadian Special Operations Forces Command) Elite Task Force. All competing participants were dispatched from different locations— seven equally proficient individuals, each having extensive training in hand combat, martial arts, and weapons, each confident in his abilities. Now they too would be in route to my exact destination. These men, who had only hours ago collaborated with each other, were now competing for the same reward. Likewise, if they did not complete their mission, their spot on the team would be lost. Since registration into basic training, each person had developed his own unique skill sets, but all were well trained in basic soldier's duties—performing any of the required tasks, should it be necessary.

My task was to coordinate the team and the missions. Sergeant Michael Parker, now the junior officer, reported directly to me. Jones took charge of weapons and supplies. David became the radio operator. Richie, Wil, and Andrew made up the rest of the unit. Since basic training, they had eaten, slept, and bled together. Although they had prepared together, each member had to wage his own battle against the elements. I intended to be first to the target to garner team respect, but a better chance at any preferred placement would be my reward.

Even though they worked separately on route to the destination, soldiers were allowed, if necessary, to work together to fulfill their overall objective— we all knew this and were prepared. This exercise was intended to encourage them to do exactly that. Navigating through hostile terrain while keeping your cool is essential, as was continually reminding yourself to always stay focused, always stay calm.

I remembered a story Dad was fond of telling. Uncle Bob had gone into a rural farm area to do a little duck hunting. The intent was to follow the river, eventually meeting up at the next concession. Uncle Bob walked leisurely beside the bank, surveying for ducks on the water. Approximately halfway through the concession, he spotted an old foundation. After probing around for a while, he decided it best to move on. As he approached a high bank in the curve of the river, it became obvious he would need to work his way around the bank, eventually coming back to the river on the other side of the rise. It sounded easy; however, after passing the same foundation for the third time, he knew he was lost. He had been travelling in circles. Uncle Bob then decided to head straight for the nearest farmhouse. Although he was becoming extremely nervous, he knew to remain calm. Whenever confronted with a major problem, Dad had taught both him and me, just take a deep breath—stay calm.

For each team member, the going would be slow, with countless deadfalls, craters, and lakes standing in their way. Judging by the topo map, I could see there was no straight-line approach. This exercise was proving to be a true test of my endurance and training. Each man knew that he would be required to live off the land—they would not fire a weapon unless absolutely necessary, for fear of being heard. As well as the C7 exercise rifle, each person carried a single sidearm with live rounds for safety.

The first day of travel seemed to be an exercise in futility. Folding the map only ten miles in, I knew tomorrow had better improve.

Regardless of how I conserved my rations, there would not be enough food or water to last the whole trip. Edible plants were not a problem. Water could be. The possibility of contracting beaver fever from contaminated lake water remained a concern. Drinkable water would be a necessity, and a supply of Aquatabs had been packed for just that reason. As a last resort, I could collect rainwater, should there be the opportunity.

With the cool chill of the evening settling in, refuge would soon be a concern; early set-up of camp was essential. The sky had remained clear; the night would be cold. Safe dry shelter, food, and water now became my highest priorities.

Perched atop a small, raised plateau, I looked out at a clear view of the surrounding area that revealed my route.

I could not risk being detected; I had to confirm the wind direction. As luck would have it, a fire was not an option. The odour of burning wood and an open flame could present a problem. The need for heat to remove the perspiration and external dampness from my clothing had become important, but not important enough to risk being detected. The prospect of roaming bears and wolves concerned me. My location needed to be somewhere with my back protected.

Several glints of sunlight caught my eye. With the sun now behind me, all reflective surfaces shone like mirrors. A piece of glass? No, it was moving. From my location, all I could think of was binoculars. At this remote location, I would not expect to see random people. It may be one of the numerous sentries that had been dropped into my area. I would not be lighting a fire tonight; I would need to hunker down under one of the numerous cedar trees. No fire meant I needed to find a way to stay warm, and I needed to do it fast.

Dense black spruce interspersed with other evergreens grew in abundance, but very few deciduous trees meant no leaves. If I worked too hard to gather adequate leaves, I would surely develop a sweat, I could not afford for my clothes to get any damper. Hypothermia had to be avoided.

To say the least, most of the usable vegetation was too sparse to be practical. Gathering these meagre findings would be futile—something more practical had to be found. Quietly breaking off cedar boughs, I proceeded to assemble what was sure to be a lumpy bed. *Not exactly the Hilton* ran through my mind as I curled up under my camouflage poncho. Although elevated off the damp ground, sleep tonight was sure to be restless.

The sun comes up early in the bush, even at this latitude. My gruelling first day had taken its toll; instantly, I drifted off. At zero-five-hundred, just like an alarm clock, the darn birds started singing. There would be no further sleep this morning. Searching through the pack, I remembered we were told there would not be enough food to last through the whole exercise. I should make use of today's pleasant weather to collect food. The rations seemed tasteless; surely, I could find something better.

Not all terrain supported edible plants. The topo map indicated some low-lying areas where sunlight and water would support such plants. With the sun shining through the trees, the spruce grouse could be seen sunning themselves. They should make easy targets.

Spruce grouse were not the brightest creatures, often standing still while they try to assess a threat. Not exactly a smart move; it took only three practice shots before my rock throwing ability was perfected. In short order, I had three birds down. The evening's dinner was in hand.

Grasping the grouse by the legs, standing on both wings, I gave a yank. I now had three perfectly skinned, eviscerated birds—no muss, no fuss. Tying string around the legs, I hung them over my pack to cool.

Onward I pressed to the next waypoint. Should the need arise to retrace my steps, I had stored waypoints in my GPS. Spots along my route that could be easily located.

I had made better time on day two, so I decided to take time that evening to prepare for the night ahead. I needed a place where the light of the fire would not show, a place protected from the wind and rain. Claiming the first usable opening in the rock cliff, I started my foraging. Even in the shelter of my little cave, the potential of detection still existed. Though my location was secluded, the smoke from a campfire could be a problem. Starting a fire would have to wait until after dark.

With so many things to consider, time passed quickly, like grains of sand through an hourglass. The smell of grouse roasting on my improvised spit teased my senses. I was looking forward to my feast. Washing dandelion leaves in a cup of water, I now had a meal fit for royalty. Well, maybe not a king, but definitely for a hungry soldier.

With two days now behind me, I could not help but wonder how the others were doing. Although each man should expect similar terrain, the perils of each route were unknown, and no two routes would be the same. I reviewed the strengths of each of the men, weighing the positives against any weaknesses. Each man had the skill and ability to succeed. I had absolute confidence in them. However, each had to independently pass this test before he could earn a place in the Elite Task Force.

Although tired and slightly exhausted, I soon developed a daily rhythm. By day, I moved closer to my final destination, collecting dandelion leaves, bullrush stems, and whatever other edible plants I could find. As long as the sunny weather held out, I could harvest the plentiful birds, then have a relaxing wild game feast each night. By consuming my military rations in the morning, I could get an early start on each day's departure, leaving ample time for a relaxing evening dinner. Eating military rations in the morning assured me that I would be getting the required nutrients to maintain my energy levels—essential energy required for the long walk each day.

Day three saw me crawling out of the makeshift bed as a noisy blue jay squawked above, swaying back and forth on the overhead pine bough. Unsure if the bird was raising the alert because of other intruders or my presence, I laid still, trying to ignore it, hoping it would go away. Postponing any movement, I listened intently for giveaway signs of what was disturbing the lone bird. Slowly moving my headfirst right, then left, I noticed a lone pair of long, furry legs. Because of its slightly elevated position, I could see the white underbelly and then the brownish-red hair along the side of a bobcat. First one, then two, then eventually three little furballs appeared on the large deadfall immediately to the left. They would pose no threat.

In no hurry to lose touch with the moment, I laid still, watching as the first of the kits walked the length of the huge log. Cautiously, the little cat leaned over the log, taking a long sniff of my boot. The small ball of fur showed no sign of alarm. Young, this feline had never smelled humans; seemingly all caution was cast aside in favour of curiosity.

Suddenly, from downwind, in a small cove of pine trees, a loud shriek permeated the silent air. All three kits, gone in a flash. It was obvious their momma knew the smell of humans or at least predators. Appreciating the moment, I wondered how many people had had such a tender experience with nature.

Munching on breakfast rations, cold grouse left over from the previous night's dinner; I relished the thought of a nice juicy steak. Mentally flashing back, I recalled the ritual that Dad conducted each Saturday in the summer. Grabbing us boys, he would hop in the car for a drive down to our local butcher. Pulling a number from the ticket machine, he would survey the freshly cut steaks on display in the glass-covered cooler. He would take great care to explain the different cuts of meat—the perfect marbling, and how it should never be less than one-and-one-quarter inches thick.

Dad would stand, like an expectant father outside the nursery window, waiting for his number to be called. Heaven forbid someone else should take his target morsels of meat, for then, the entire process would start over. I smiled to myself, recalling how proud Dad looked when he went up to claim his freshly wrapped chunks of beef and then gently place them in the cart. But wait, this exercise was not over yet. The perfect salad accompaniment had to be chosen, for a steak without a salad would be sacrilegious. He had to squeeze and smell each vegetable before placing it into the cart. At the time, I could never understand the need for such detail. After all, it was just a hunk of meat with some vegetables. Looking back now, I realized that my personal need for perfection in everything I attempted was partly due to the meticulous effort that my father displayed in the simplest of things. For a split second, I could smell these steaks of the past sizzling on the grill. All the while, my mouth watered. I realized these sweet memories would have to sustain me for now.

Traversing a large, flat, sun-covered plateau, I decided to take a small detour to investigate what appeared to be a minor clearing west of my present course. Dropping my pack, I prepared to take inventory of my food. As I suspected, rations were running low. If I were to maintain the present rate of travel, I would have to round up some additional grub pronto. Approaching the clearing with a rock poised and ready to fling at any unsuspecting bird, I stopped in my tracks. Immediately ahead, almost totally concealed by the greenery, sat a plump, oversized black bear.

I could see the bear casually eating—what? I was not yet sure. Startling an animal that size was not an option, I pondered my options. I stood motionless, waiting, watching intently as the rather large adversary continued to dine. No time to waste I had to decide to move, risking attack, or startle the bear without advertising my presence. Kneeling, I slowly grasped two fist-sized rocks. Underhand, I whipped one off to the right of the bear. Almost at once, squirrels and birds started to fuss. Disconcerted, the bear stood; erect on its hind legs, it blocked out a lot of skies. This carnivore appeared much, much larger than I had first thought.

Standing motionless, the taller grasses waved in the breeze. The rich blue of the northern sky perfectly accented the bear's sparkling, midnight-black fur. I stared, wanting to burn into my memory the beauty of the moment.

Inwardly, I gave thanks for seeing for the first time the true majesty and beauty of one of God's wild creatures.

Satisfied there was no immediate danger, the bear promptly lowered onto all fours and sauntered away. Quickly newfound courage pushed me forward as the bear headed in the opposite direction; bravely, I stood. I thought one more rock should guarantee the bear's continued departure, but this time I would throw it toward him. Scurrying upward, the bear slowed to a walk before disappearing over the crest of the hill.

To strengthen my courage, I mumbled to myself, "There you go. It should be safe now to approach the clearing."

Curiosity got the better of me. I needed to see what that big bruin had been eating. I could not believe my eyes—a huge patch of plump wild blueberries. With little concern for my safety, I plopped down to the ground, gorging myself with the very abundant stash of berries.

In every direction around me, the plump berries dangled from the stems, just waiting to be picked. Grasping the stems from beneath, my open fingers functioned as a bowl. I drew the berries away from the plant, handful after handful, funnelling the sweetly succulent berries into my mouth. Not even caring about the leaves, I continued until I could eat no more. What a find.

Not sure how long I had been there, I knew I had better get moving. In the distance, large, ominous clouds blackened the sky. Night would soon fall; I needed to hike a few more miles. With a bag full of berries, a smile, and a full belly, I returned to my charted course. Are the other team members having fun like me? Some may consider this work; I gave thanks for all these magnificent gifts. I walked, stopping occasionally to admire the scenery, to cleanse my soul.

Hill after hill, I hiked toward my destination; the clouds were getting darker and more ominous. I would need to find a safe, dry place to spend the night. Observing many large crevices, I was hopeful of soon finding a suitable spot. A small cave would be nice. The thought of sitting under a poncho in a downpour certainly held no appeal.

Ascending a steep hill of slippery rock, I peered over the edge. To my amazement, I stood staring at an old trapper's cabin. A little rundown, but still standing. Cautiously, I approached the front door. After snapping a small twig, I stood in silence, waiting to see if anyone was inside—a sentry, possibly? I had come too far to lose at the game now. Minutes went by with no response. Hesitantly, I knocked—still no response.

Finally, I called out, "Anyone home?" Gently, I pushed on the door, the dry, rusted hinges creaking as they moved.

The cabin had not been occupied in some time, though there were signs of raccoon and bear visitation. Closing the door behind me, I approached the old stone fireplace. With the expectation of heavy rainfall tonight, this would be my best chance of staying dry. I grinned. What a stroke of luck. With heavy rainfall, there would be little chance that the spotters would stay out in the open. A nice fire would provide me warmth—a chance to remove the dampness from my clothing.

Hurrying around to gather the necessary firewood and grasses, I held little concern for being detected. With no need to use my poncho, that night I could string it across a couple of pine boughs to collect some much-needed drinking water. By deflecting the freshwater into my open canteen below, I wouldn't need treated water. If it rained all night, I should have more than enough fresh water for the following day.

With my dinner of dandelion leaves and blueberries completed, I sat back, peering through the window at the beauty of the approaching darkness. Raindrops tapped on the roof, relaxing my tired body until, finally, I faded off. Safe and warm, I quickly drifted into my first peaceful sleep in days.

Ka-thump! Noises from outside, I stirred to the sound of footsteps. Human? No, I thought not. Light sniffing sounds as it walked—it had to be a timber wolf or bear. Swallowing deeply, fear enveloped me. Cautiously, the animal worked its way around the porch, sniffing and probing each opening or crack in the wallboards, the old porch creaking with each step.

The prowler was now behind the cabin, I grasped my sidearm. Rising to my knees, I slowly peered out the window. Lying on a rock ledge facing the cabin was a lone wolf. Its large grey head lay motionless, staring intently toward the cabin door. Poised, ready to pounce, the animal sentry patiently watched, waiting to detect any fleeing prey. The prowling wolf currently out of sight behind the cabin—meant an escape in either direction was impossible.

With the door bolted shut, I needed only to watch the windows. Motionless, with my hand on my loaded firearm, I grew increasingly anxious. Darkness was falling around the small cabin; with every minute, it became harder to make out the motionless form. Were there only two, or were there more?

Perched atop the ledge, the supreme killer monitored the cabin. In all the trips I had taken with Dad, never had I been confronted with such a situation. Concern wrinkled my brow. Did the wolves know I was there? Were they stalking me? Were there more of them? If so, what could I expect them to do next? Tension mounted.

Growing more restless by the minute, I took a deep breath, mumbling aloud, "*Stay calm.*"

I had to occupy my mind. Looking around, I started taking stock of the situation. I had the door locked. To get at me, the wolves would have to break through the glass-filled panes of the windows—not likely. Most important, I had my handgun.

Sitting in the corner, the handgun lay across my lap. Tightly wrapped within my fingers, the cold of the grip gradually warmed from my touch. If I fired it, everyone within miles would know I was there. I did not want to exercise this option but would if needed.

Slowly, the hours crept by; twenty-one-hundred, twenty-two-hundred hours. Straining my ears and listening for the slightest sound, I finally succumbed to the warmth of the cabin and the darkness of the night. The pitter-patter of rain on the roof lulled me into a deep sleep. That night I slept, and for the first time in days, I was even permitted to dream.

Honking of geese flying low overhead, the anxious yelps of the older birds encouraging the young ones to speed up, eventually stirred me from my slumber. Just five more minutes of sleep was all I wanted. Stiff from the hardness of the old wooden floor, I rolled over, supporting myself on one knee. With a yawn, I slowly stood erect. Peering through the foggy glass, I could see that the ledge was no longer occupied. The wolves had had enough, departing in search of easier prey. A glance of the surrounding bush, and the small cabin, convinced me the wolves had indeed left. I could now get on with preparing for the coming day.

Still groggy from the short night's sleep, I staggered toward the lake. Kneeling on a rock, I reached both hands into the clear, chilly water and grabbed some instant awakening. Icy water splashed on my face promptly erased my sleepiness. Four days without a shower, I could detect my musk and eagerly welcomed the thought of a nice, hot shower.

A quick breakfast and I could be on my way. Yuk, it tasted awful. Peering at the black ink etching on the side of the chow pouch, I could see that it was outdated—by two years! Was someone trying to kill me, or was this just another test? If not a test, then someone was going to get hell.

A quick look at the remaining chow packets proved equally disappointing; they had the same stale-dated marking. Without the proper nutrition, I would not make it through the next couple of days, nor would I be able to complete the mission.

Protein and vitamins were what I needed. *OK, what did I have at hand? Vitamin C, I could get from pine tea. Protein, from meats. I had no more grouse to eat, and the sky was overcast, so the birds would not be sunning themselves. Hunting them would not come easy. Looking out across the small lake, it became obvious. There sat a beaver dam: sticks and debris, piled high above the water-line—a beaver dam means meat.*

Walking down to the dam, telltale signs of recent activity lay all about. Based on the muddy trail to the water's edge, the channel to the dam opening would lie concealed below the water surface. Quickly, all I needed to know became clear. Moments later, a furry resident surfaced, heading up the bank. If I set a trap while the varmint was gone, capture upon its return should prove successful.

Aligning the lower log with the balanced, heavier log overhead, the trap was set. When the beaver would pass under and bump the horizontal trip stick, the overhead pole would drop, supplying the crushing death blow. All I had to do now was wait. Two hours passed before the waddling inhabitant made its way back to the water's edge.

Cautiously, the beaver approached the trap. It could smell the human activity and did not appear to like it. Slowly, it passed under the trip stick, dislodging the support—down came the executioner's log! From across the little bay, it was easy to see that the weight of the log had snapped its neck. After a quick retrieval of the carcass, I went back to the cabin ready to cook breakfast.

The embers of last night's fire still glowed; in no time at all, the backstraps were sizzling, ready to eat. With a nice hot cup of pine tea and a belly full of beaver meat, I would have sufficient nutrition for the day. Tomorrow, I could eat the remainder. Although I had never previously eaten beaver, I found it quite tasty. I chuckled to myself. That remark could have taken on a completely different meaning if the rest of my team had been present.

Day five: what challenges lay ahead for the day? Aligning my site and go path for the day, I set out. According to the topo map, there should have been a lake ahead. It looked as though the terrain would be flat up to the lake, but a significant elevation change was indicated just short of the lake. This could mean only one thing. I would have to rappel a cliff or waste considerably more time circling the lengthy cliff that lay directly in my path.

I reached into my pack for the rope. I hoped the hundred feet of rope would be long enough; if not, my day would be a long one. I would be forced to do a lot more walking. With all my time alone, I had become accustomed to talking to myself and chuckled once I heard the sound of my voice.

Over the edge, I could see the drop-off to the lake, and beyond that, the distant shoreline. It would take me about an hour to circle the end of the lake; after that, I would be able to see what tasks remained for me today. Shortly, I would find this would not be my lucky day.

Checking my GPS, then the map, it appeared that I would be able to complete my travels the next day. As long as I could get down the cliff by sundown today.

My mission briefing had been clear, reach my objective, find the terrorist, then execute a killing shot—all of it needed to happen without being detected.

It sounded simple, but I knew there would be more tests for tomorrow. For now, I had to get down to the bottom of this cliff. Tied to the nearest tree, I lowered the rope to its full length, noting it was about twenty feet short. That distance would be too much of a drop. I needed to do something to get myself closer to the bottom. Removing my pack, I looked about for anything that would help. If only I could find some wild vines, I could lash them together to make a rope. Around home, we had all kinds; here, I could see none.

How about deadfalls? Black spruce trees lay scattered around. Winter here was hard on the forest. All the fallen trees were too rotten to use; I would need a live tree. Grabbing onto the top of a partly uprooted tree, I angled it toward the cliff. The additional length was only going to gain ten feet, I would need to find the other ten. If there was nothing to hold onto near the bottom of the cliff, it would mean a ten-foot drop.

If I secure a clove hitch around the tree, then pulled with all my might, I should be able to assess the holding capability. If luck was with me, it would hold my weight; I could not afford for it to let go when I was halfway down. Confident that the tree and knot would hold, I donned my pack then slung my rifle across my back. The decisive moment arrived as I crawled over the edge.

The thought of extra strain on the tree concerned me. The standard rappelling practice of pushing off the wall then dropping down would surely cause a jerk. With each push off from the rocks, the risk would increase. I could not take that chance. I would need to keep constant pressure on the rope, avoiding any jerking actions.

I cannot afford a fall, not from this height, flashed through my consciousness as I relaxed my grip. As I lowered cautiously, the rope stretched. With each foot I dropped, the palms of my hands grew hotter. Two hundred pounds, plus a fifty-pound pack, plus my gun—that tree was under considerable strain. The shallow root base had already been damaged when the tree had blown over. I sensed danger. I knew I had to take time to stop and further assess my situation. Moss and slime were all over the rock face; there wouldn't be any solid footing. I would need to rest occasionally on the way down—couldn't risk a fall.

With all this weight, my arms tired quickly. Stopping partway down, I rested. Briefly, I looked out across the forest below. The song "What a Wonderful World" by Louis Armstrong came to mind as I beheld the vista below. Mist from a waterfall billowed upward across the rock face, casting a rainbow across the dampness that covered every crevice. On the lake below, a pair of northern loons called their echoing cry as they drifted peacefully about.

Wow—what a morning. Every one of my senses tingled, filling me with awe as the sunlight glistened off the rocky face. For a moment, I thought of Dad—how he loved to lean against the base of a tree, trying to describe moments just like this to me. At that early age, I did not quite get it, but now with no distractions, I could finally smell, almost taste, those very feelings.

I wished the embassy bombing in South Africa had never severed Dad's spine, never destroyed the chance of his ever again enjoying moments like this. The ever-present hatred and contempt—the same emotions that had driven me on—crept back into my consciousness, pushing away my moment of pleasure.

Instantly I became aware of my current predicament—I hung on tight. Cross-legged around the rope, my boots squeezed securely above the large knot; the only thing between me and the rocky ground. Ten feet of free air; between me and the ground below. Standing erect, I hung precariously onto the rope. I must now decide what to do, a jump from this height could result in a sprained ankle or, worse yet, a broken one.

I gazed across the rock face, a handhold, a hole in the rocks. *Not a chance.* Andrew James's incident with the rattlesnake provided an easy decision: I was not going to reach into any hole, safe or not. The only option would be for me to drop hand over hand down to the rope knot. Once there, I would have to free-fall to the rocks below. With a leap of faith, I opened the space between my boots descending downward. I squeezed tighter on the rope, moving slowly downward until both hands gripped the bottom knot. I now hung helplessly. I had no other choice but to find a soft landing spot. *If I can only push out a couple more feet away from the cliff, the softness of the grass should break my fall*, I hoped.

Pushing off the wall with both feet, I expected to be able to let go of the rope and fall to the grass below—all I heard was a snap, and, seconds later, a thud as my head hit the ground below. Flat on my back, lying face-up on top of the backpack and rifle, I watched a hundred feet of rope drop from above. An intense ringing began in my head.

I lay motionless, afraid to move; fear set in. The pack and rifle had taken the major brunt of my fall, while my head felt like it had taken the rest. Wiggling my extremities one by one, I checked for broken bones. Everything seemed OK. As I rolled to the right, a trickle of something warm ran from my ear and down my jaw.

Testing with a glove-covered hand showed a smear of red, which meant only one thing: I had cut the back of my head, or worse, incurred a concussion. This was serious—a short rest was in order. I needed to assess the situation and my physical condition.

Leaning against a nearby stump, my situation became obvious—acute personal damage had occurred. My pack looked fine, but my rifle; destroyed.

The scope and laser unit were smashed. Even if I made it to the destination, I could no longer complete the mission, at least not alone. Testing all my extremities could find no further injuries. Rolling up the rope proved a little more painful than I hoped. Even pondering my options hurt.

Two hours passed—still, the back of my head throbbed. With each pulse of blood passing to my brain, intense pain shot upward through my skull. Sharp, excruciating pain that hurt like hell. I sorely needed to take a pain-killer, but I feared a possible concussion, and the painkiller could do me more harm than good. Just going slow and resting frequently seemed to help. *Oh boy, Spencer, this is another fine mess you've got yourself into.* Humour was the only thing that helped diminish the pain, but the throbbing continued.

The last leg of the mission lay ahead. What should have been the easiest part of the trip had quickly turned into the most difficult. This final leg of the journey was working out to be more draining than I ever could have imagined. With the C7 rendered useless as a weapon.

Adapt and overcome. Quickly my options flashed through my aching head. Tie a tree branch to the rifle barrel, it should make an adequate crutch, walking over the rough terrain, I would now need one.

Extracting my knife, I proceeded to cut strands from my rope, securely assembling my temporary support. Considerable time had been lost, time I could not make up.

Damn, why did this have to happen now? I am so close.

Taking another of my frequent breaks, I worried. I could not fail now. I knew today was going to be a long, painful day and I needed to re-think my plan. More importantly, I needed to heal. Confident that the others would be nearing the site, I knew my options were limited. The painful realization became clear. I could no longer do it alone. I needed to devise a plan to get one of the others to collaborate with me. With help, I could still achieve the desired outcome. For me, it appeared the only workable option.

Resting, trying to get my bearings I peered through my binoculars, There, behind a cluster of tall trees. The makeshift camp stood alone on an island.

Clearly the planning team had picked the spot well. The cabin stood just over the brow of the rock edge, partially hidden behind piles of downfall and wooden debris. Without my GPS to alert me that I had reached my destina-tion, I may well have walked right past it. Approaching from this direction, the cabin lay well concealed. Nearby the river split, creating an island with two faster-flowing and treacherous bodies of water. One more obstacle to overcome. Closing in on the encampment, I suspected additional sentries may well be present, or at least they would be more alert.

With each step, stabbing spears of pain shot up the side of my head. Still hurting like hell, I had to ignore the pain and focus on the objective. My reconnaissance of the site revealed no other human movement. Glassing through distant trees, I felt confident I was the first to arrive. To this point, it appeared there were no other identifiable hazards. Dropping my now useless rifle and heavy pack to the ground, I sat to rest. The others would also work their way around the area before attempting an attack—they too would be just as cagey.

My pack and rifle would be of no further use,. I could not afford for any of the other team members to find my discarded gear. Except for the poncho and rope, I would have no further use for the extra items. I would have to conceal them. Essentials aside, I covered the remainder with branches and debris.

My best plan appeared to be to wait until after dark to traverse the river, approach from the north end of the island, then climb onto the island. I would need to use every trick I knew. With the prevailing winds coming from the west, a crosswind would blow my scent away rather than into the camp, where it could potentially alert the awaiting enemy.

Covered in leaves, I concealed myself on the forest floor. Tucked in under a large downfall, I monitored the site. From here, I could see the river below, and any individuals should they wander by. The log had fallen across a heavily used moose trail. This would be the logical spot for anyone else to survey the cabin. Just as I had done, they too would probably follow this route.

Mission rules did not prevent me from taking out or immobilizing other competing members. Without a weapon, I would have to depend on this option. My plan seemed solid. At best, I will have to surprise one of my rivals, execute their capture, then solicit their help. *Yep, it seemed like a good plan.*

My concealed rope tied to a nearby tree would provide an ideal trip hazard for any unsuspecting adversaries. Laying motionless under my green poncho, I held onto the loose end of the rope, ready, waiting for the moment when I could pull it tight, and making the first unsuspecting soldier a captive and ultimately my accomplice. That was assuming that my prey would be accommodating.

Half asleep, I could hear the soft crunching of leaves—footsteps approaching from the east. Unable to see what it was, I readied the rope. Blocked by the fallen log, I lay motionless, not able to tell if it was animal or human. Slowly, the crunching sounds approached. Unable to move for fear of detection, I lay waiting. Whatever it was, it did not appear to be in a hurry. *Oh shit, it's right on top of me.*

Perched on top of the log directly above me, the sounds stopped. In the fading evening light, I suddenly realized my rope trick would be of no use. I would need to improvise. I dared not move. The ensuing seconds seemed like an hour. The throbbing in my head increased as the tension built.

Confident I had the upper hand, I lay waiting for some sign of who or what stood perched above me. Almost without sound, a black army boot descended from above. Relieved that it was not a wild animal, I grabbed the leg and pulled backward. The near-silent intruder fell face-first onto the ground. Leaping forward from under the log, I clasped my hand around the intruder's shoulders, covering his mouth. I did not know who it was... but I needed to avoid any outcry or excessive noise.

In an instant, the form found his legs and raised both him and me out of the mud.

"Private James, is that you?" I asked.

I held tight as my victim cleared the mud from his face. As he nodded acknowledgment, I released my grip. With a gesture of silence, we knelt. "Lieutenant, I would have expected you to have already made the kill."

I smiled. "I would have, but I had an accident. My weapon is broken, and I am hurting. The rules allow us to team up. You in?"

I already knew he would accept, for if he refused, he would be out of the game. Should he refuse, Private James could still graduate; however, he would not have the accomplished accreditation mission in his file. After all, that's what this was about. Tucked in beside the log, he pondered my offer.

Quietly, I proceeded to outline the plan to the private. "If you have a better idea, let's hear it; otherwise, we should get started."

Private James had come to respect my decisions. Though he knew the chain of command and would have to follow the orders anyway, he could see that his opinion was valued; we agreed the plan was workable.

"OK, let's get started."

It felt gratifying as again we were acting as a team, increasing our odds of completing the mission. Darkness arrived as we stripped down to our underwear and boots. Wrapped in our rubber ponchos the clothing should stay dry. Private James quickly tied the rope around his waist. We both knew in my weakened condition I would need help, something to hang onto as I traversed the river; an uncontrolled slip could mean sure disaster.

"Damn this is cold," both of us simultaneously exclaimed as the water enveloped our legs and up past our waists.

Both of us were very aware that extended exposure to this extreme cold could cause heart failure—our hearts raced, our lungs gasped for air. Once our bodies adjusted to the temperature, we started to move into the current. With the private's rifle and our clothes above his head, he let the northbound current push him slowly toward the island. Securing the rope to a nearby tree, he signalled for me to come over. The extreme cold of the water now turned my skin blue. With my recent likely concussion, I needed to get out of the water fast—shock or hypothermia posed a considerable risk.

Shivering uncontrollably, I navigated the muddy bottom, sinking inches into the soft silt with each step. Like a suction cup, the mud held onto my boots as I strained to walk forward. With each second in the water, spikes of pain shot through the back of my skull. I could feel my energy being sucked away. Pulling firmly on the rope, Private James rushed to get me ashore.

There could be a problem. Now he had to get me out of the water. Steadily, as mud gave way to the rocky shore, the walking became easier. Cold, exhausted, I crawled onto the rocks.

"Lieutenant, it's just a short crawl up the rocks to where you will be on the soft grasses. Can you stay with me? I will get you warm once we are there. OK?"

"Private, my head is killing me."

"Lieutenant, I need you to focus. I do not have anything to give you, but when we reach the top, I will get you warm. Hopefully, then the throbbing will stop."

Out of the water, even the cool night air felt warm. The rocky surface, although slippery, remained the best approach to the small meadow above. Lying at my side in the tall grass, Private James wrapped his arms tightly around me. Our body contact transferred heat, stalling hypothermia and shock. Boots removed, we proceeded to dress into our warm dry clothing, regaining colour gradually as our warmth returned. Now protected from the cool west wind, we warmed rapidly.

Tonight, would be our only chance to sneak up on the target and execute the kill; continuing had become our only option. With no food or protection, the need to keep moving had quickly become our primary concern.

There had been no other movement near the camp. It did not appear that the other members had arrived yet, but we expected them shortly—at least by morning.

As midnight approached, we cautiously crawled toward the debris pile. Peering toward the wooden hut, I could see flickering light from a Coleman lantern. Someone moved about inside. Someone was exiting the cabin.

Slowly, Private James switched on his rifle laser. Each soldier had his gun equipped with a laser beeper and wore a red flasher light. Whenever the rifle trigger was pulled and the gun aligned, the red light of the beeper badge would flash, and the alarm would beep. We waited for the would-be terrorist to turn around—providing a clear shot at the target. Any second Private James would fire, I waited for the alarm to sound.

The private readied to shoot, the boom of a Browning handgun exploded, breaking the silence of the night. The target flung open the door, stepping out into the moonlight. Although I knew something was seriously wrong, we were trained to let nothing distract us. The shooter must make the kill to complete the mission. As soon as the moonlight reflected off the target's badge, Private James pulled the trigger; the red shining light confirmed a hit.

Simultaneously, another shot rang out—the sound of a live round echoed throughout the darkness. Someone was in trouble. Running up to the target, I shut off the light and removed the beeper alert; Private James and I both ran for the south shore. A second shot rang out, confirming the direction we needed to follow. We hopped into the boat, screaming could be heard. Running toward the sounds, we both unholstered our sidearms. Approaching, we could see a large bear mauling someone, the sound of bones cracking, flesh being torn away, and screams filling the air. With each bite of the bear's jaws, a new scream rang out, again breaking the silence of the bush. Quickly, we aimed, both discharging our weapons at the black object. The bear turned to face us, rising onto its hind legs it leaped forward. Two more blasts rang out as the bear collapsed at our feet.

As we had suspected, other members of the team were indeed there; the bush came to life as each member of the team yelled out to report their position, each trying to establish what had happened. Jones, David, Richie, and Andrew reported to the attack site to find me kneeling beside Wil. It appeared, Wil had attempted to protect his face from his attacker. There was blood spewing out of large gashes made by the bear's powerful claws, and numerous bite marks were visible where its powerful canines had punctured the skin. Broken and mangled, Wil's arm hung down beside his body, blood spurting profusely.

An artery has been severed. "Jones, hold pressure on the wound, while I check the other his right leg."

Afraid that the femoral artery was also severed, I removed Wil's shoelace and swiftly applied a tourniquet. Just as Wil took his last breath, Private Dunsmoore returned to the attack site. The first aid kit would no longer be needed. Twenty minutes passed—CPR, unsuccessful. The loss of blood had been too severe.

"Set up a perimeter, we need to protect the site until morning" I ordered. "A full investigation will be launched after day-break."

The radio located in the cabin crackled, emergency personnel would be dispatched shortly. The mission had been completed; however, not one of us wanted to celebrate. The thrill and intrigue of the night exercises had just lost their appeal. We all dreaded the coming of sunrise. We knew the light of morning would present a more gruesome picture.

THE FUNERAL

Sadness overwhelmed me as I gazed out my office window. Although the sun was shining, and it was in every way a beautiful day, I could not bring myself to smile. In front on the desk sat the incident folder for the accident with Private William Wright. His name was written in bold letters, and below it, in red, the word "Deceased."

Slowly, I turned my chair, facing the old, weathered desk. Methodically, I started reviewing the autopsy and incident report. From the evidence present in the light of day, it was found that Wil, under the cover of darkness, had inadvertently wandered between a sow and her cubs. The combination of small and larger paw prints showed there were at least two cubs. Without any warning, the sow attacked, easily killing Private William Wright. Unknowingly, Wil the predator had become the prey.

The rest of the report was filled with medical facts and terms, terms that only further reinforced the fact Wil was dead. Slowly, I closed the folder. Placing it in the file cabinet, I saluted Wil, my friend.

Tomorrow, along with our commanding officer, I would have to travel to Private Wright's hometown to inform his parents of the tragic accident resulting in the death of their son. This I did not look forward to. We had been friends since grade school; this would not be easy. Staring at a four-by-six photograph, my eyes welled up, tears running down my cheeks. I stood, recalling the many times Wil's sense of humour had brought joy to the team, how his down-home humour had made them laugh. I already deeply missed him.

Standing at the door, we waited. Having pushed the doorbell once, to no reply, I pushed it again. Moments later, footsteps could be heard approaching the door. A tall, heavy-set man opened the door. "Can I help you?" Mr. Wright stood motionless in the doorway.

With a sombre tone, the base commander introduced himself. "Mr. Wright, do you mind if we come in, sir?"

A brief smile passed over Mr. Wright's face when he recognized me, but it was obvious he knew something was wrong. I could see the colour draining from the face of the elderly man as he ushered us into the small, tidy sitting room. Deliberately, the base commander directed me to sit in the chairs facing the sofa. Mr. and Ms. Wright would need to be near each other when the sad news was delivered. Wil was an only child; this was going to be difficult.

I strained to find the words. Breathing deeply before each sentence, I informed them that their son Wil had been killed during a nighttime exercise.

With tears running down her cheeks, the fragile woman tried to push the words from her now dry lips. "How did it happen?" were the only words she could force out.

As they consoled each other, both stared teary-eyed across the room. On the mantle sat an eight-by-ten framed picture of Wil in his dress uniform, smiling as usual. Looking directly at the sobbing couple, I proceeded to explain the events of that fateful evening. How Wil had reached the destination, how he set out planning his final approach to the island cabin. Inadvertently, he had slipped between a sow bear and her cubs. Mauled by the bear, Wil eventually succumbed to massive blood loss.

Although very thorough, I could not bring myself to provide all the gruesome details. We could feel their pain and did not wish to make it any worse. If requested, they would be given a copy of the autopsy report, but for now, the slightly watered-down details would have to be sufficient.

Quite sure that his parents already knew, but for some unknown reason, I reminded them that Wil was a good soldier. He loved what he did with every grain of his being.

I stood staring into the full-length mirror in my drab motel room, knowing full well that the next time I put on my dress uniform would be for Wil Wright's funeral. In officer training, they had tried to prepare us for death, even the loss of friends. Somehow, at this moment, it did not seem to help.

The team arrived at the funeral home early that day. In full dress uniform, we all stood at attention beside the flag-covered coffin. After the minister completed the service, friends and family were asked if they would like to say a few words.

I had been elected to represent the team. Approaching the microphone, tribute in hand, the emotion started welling up inside me. I, personally, had never lost a close friend. Opening the pages, my mind flashed back and forth between our many memories. The time spent together—the laughs of the good times, the tears of the bad—all came back as pictures of Wil flashed continuously on the projection screen.

Clenching my teeth together, the tears dripped down my cheeks. Trying hard to collect myself, I just stood there, not knowing how long. I had practised this speech many times, confident I could manage the task, yet not truly knowing how hard this was going to be. I knew this would be tough, but I didn't realize just how tough.

A sniffle from the front row jerked me back to reality. I had to complete the tribute before I lost it completely. With a deep breath, I sighed, continuing, as more pictures flashed steadily across the screen. Such intense feelings of loss—feelings I hoped I would never have to repeat.

Wil's death had placed a hole in my heart, one I expected could not be repaired. Oh, how I would miss my dearest friend. Reluctantly I completed my tribute, the team saluted Wil. Six individuals who had laughed and cried with Wil now carried his casket. To the sound of bagpipes, six sombre men placed Wil at the site: his final resting place. Family, friends, and all the base personnel circled round, paying homage.

"Ashes to ashes, dust to dust..." I fell sobbing to my knees as the casket descended almost out of sight.

Back at the Quonset hut the team raised their glasses, "To Wil." Each offering up one last toast, acknowledging their friendship—a tribute to the time they had spent together.

Reaching into my mail slot, I pulled out an inter-office memo signed by the base commander. This looked important. "Your team's attendance is required in the auditorium at zero-eight-hundred tomorrow."

Stepping sharply into the auditorium, the team stood in their CADPAT fatigues. At attention, they waited for the commander's arrival.

"Room," I called out. All conversation ceased. Promptly, I saluted.

With a snappy salute, the commander directed the men to be seated. "Gentlemen, warning orders.

"Your pre-orders are as follows. We have been requested to create a Special Forces Branch to assist the allied forces in infiltrating and destroying Taliban terrorists now situated in Afghanistan.

"Numerous teams from across Canada, in all branches of our armed forces, are being assembled as we speak.

"Due to your outstanding performance, I am pleased to announce, that your team has been selected from our base to join the JTF 2 Elite Forces Branch. Your training will commence immediately. As of today, your team code is Alpha.

"Recently, the Taliban have gained in numbers as well as financial backing. They have currently taken up residence in Afghanistan's northeastern region, near the Pakistan border.

"As you know, the terrain is rugged, and the weather harsh. To enable us to weed out the resistance forces, your team will need to undergo more intense training. To take down the Taliban, top physical conditioning is paramount. Training will be harder and longer in some of the harshest environments you can imagine. In short, you will need to toughen up.

"Lieutenant Cook will be the point.

"Lieutenant, would you please stay behind so I can fill you in on the details."

Waiting patiently for the room to clear, a rush of excitement and anticipation came over me—not because of the fact that we were going to war, but because I could sense I was about to make a difference.

PART FOUR

THE NEW THREAT

The base was a beehive of activity as increased effort became directed toward the defence against terrorism. Studying movements of known dissidents, their associates, and their communication techniques as well became a daily routine. A new task force of local police and RCMP anti-terrorism forces was established. Temporary headquarters were established at the base, and the presence of armed guards at airports and large gatherings stepped up.

I remembered the incident in Toronto during the spring of 2006. Individuals were apprehended partly due to a tip given to the Greater Toronto Airports Authority police. The security report indicated a civilian noticed a suspicious individual loitering around an airline check-in. This individual would approach passengers waiting at the check-in terminals. He would then engage them in a conversation while scanning the check-in area, watching how passengers were being checked through security—apparently looking for weaknesses in the system.

At this particular check-in location, a middle-aged couple waiting for a friend to arrive noticed a man about to check in for their flight to Mexico. The husband became suspicious when the individual informed them, he had just arrived on the red-eye. The husband noticed this individual had no luggage, not even a carry-on. The husband was unsure if red-eye flights even arrived at Pearson.

As they were chatting, the husband noticed the young male moving about, always keeping the husband between himself and the armed security guard. Not thinking any more of it, the husband said farewell to his wife and friend as they checked in for their flight to Mexico. On his drive home, the young male's behaviour started bothering the older man. The following morning, he decided to call the airport police. Upon calling, he notified the officer of the suspicious behaviour and was immediately questioned as to why he had not alerted security officials at the time. His response: his sister was terminally ill, and the airport issue was not foremost in his mind. Only after a night's sleep did he give this puzzling activity any further thought. All the threats and bombings going on, linked with the fact that his wife was on the airplane being suspiciously scrutinized he felt it was his responsibility to report his observations.

In the following weeks, the Canadian media was all abuzz when a group of eighteen Muslim extremists, dubbed the Toronto 18, were captured and charged. Among their planned crimes—detonating truck bombs, open firing on a crowded area, bombing buildings in Toronto's business community—all became public knowledge. Threats of beheading the Canadian prime minister added to the list of charges. Shortly after, two men accused of plotting to derail a VIA Rail passenger train travelling between Canada and the USA were arrested, as were eight others from the airport incident. These men were also found guilty of a whole series of terror-related charges—murder for the benefit of, at the direction of, or in association with a terrorist group topped the list.

The Canadian government had just received its first taste of terrorism. The political landscape across Canada was changing, but not for the better. Leafing through the inter-office mail, I flipped open a memo. A special meeting had been arranged: "All officers to report to the drill hall for ten-hundred hours today, October 1."

The room was abuzz with activity. All base officers from corporals up were milling around. The rumour was the Canadian military forces were being deployed to Afghanistan.

The commanding officer stepped up to the microphone; swiftly, the men saluted.

A salute, followed by a light blow into the microphone, confirmed he could start. "Have a seat, gentlemen."

Quickly, each grabbed a chair, anticipating the news.

"9/11 marked the start of a worldwide push against terrorism. I know you have all seen the footage of the World Trade Center attacks—numerous times, I am sure.

"We have witnessed senseless slaughter of thousands of innocent people and the needless destruction of millions of dollars of property. NATO and our allies are outraged.

"As part of NATO, we will be committing troops and equipment to Afghanistan immediately. Starting December 1, we will be sending six Aurora patrol aircraft as well as Hercules and Polaris transport planes to the Kandahar area of Afghanistan.

"Air Command will also be patrolling the waters off Southwest Asia for surveillance as well as troop support.

"The first of our troops to be deployed will be our JTF 2 Elite Task Force. Working in conjunction with the American and British special forces, it will be JTF 2's job to clear the area of Taliban insurgents in preparation for larger troop deployments.

"Ground troops will be leaving in January. From that point forward we will be focused on eliminating any confirmed or suspected terrorists. The intent is to return political stability to the area. Gentlemen, make no mistake: this is war, and we will lose good soldiers.

"Troop equipment supply lists have already been prepared. They can be picked up on your way out.

"Your orders will be issued shortly; you are to report with your teams as directed. Good luck, gentlemen.

"Dismissed."

We needed to prepare; we needed to tell our families. Each officer was aware that in the coming days, we would be shipping out. The safety of home would soon end.

PART FIVE

CAMP NATHAN SMITH, AFGHANISTAN

Two days later, deployment of the Canadian troops to Afghanistan saw us thrust into the heart of an active conflict. No more schools or practice drills—this was the real thing, a place where people were crippled and killed. As the troops would soon learn, in this type of guerrilla warfare, the enemy had no rules of engagement. The boys would soon find out the Taliban were ruthless and determined adversaries.

Puffs of dark smoke rose, and rubber squealed as the Hercules aircraft touched down on the dirt runway. Taxiing around huge clouds of sand, the plane headed toward a cluster of tented structures near the north end of the runway. "Camp Nathan Smith" stood out in bold black letters at the end of the runway.

Located on a flat area of land far from the desolate, low rolling hills, this tented community housed the Canadian troops in Kandahar. In 2002, Canada had seen its first casualty; the camp had then been renamed in honour of their fallen comrade. The name stood as a constant reminder that they were at war. The tented barracks, nestled behind concrete barriers, awaited our arrival; this was to be our home for the coming months. A place of safety—a place we would all grow to hate.

Deliberately making direct eye contact with each of my team, I said, "This is it, boys. Put on your game faces.

"Sergeant, take the men over to the barracks. Wait for me there."

"Aye, sir."

Squinting, my eyes nearly closed, I walked into the blowing sand. Here for not even five minutes and already I had sand in places I did not know existed. The realization soon befell me: this would not be a walk in the park.

Standing at attention, I waited for the commanding officer to raise his gaze. "Alpha Team reporting for duty, sir."

"Welcome aboard, Lieutenant. I assume you had a pleasant trip over?"

Jokingly, I replied, "Slept like a baby all the way here." Actually, I was exhausted. I hadn't slept a wink. Day one proved interesting. All but one of us had the "Kandahar Kurds." Frequent trips to the latrine helped, while Imodium took care of the rest.

"Lieutenant, our mission, dubbed Operation Medusa, will involve one thousand Canadian troops. The objective is to eliminate the Taliban forces in the Panjwai district.

"Our first mission will be to purge the Tajikistani section of Kandahar City. As you can see on the map, there are a total of five districts within the city perimeter.

"We will be methodically working our way through the different districts. There continues to be a lot of rooftop activity, so we will need your sniper team to assume position on the key rooftops here. From these buildings, your boys will have a clear view of the rooftops, as well as the streets below.

"Bravo and Charlie teams will have their snipers set up here and here." The red laser pointer moved about the map, circling the points of interest.

"From these three buildings, they should be able to protect our boys on the first two full blocks. Your snipers, as well as two men on the ground, will remain at the starting point until the sweep is complete.

"There is a chance they will try to circle behind our boys on the ground, so keep your eyes peeled.

"When these two blocks have been cleared, your sniper teams will relocate to the next three buildings here, here, and here.

"Once we have cleared the first two streets, Charlie Team will remain in place while Alpha and Bravo teams relocate. The plan is to have the five full blocks cleared by nightfall.

"Alpha, Bravo, and Charlie teams will run parallel to each other. As you can see, the streets all converge to a central market area near the north end. You will be executing a door-to-door search. Your orders are to eliminate anyone of military age and anyone who poses a threat. As soon as we have completed our mission, the UN security forces will take over to maintain order and keep the Taliban forces from returning.

"Since Alpha Team does not have an experienced medic, I have assigned you Lieutenant Renner. Lieutenant Renner has been here from day one. He will no doubt be an asset."

Driving along the bumpy street, Alpha Team could hear bullets bouncing off the outside of their troop carriers. Already their arrival had been relayed to the local resistance; it seemed obvious that our soldiers were not wanted here.

"Private, why don't you let them know we also have bullets?"

Standing erect through the top of the armoured patrol vehicle, Private Dunsmoore cocked the fifty-calibre machine gun and returned fire at the approaching rooftops. Bullets bounced off the reflector plates. For a brief moment, he was glad that these peasants were lousy shots.

Three armoured vehicles turned down each of the streets. By the sounds outside, Bravo and Charlie teams were meeting with the same resistance as Alpha Team. The three APVs slowed to a crawl, bullets from the two machine guns and the single grenade launcher scattering fire into the surrounding doorways and rooftops.

In the distance, locals could be seen scattering from building to building as the machine-gun fire increased. Repeated blasts from the fifty-calibre machine gun cast holes through walls and roof edges, keeping the would-be snipers away from the roof edges.

As the turret spun back to the left, a yell came from above. "Lieutenant, you can get out now."

As the tailgate swung upward, I jumped from the rear of the now stationary vehicle. I was anything but a coward, but at this moment I was scared shitless. Even though there was an increased danger for the first man out of the APV, I knew the team gained strength from my willingness to lead the way. One second the door was opening; the next, I was out and against the closest wall.

Gusts of wind swirled around in every direction, blowing razor-sharp particles against my face. I did not like wearing goggles, but today I was glad to have them. Ushering the rest of Alpha Team toward the door, we readied to enter the first building.

"Two men clear the building. We need our spotter and sniper on the roof now—we are too vulnerable. Hustle, we need his eyes, now!"

Gunfire rang out, distant this time but still too close for comfort. Everywhere, I could see signs of previous battles. Concrete walls sprayed with bullet holes. Spent cartridges everywhere. All along the abandoned street, vehicles lay destroyed, burned out, useless. They were broken-down relics, witnesses to prior battles, and examples of futile attempts to overtake this Taliban stronghold.

"Dunsmoore, you and James cover us from the alley. Sergeant Parker, you take Miller—get this building cleared. We need Jones up on the roof.

"OK, you all know the drill, sweep each building room by room. Keep blind spots covered, watch the rooftops. For God's sake, watch for bloody booby traps."

Private Dunsmoore hustled into the alleyway. From there, he could see Bravo Team running from their APVs. Two quick bursts of gunfire from an adjacent rooftop struck a soldier square in the chest. The distinctive thud of the bullet hitting flesh was unmistakable.

He stopped, rigid, in his tracks, as two more rounds pierced his vest. Mouth open, he fell back against his team member, tumbling into the dirt as his blood sprayed the men around him. Dunsmoore instantly froze in his tracks. Wide-eyed, he stared as Bravo Team members wiped the dripping blood from their goggles. Never having witnessed a man die, Dunsmoore stood frozen in his tracks. Gunfire cracked from above; instantly, a body fell into the street below. The single fifty-calibre round was evidence enough; Corporal Jones was in place and had their backs.

Thanks, Jonesy, was all I had time to think.

"Get down, you fool."

Grasping him by the vest, I yanked him into the open doorway. "Dunsmoore, are you all right?"

Fear had frozen him stiff, to the point where he had become unable to move. An open-handed slap to the face brought the private out of his daze.

"You have been trained to fight. Now suck it up! Fight! We need you. Private, do you hear me?"

The glazed look in Dunsmoore's eyes disappeared as he moved tighter to the wall.

Staring into the private's eyes, I screamed, "Are you with us?"

As his fear subsided, he lifted himself to his knees. "Sorry, sir. It won't happen again."

Working our way toward the entrance of the next building, Dunsmoore drew his rifle up to his shoulder. As we inched slowly forward, the makeshift curtain hanging limply across the doorway concealed little. It was obvious that someone was behind it. The shadow looked large enough to be a male, but confirmation was not possible. Pushing aside the curtain door, Private Miller stood staring down the muzzle of an AK-47. *Click* was all he heard. Lunging forward, he drove the barrel of his rifle into the motionless form.

Just a fucking kid, barely fifteen, he could be my brother—the terrifying thoughts flashed through Miller's mind. *Young or not, no one sticks a fucking gun in my face.*

Frothy blood spurted from the youth's mouth as the metal-jacketed bullet ripped through his lungs, shattering the door frame beyond. A second later, he lay sprawled out on the dirty floor, motionless, dead.

There was no time to contemplate what had just happened; we needed to clear the second floor. Tremors of fear ran up my spine as the adrenalin pushed us upward. Around every corner, we were expecting the worst, thankful for now that all we found were empty rooms—empty of all but the simplest of furnishings.

From the rooftops, the teams could be seen sneaking along the narrow passageways, clinging close to the walls like rows of ants. One by one, they would disappear from the alleyways into each open door, only to reappear moments later. As they neared the end of the street, more shots rang out, followed by that all-too-familiar thud, or screams of agony. Adrenalin raged. There was still danger ahead.

Blackhawk helicopters could be seen popping up and down like gophers in a clover field, sweeping gunfire across the rooftops, eliminating everything in their path. The hot cartridges fell to the ground below as the bullets ripped through concrete and steel with the ease of a knife through butter. Brass casing clung to the edge of the holes left in steel plates, evidence of the massive heat generated as the bullets travelled from muzzle to target.

Scanning the streets below, Private Jones watched as a rocket-propelled grenade swung around the corner. Private James stood only feet from the open door of his APV. Only fifty yards from the target—it would be near impossible for the RPG to miss. Jones dropped the crosshair square onto the centre of his target. With a gentle squeeze of the trigger, the fifty-calibre bullet exited the muzzle, pushing the rifle stock backward into his shoulder. The whistling sound of the brass and the immediate thud of the exploding shell meant only one thing: another threat was removed. Both the RPG and its host fell heavily to the ground. The repeated sound of one more round into the body of the RPG rendered it useless.

James looked back and smiled, thankful, for he knew that their guardian angel was watching over them. Without his protective eyes, any one of them could be next to be sent home in a silver casket.

Explosions and bursts of gunfire continued into the early afternoon before Alpha Team had reached the end of their street. While countless fires burned, the town centre stood bare, void of activity.

I quickly glanced at my watch. The mission time was estimated by our team to have been four hours. Now already in the sixth hour, it was obvious that the Taliban did not want to be pushed out of the city, for they too knew it would be harder to fight their kind of war in the open hills. Earlier briefings indicated that the resistance would be considerable. "Considerable" seemed to be an understatement. Bravo and Charlie teams completed their sweeps just as the support teams were arriving.

I pulled my men aside. "Gentlemen, we will be moving over to the next block. At this rate, we will not be complete before dark. Let's see what we can do to speed it up. I do not want to be here, especially after dark.

"Sergeant, you take James and Dunsmoore and clear those two buildings. We will secure this corner and watch your back.

"Jones, are you in place yet?"

Nothing came back, only silence.

"Miller, come in."

Anxiously awaiting a reply, I could not have the men risk stepping out, leaving the security of the small corridor without confirmation—not until they had eyes from above. No reply: only two microphone clicks resounded in my ear. Two clicks meant Jones and Miller had met company on their way to the roof. No shots or commotion could mean only one thing: Alpha Team would have to stay put and wait for the snipers to get in place.

Inching his way up the stone stairs, Miller stopped, standing motionless. First touching his ear, he then pointing up toward the shaded doorway. Jones strained to hear what Miller had detected.

Faintly, from behind the cloth door, the whispers of two people reached Jones's ears. *We've got company on the roof.* Slowly, he pointed upward.

Lightly brushing aside, the small stone pebbles from the step, Miller dropped to one knee. Peeking through the bottom corner of the doorway, the small, tattered corner of the curtain slowly moved in the breeze, allowing him a partial look at the activity outside. Across the roof, peering down to the street below, two males readied an RPG while a third faced the roof access. Not thirty feet away, the muzzle of his 9×18-mm Makarov submachine gun pointed in Miller's direction. Holding up three fingers, he mouthed, "RPG," then pointed toward the roof. There was no chance that he would be able to charge through the doorway without getting shot. He had to find another way to disarm the men on the roof before his team below got blown away.

Reaching down to his vest pocket, Miller extracted a grenade. Easing the pin from the handle, he readied to toss. The weight of the curtain would surely be a problem. He could not throw the grenade far enough as long as the curtain was in the way. Jones would have to whip the curtain aside while Miller tossed the grenade—not exactly a safe thing to do while the Makarov pointed their way. Seconds felt like an eternity as Miller watched the activity on the roof. It was apparent that the RPG was pointed toward the hallway across the street, just waiting for someone to step out.

Although Miller hated the damn sand, he was at this moment thankful. Straining to see through the cloud of dust, he could tell the rooftop killers had knelt to protect themselves from the razor-sharpness of the blowing sand. Crouched low to the roof, their lone sentry looked away, shielding his eyes from the swirling dust. Now was their chance. Miller waved frantically to Jones. With two quick steps, Jones was across the doorway and pulling the curtain aside while Miller tossed the grenade. The thud of the grenade hitting the sandy roof immediately brought gunfire in their direction, punching holes through the curtain and splattering stone chips from the stairway wall. Only seconds passed before the blast rang out. Gunfire from the roof ceased.

"Jones, are you OK?"

"Roger that, sir. Securing our position, sir."

Whispering softly, Jones directed Miller, "Allow me to glass the rooftops before you exit."

The roof they had chosen was ideal. From behind the ornamental openings of the parapet, Jones could see all the neighbouring roofs. Peering out toward the city centre, Jones could hear the gunfire. By the sound of things, the fighting would continue for quite a while.

Armed males scurried about the neighbouring rooftops from corner to corner, peeking down at our oncoming soldiers.

"Lieutenant, I have multiple targets on rooftops. Are you in a position to move?"

The response came back immediately. "Jones, take out as many as possible, but clear anyone in our immediate area first."

Lying in a prone position behind the small wooden table, Jones steadied his bipod, scanning the roofs below. Jones could tell this location had been used by other snipers; it had perfect concealment with wide-open shooting over most of the market buildings. Miller watched as the barrel of Jones's rifle swung from right to left.

"Miller, I need a range on the rooftop directly below the tallest building, lone male looking our way."

"Set, three hundred yards, crosswind three miles per hour."

Jones dialled the scope down and focused the crosshairs. There would be no need for him to be dialled way out today; most shots would be under four hundred yards. Lifting the bolt, the familiar sound of extracting the shell from the magazine shattered the momentary silence. Seconds later, the sharp sting of the fifty-calibre shell reached the unsuspecting target.

"Miller, tell the lieutenant that he is clear to go. I will continue sweeping the rooftops."

Without hesitation, Jones swung the rifle again. Shot after shot could be heard from the street below.

Miller lowered his binoculars. "Jones, do you realize that you have seven kills today? One more, and you will have the record for the whole base."

Jones blinked to remove the sweat and sand from around his eyes. "I am not concerned about records. Stay focused. I think I saw movement in the little window."

Miller rose to his knees to peep over the wall just as a solitary round smashed through the side of his helmet. Instantly, Miller fell.

"Lieutenant, we have a sniper in the tower to the east. Can you exterminate? Miller has been hit—I can't get a shot."

"Sergeant, you and Dunsmoore circle back. Sweep that tower. Radio me as soon as you get him. He may be trying to relocate. Go carefully."

Already past the tower, Sergeant Parker turned, heading back along the narrow street. "Why did we not clear the tower? We are already well past it!"

Dunsmoore just shrugged; he could not answer the question, except to say, "I couldn't find a door into the tower."

Except for a small pile of debris, the base of the tower seemed void of any entry. The area around the tower showed no signs of activity. There was no way to access it from the street.

"Lieutenant, I cannot find any way in. Access must be from an adjacent building. We need a sweep on these three buildings again."

"Roger that. I will search the smaller building first," the sergeant replied.

Another shot thundered from above.

"Lieutenant, the sniper appears not ready to leave his little nest. This could take hours before we find our way in."

"Sergeant, clear the area. I am going to call in an airstrike. We will take the tower down.

"Base, this is Lieutenant Cook. Requesting artillery hit—Market Tower. We will exit the area and light it up for you."

"Roger that, Alpha Team. Arrival time, two minutes."

Extracting a small laser ball from my backpack, I tossed it at the base of the tower. In the distance, the soft drone of the plane could be heard as the sergeant and Private Dunsmoore retreated behind a nearby building.

"Alpha Team here. Target marked; site clear."

The top of the tower crumbled downward toward the street. Rock and mortar sprayed in all directions. Buried under a pile of stone and dust, the sniper no longer posed a threat, or so we assumed. The tower now in pieces on the ground, we prepared to complete our sweep of the remaining buildings.

"Lieutenant, something is up. The pile of debris is moving."

The sergeant prepared to raise his rifle when a crack rang out from above. With the crosshairs still on the target, Corporal Jones watched as the lone male rose from the dusty ground, only to collapse as the shell from the fifty-cal hit its mark.

"Nice shooting, Jones. I doubt I would have had time to get a bead on him," commented the sergeant.

"OK, boys, enough chit-chat. Let's get the sweep completed." I replied.

Reaching the centre square had not been easy. Thankfully, Alpha Team sustained no fatalities or injuries. Bravo Team, one fatality, Charlie Team, two facial injuries. Exhausted, Alpha Team awaited direction to return to camp. UN forces had been dispatched. They would sit vigil until morning.

Scurrying into the safety of the APV, I congratulated the team. "All in all, a good day, gentleman. We can all go back and chase down a cold one."

As I did every night, I knelt beside my bed, bowing my head with folded hands, giving thanks.

"Dear Lord, please take our fallen brother into your fold. Forgive his transgressions. Please continue to watch over Alpha Team as we continue in this awful war."

That night, I ate my dinner alone. I needed to come to terms with the things we had done today, the things I knew we would have to do every day henceforth. As "thou shalt not kill" echoed in the back of my mind, I felt unsure if I would ever find the strength to forgive myself. For now, I had to unwind, to try and forget my first day. As I rolled to face the wall, the words *I hope Dad would still be proud of me* flashed through my mind.

This bunk, which at first looked so cold, so uninviting, now seemed so comfortable, so safe. I was unable to rest. My mind drifted back to our peaceful home, to the family I loved. Rolling backward, I laid face up, torn by conflicting emotions. I was sad for the family of the soldier that had been killed, yet thankful that all of Alpha Team had returned in one piece. Eyes closed, locked in my darkness, I lay, experiencing feelings of loss, guilt, and especially loneliness.

Morning came early. Stretching to silence the alarm, I moaned aloud. Contrary to what I expected, I had slept soundly; not once had I stirred. Today the War Room was especially full; as usual, all three teams had arrived early for the morning briefing. Sitting with the other five team members, we listened to the base commander describing the next phase of the operation.

Re-populating the ruined city will be the next step to securing stability in the area. Bomb disposal teams would sweep the streets and buildings. The UN security forces would be present to maintain peace throughout the city. We were not fooled; the threat was still present, and we needed to stay vigilant.

"Gentlemen, before allowing any civilians back into the area, Alpha, Bravo, and Charlie teams will take the three bomb robots into town.

"Starting at the south end, we will commence with a more intense sweep of the previously cleared areas. Until the operation is completed, two APVs with fifty-calibre machine guns will accompany each team. Snipers will set up as usual."

I peered out the narrow window as the second APV rounded the corner. The town looked the same. Piles of debris littered the streets, garbage everywhere; perfect spots for bombs to lie concealed. The teams would be here for hours, possibly days, sifting through all the potential hiding spots. Today would be just a little different, for instead of room to room, they would be searching pile to pile.

"Gentlemen, please remember this threat does not shoot back, but it is even more deadly. Keep eyes and ears open. More snipers could still be out there."

Outside, the teams waited; vehicles stood ready as men hustled about making sure they had all they needed.

"OK. Lock and load."

Clouds of dust rose as the rubber tires of the APVs rolled past the camp gates.

"Cook here, Sergeant. Is the Guardian in place?"

"Yes, sir, and the streets are clear."

"All right, gentlemen, if anything looks out of place, we stop. We need to be thorough. Let's do this right."

I watched intently as Private James lowered the headcover of his bomb disposal uniform, covering his head. I respected James—the courage it took to walk up to a live bomb, knowing that at any minute it could go off. Outwardly, James seemed to have nerves of steel.

"OK, you all know the drill. Once the excess debris is cleared by the robot, Private James will move in to disarm the ordnance."

As Private Dunsmoore pushed the thumbwheel forward, the robot moved toward the small pile of garbage in the centre of the square. Dunsmoore had become quite proficient in the use of the robot; if somewhere needed to be cleared, he could do it. The sun glistened off an exposed silver tip. Everyone paused, not yet sure if the object was indeed a bomb—no one wanting to be the first to find out. Concealed behind the APV, they watched, all the while scanning left, right, then up to the rooftops.

"James, are you transmitting?"

"Yes, sir," came the reply.

"Stay put. Dunsmoore is checking out a suspicious pile of debris. Hold steady until he is finished."

Just a little right and down—there we go. The robot arm squeezed the corner, slowly elevating the plate to expose what was indeed part of a hidden bomb. Holding tightly with metal fingers, the robot lifted the plate up and away. Almost flush with the ground, the charge appeared sizable. Focusing my binoculars, I strained to get a better look.

"James, the ground looks disturbed. Two metres around the shell have been moved. This could be a big one."

With that much disturbed earth, someone had spent a considerable amount of time setting this trap. A bomb this size would cause widespread destruction.

"James, you're to take your time going in. Dunsmoore, are we ready?"

"Sir, I would like to relocate the robot to the other side. I need to know what else is there."

"Roger that, Dunsmoore. Get it done."

Skirting the edge of the disturbed earth, the rubber tracks of the metal man manoeuvred around to the opposite side of the pile. With each new position, the camera mounted atop the robot zoomed in and out, looking for any telltale signs of how it had been wired, or how they planned to detonate.

"OK, Lieutenant, I don't see any visible trip switches. I suggest that James walk in on the same path as the robot. No sense taking any chances."

Dragging the metal plate, the robot retreated to the APV.

Tapping lightly on the helmet, I gave one last instruction. "James, as soon as the robot is back to the APV, you can go in. Stay inside the drag marks."

Private James trod forward clothed in the bomb disposal suit, looking like the Goodyear Blimp. Slowly, he advanced toward the newly exposed explosive. Walking with his legs spread wide, I imagined he must feel as if he had just shit in his pants.

Even though the suit was equipped with a small, battery-operated fan, droplets of perspiration trickled down his brow. The putrid, stale smell from hours of sweat had soured the inside of the suit. I tried to think about what Private James must think each time he put the suit on. It always reminded me of the damp, musty smell of a school gym locker room.

Across the open expanse of the city courtyard, the dark-haired, rather skinny man stood looking at Alpha Team as they prepared to deactivate the bomb. One leg over the crossbar of his bike, he stood there, watching. He did not look armed, but the carrier on the bike overflowed. Something heavy filled a white cloth bag. Private James knelt beside the bomb while never taking his eyes off the lone male.

"What is up with that guy on the bike?"

"Lieutenant, does the Guardian have eyes on that guy? I am awfully alone out here."

"Jones, do you see the biker?"

"Affirmative, Lieutenant. I will take him out when he moves so much as a finger."

Private James sighed, returning his gaze to the two red wires. "Lieutenant looks like only one explosive with a simple pressure switch. Why it did not go off when the plate was lifted is unknown."

I watched intently. "Private, get your ass in gear. You need to disarm that bomb.

"I'm not getting a good feeling about this situation. You are far too exposed," I remarked.

Private James tugged gently on the trigger wires; wires that should have gone to the bomb appeared to be heading in another direction, toward the other side of the courtyard. This could only mean one thing. It took only a second to realize that the biker was the detonator. Adrenalin flowed like water as Private James stood clumsily trying to run away from the explosive. He would have only seconds before the trigger man would be aware he had figured it out. The pressure switch was a decoy. The intent was to activate the bomb and kill James while he attempted to disarm it.

The biker raised his right hand, reaching into his left shirt pocket just as the single fifty calibre bullet ripped through his chest. Private James, still only fifty feet from the bomb, stumbled and fell to the ground. Almost sure the bomb would go off, he expected to feel the blast at any second. Seconds passed as he lay facedown in the sandy street, gasping and clawing to get away. When would the pain start? But the blast did not come.

"Private James, you can get up now. Your job is complete for today. The Guardian has taken care of the detonator. Still, out of there ASAP.

"Private Dunsmoore, secure the switch from the biker's jacket. Once all our team is clear of the blast area, detonate it.

"Jones, do you see the white package in the bike basket? Put a couple of rounds through it. Whatever is in that bicycle carrier, I want it destroyed. I do not like the look of it."

A loud crack from the sniper rifle followed by a huge blast confirmed my suspicion. The sneaky little coward was ready to blow himself up.

"Dunsmoore, get over there and secure what may be left of the other switch. Jones, you and Miller keep an eye on the rooftops while we clean up here.

"Nightfall will soon be on us. Speed it up."

Standing concealed behind the APV, Alpha Team watched as the private yelled, "Fire in the hole!" and closed the trip switch.

The blast shook the vehicle, cracking the windshield, blowing stones and metal debris in all directions. Behind the APV, a scream of pain rang out. Startled by the sound, I glanced to my left. Sergeant Parker lay on the ground grasping his left ankle. The blast had been so powerful that it had blown a fist-size stone clear across the sixty feet, under the APV, then broadside into the sergeant's ankle.

"Doc, get over here. Dunsmoore, help me drag the sarge inside the APV. Doc can work on him in there."

Within seconds, Sergeant Parker was lying flat out on the floor of the APV. Chunks of stone had cut through the leather of his boot, ripping into his ankle.

"Lieutenant, I cannot risk taking off his boot here. The foot will swell up like a balloon. He needs to return to base ASAP."

I knew the doc was right. "Dunsmoore, get on the radio. Advise base we are coming in. The rest of you load up; we are pushing back to camp. I believe we have had enough excitement for one day.

"Jones, Miller, hustle down here. Dunsmoore will stand guard and ride back with you. We will wait for you at the corner."

Heavy footsteps could be heard exiting the doorway as the lead vehicle pulled away. The scorching sun of late afternoon beat down on the APV as the remainder of the team jumped in. Not a perfect day, but still they were all going back to base, alive. The ride back was filled with tension for everyone, especially Sergeant Parker, who was painfully close to death. While we all dreaded the thought of what might have happened, the rush was exhilarating.

Three weeks of pampering and sitting around doing nothing followed. As Sergeant Parker listened to the injured men recall their stories, each day became harder—worse than being out there. The sergeant had had enough. Luckily, only the skin had been peeled back; no broken bone, no severe damage had occurred. Turning his head toward the approaching sound, he could see me rounding the corner, heading toward his bunk.

"Lieutenant am I ever glad to see you. I need to get out of this bed, get back with the men. I can't take this lollygagging."

"Sergeant, the doctor said it looks like you will need to spend another couple of weeks here before they will let you put your boots back on. Be patient. You will be out of here soon."

Day after day, the routine continued: ride into town, isolate a threat, then take it out—every day there were new bombs, lone shooters, suicide bombers. When would it end; when would they stop this nonsense? Everyone was wearing down, like a bad job where nothing ever got completed.

To all, it seemed so senseless. This whole exercise, going nowhere. Allied forces, all good men, were being killed, but for what? Tonight, Alpha Team would relax. Tonight, the men would indulge with a few extra pints. Their tour was up today—all had survived.

Private James intended to forget; he needed to get pissed; he needed to come down from the painful high of his last day. He had survived his last day. No more bombs, no more snipers to worry about. Tomorrow he would be going home.

I bellied up to the bar, smiling. Alpha Team had lived through yet another tour, but before they went home, they all needed to let their hair down. To blow off a little steam. They had performed their jobs exceptionally well, day after day. Tapping each team member on the shoulder as they entered the pub, I congratulated them, stating how proud they should be of their service, and for them to be happy as well, to hold their heads high. The bond that now existed toward my men was indescribable. At deployment, I sensed each member of our team had become as close as brothers. Now it stretched far beyond that.

For the first time in a long time, I felt clean. Possibly it was knowing that I would not have to face another day here. I could not be faced with the torment of placing my team in mortal danger, just to execute another useless raid on unsubstantiated intel or face some stupid peasant blowing himself up. I sat trying to convince myself that it had all been worthwhile and soon I would be going home. Operation Medusa had cost the lives of twelve good Canadian soldiers—thank God, none from Alpha Team.

Across the room, and all alone at a small table sat Chuck. Not a particularly sociable guy. Chuck gazed toward me, waving me over. *I wonder, what's up?* Although I had seen Chuck around camp, we had never once spoken, through the two full tours at Camp Nathan Smith. The US teams tended to keep to themselves and were usually very secretive about the activities they had on the go.

Chuck was rumoured to be a spook, CIA or FBI—one of the guys that always seemed to be alone. Chuck acted especially friendly tonight. In fact, he looked like he just might be three sheets to the wind.

"Sit down, Lieutenant, let me buy you a beer. You know, Lieutenant, happy hour started two hours ago, but… I… I… I got an early start."

Chuck reached into his pocket for cash. "Waiter, bring my friend and me a pitcher of beer?" It was obvious that Chuck was intending to get more wasted. His reason was not yet known, although I sensed I was about to find out why.

"What is your name, Lieutenant?" Likely my name was known to Chuck; his absence of recognition was obvious.

"What is your name, Lieutenant?" he repeated.

Reaching out, I grasped Chucks hand. "It's Spencer Cook, and yours is…?"

"My name, dear sir, is Ch… Ch… Chuck."

Noticing a slight slur to his words, I could see this was going to get interesting.

"Well, Spencer, my friend, I must tell you that I am more than a little pissed off."

I just had to take the bait. "Why is that Chuck?"

"You know, Spencer, I have spent the last two years working a source, feeding the CIA countless pages of intel. My intel has been proven accurate, yet they fail to act. I have fed them accurate data on high-level targets, yet they do nothing."

This was my cue. "What info do you have?"

"Well, sir, I can tell you that bin Ladin's chief advisor will be travelling the northeast road from Kabul to Baghlan, then up into Pakistan on Thursday. How is that for intel?"

Grasping the moment, I sipped on my beer and inquired, "So, what is it you want from me?"

"Well, Spencer, my dear man, I can hand you a key target. All you need is to be there. How does that suit you?

"Spencer, old pal, I tell you what. I have an informant that wants one hundred thousand dollars to provide the locations and times of the advisor's travels. I will get the money if you are genuinely interested. I will feed you the intel on when and where they will be. All you must do is have your shooter take the target out.

"I hear that your Corporal Jones has acquired quite a reputation for long-distance kills. This should be right up his alley."

I thought for a second. This decision, I could not make on my own. I would need approval.

"Chuck, how will you swing this past the US troop commander?"

"I already have. He does not believe that my intel is accurate; he refused to send any of his troops on a wild goose chase. He just scoffed at me when I said I would get you Canadian boys to take care of the op."

"Well, Chuck, I will have to take this up the ladder. If I can get approval, would you be willing to accompany my team and see this through?"

Without hesitating, Chuck leaned forward, "Damn right I will."

Emptying the pitcher into Chuck's glass, I was elated with the prospect of finally acquiring a high-value target—a target worth pursuing. Judging by the conversation, Chuck seemed confident in what he was talking about. With this offer, there should be no way my command would refuse.

I rose, commenting, "I will get back to you tomorrow morning, say zero-eight-hundred, in the mess tent."

Before rushing over to my base commander, I would have to review the maps and enemy troop movement reports. To look over that much information, I could see it would be an awfully long night.

Sifting through the daily unmanned drone reports should be a good start, then I would confirm where a night drop could be executed along the intended travel route. I was once again becoming interested. Finally, a worthwhile target, a solid reason to stay in this hellhole.

Hastily, I called my team together; they would all have to agree before their flight lifted off for home. The men would have to extend their tours to make this happen. I hoped all would accept, but deep down I knew it would be each man's decision. I could not make it for them. I could not make them stay.

Alpha Team sat in the briefing room wondering what was going on. The team had been called to an urgent early morning meeting—for what, they did not know. The team should all be back in the barracks packing to go home.

"Well, gentlemen, last night I had a rather lengthy conversation with one of our neighbours. He made us an interesting proposal.

"We have the opportunity to neutralize a very high-value target. Your participation is voluntary. I fully understand if you decline.

"We have been authorized to proceed with this special mission as long as I have adequate team resources.

"The base has no one to spare. We are the only team available. I ask you to come with me into the northern region to take out this target."

"Hell, we can all take leave after we return." Commented Dunsmoore. In unison, all stood and agreed.

"Great, now that we have all agreed, I would like to introduce you to Chuck.

"Chuck is a CIA operative who has a special informant willing to disclose the movements of a high-level advisor to Osama bin Ladin.

"Team, this is Chuck. He will be guiding us into the hills to where we will set up."

Chuck looked a little bedraggled as he stepped up to the map. The previous night at the bar, although tiring, had not dampened his enthusiasm. Finally, someone was taking all his hard work seriously.

"Gentlemen, the target should be in place on Thursday. I have confirmation he has left Kandahar in a small grey pickup. A tracer has been secured to the vehicle; their movements are currently being tracked. We may not be able to get close to the road due to the low terrain in the area. We may not get another opportunity if the target reaches the Pakistan border.

"Corporal Jones, you will have to make a very long shot."

Looking at Corporal Jones, Chuck smiled.

"We are expecting heavy cloud cover tonight. Parachuting under the cover of darkness should guarantee we can get into place well before the target arrives on Thursday morning. We may need to go mobile—five-day rations, complete armament pack.

"Mr. Dunsmoore, please make sure the radios are shipshape. I expect a hasty extraction will be necessary."

I rose as Chuck stepped away from the map. "OK, get moving. We depart in six hours."

In the air, three hours north of Kandahar, the amber light blinked as the rear cargo door opened. Each man, in turn, stood and hooked his lanyard to the steel tether line. In moments, they would be free falling into the cold darkness. Thick grey clouds blanketed the sky, making visibility poor—so poor we would have to be at three thousand feet before breaking through. The butterflies raced up my spine, subsiding only after I was out and stabilized in flight.

"Thirty seconds. Green light—GO!" Each man in turn awaited the thrill.

Thick, rain-filled clouds enveloped us like a heavy blanket. Free falling from five thousand feet, racing into the pitch black of night, not a light in sight… WOW! What a high.

Four thousand, three thousand—chute time approached as we shot out of the clouds. Below, distant white specks of lights sparkled like tiny stars in the sky. Moving slowly along their northerly path, vehicles stood out like lanterns against the blackness of the northern night.

The sparse late-night traffic gave the team a bearing. Distance would be our friend tonight. We had to stay far enough away to remain undetected. Opening our parachutes in unison, we jerked backward, rapidly slowing our descent. Slight pulls on the parachute ropes changed our direction, quietly drifting us northward, parallel to the distant roadway.

Silently gliding toward our intended landing spot, I flipped down my night vision glasses. Scanning the surrounding hills, I observed no thermal images, just the small spots from the distant cars. Rows of rocky cliffs lay out before us; any one of them would provide a secure landing area. However, we needed one that would also conceal our landing and still allow easy access to the flatter land nearer the road.

I signalled to the others. Pulling lightly on the left parachute line, I steered my team toward a north–south gorge, just one kilometre west of the desired road. One by one, we descended into the narrow depression. My feet touched down lightly onto the gorge's rocky floor. I appreciated how easy these new chutes were to use. No more hard landings; little chance of broken bones. After folding and stashing our parachutes under nearby underbrush, the team gathered, silently awaiting orders.

"Private, radio in and advise base that the falcon has landed. We will report back once we have located a viable vantage point. Lock and load. If possible, do not fire your weapons. We do not want to awaken any of the locals.

"Sergeant, you take point with Chuck. Find us a suitable place for Corporal Jones to set up the fifty-cal. No time to waste; we must be in place before sunup at zero-five-thirty."

Navigating upward through the sandy, stone-covered gorge proved treacherous. Ascending from the valley below, countless slips and falls slowed our progress. Peering over the rocky edge, Sergeant Parker readied his rifle. Although we had seen no sign of locals, I was not taking any chances. Being less than two kilometres away from the road, we needed to gain elevation—a vantage point from which we could see the entire area, somewhere where I could better assess the terrain and ambush options.

To the east, I could see a large rock outcropping. Following the gorge for another hundred metres should bring us out at the bottom of the rise, straight in line with the roadway. Not more than thirty metres vertical, it appeared to be the only high ground available. It would have to do.

"Sergeant, once you have set up, we need to secure a perimeter. Sunup is in sixty. Hurry.

"Private, radio the base. Advise them we have arrived, and that we will confirm set-up shortly."

"Sir, I have the base on the line. They want to talk to you."

Walking, I held my hand over the phone as I whispered, not wanting the sound to carry across the silent night air. "Cook here, over."

"Lieutenant, we have the target on satellite. At his current speed, ETA to your position zero-eight-hundred today."

Chuck glanced at me. "Lucky the plane was ready, and we were able to get away early."

The target had not stopped for a night in Kabul as expected. There would be no time to relocate to a better location. Corporal Jones would have to take the first available shot. Glassing across the wide-open expanse toward the roadway, Private Miller and Corporal Jones looked for a suitable position for the fifty-cal.

"Sir, there appears to be a small rest area alongside the road. Hopefully, they will stop there, allowing for a stationary shot—distance 2.4 kilometres. At this distance, a moving shot will be near impossible.

"You know as well as I, there has never been a confirmed kill over two kilometres."

Jones withdrew a shell from his upper pocket, blew the dust off the head, and inspected it for scratches. The slightest imperfection could cause the bullet to fly off course. Smiling at Private Miller, the corporal chambered his round, glanced to his right, and promptly requested the status.

"Sir, the wind is directly into our face at the moment. I will update you every minute until the target arrives."

At takeoff, the weather forecasts had shown the possibility of gusting easterly squalls, which usually meant sandstorms. Gusty winds increased the possibility of another sandstorm, making me even more anxious.

Scanning the area looking for potential targets, Corporal Jones practised his shot rehearsals: setting the crosshairs onto an oncoming vehicle or stationary object repeatedly requesting windage and distance. Each time Miller would relay the data, the corporal would go through the routine of adjusting the scope while practising his breathing; it had to be routine, right up to the bullet hit its mark. With this distance, he could not afford the slightest hesitation or flinch.

"Sir we have the satellite tracking showing the target vehicle two clicks out, travelling at sixty kilometres per hour."

Corporal Jones whispered, "OK, Private, at the ready. If they do not stop at the rest area, we will only have one opportunity. I will need an update as the vehicle rounds the bend, by that large rock pile."

Chuck and I moved on top of the rocky ledge. Lying prone, we steadied our binoculars. From our elevated perch, we watched as the grey pickup wove its way along the dusty road. With a snap of his fingers, Chuck motioned— here they come. From our slightly elevated vantage point, we watched the approaching pickup; Jones and Miller would have eyes on it a minute later.

"Private, radio Jones. Tell him to get ready, the target vehicle approaching—just cresting the hill."

Clouds of dust billowed up behind the pickup as it headed toward the small roadside building. Chuck smiled as the pickup slowed to a stop. It appeared that we were about to catch a break. Almost immediately, the cloud of dust rolled forward, obscuring the target. The Leupold 16×40 scope rested motionless. Crosshairs set where the target should be, Corporal Jones waited. At this moment, he sat helpless, waiting for the dust to clear. With the wind coming directly toward them, the cloud seemed to hang over the pickup as if protecting the inhabitants.

"We cannot see. Too much damn dust," came over the radio. "OK, I have eyes on, ten metres to the left of the pickup, heading toward the small building."

With only a few metres before they reached the building, the target had to be taken now, or we would lose the only opportunity.

Slowly, the dust dissipated. "Distance, Private?"

"Two thousand, four hundred and thirty metres, sir. No crosswinds."

Adjusting for the added thirty metres and headwinds, the corporal exhaled. Ever so slowly, he pulled the rifle butt snugly into his shoulder. The crosshair sat steady, just in front of the target's head as the resistance of the trigger gave way. The familiar pressure of the rifle's recoil pushed back into his shoulder. Mere seconds passed before the puff of dirt could be seen. Miller reported the miss. Holding the crosshairs on the target, he could see the subject still standing. The two males seemed dumbfounded as sand and stone sprayed all around them.

Swiftly chambering another round, Jones delivered a second shot. By the time, the reality of what was happening had sunk in, the second round was already on its way. Unable to move fast enough, the two men stood still in their tracks as the bullet exploded mid-body on the target. Confused, the driver ran back toward the vehicle. Stopping to open the driver's side door, he was introduced to the third bullet as it hit the car, exploding the gas tank.

After shaking Chuck's hand, I rose to my knees then backed away from the edge of the ledge.

"Dunsmoore, get on the horn. Confirm mission complete, then get us the hell out of here. I suspect we will be unpopular very soon. We will rendezvous at the drop point in sixty minutes."

Off the ledge and down the gorge Alpha Team hustled at double time, not one of them wishing to stick around any longer than necessary.

Back at base, the helicopter dropped down to rest on the sandy pad. Only after they were back behind the security of the base walls did Alpha Team relax. Adrenalin still pulsating through their veins, so intense they thought their hearts would burst. Debriefed and showered, the team awaited the next flight home. The camp was now abuzz with the news of the mission's success. Six tired soldiers finally knew our time there had accomplished something, something worth risking our lives for. Now, we all awaited the comforts of home.

Having taken the latest intel to forces other than his own, Chuck had created a shitstorm for himself. He shook the hand of each of the team members and bestowed sincere gratitude for their efforts, knowing full well that his assignment here would be stopped—he would be returning home on the next available flight. The FBI and CIA did not take kindly to involving outsiders in what was perceived to be their business. Chuck smiled, knowing it did not matter now. His demanding work had paid off; another link in the Taliban chain had been broken, no thanks to his people.

Tonight, we all sat around the bar and raised a glass to say goodbye to our newfound friend. Lieutenant Renner would not be leaving with us. Assigned to another team, he would be staying—another gruelling six months before he could leave. As for Chuck, rumour had it that he had already been confined to his barracks.

His superior was not impressed that he had been made a fool of. Everyone knew he would make it look like Chuck had stepped outside of the chain of command. Worse yet, Chuck had been correct. I did not envy Chuck at this moment.

PART SIX

2011, BACK HOME—OTTAWA, ONTARIO

2011 saw me and my team of five returning home. Each was glad to be home, but at the same time worried, for he had looked into the demon's eyes. It was only a matter of time before each man would meet the demon again, but not knowing when or where. I feared the next time it would be at home. For now, we were all happy to leave that God-forsaken place. We would eventually need to decide whether to continue with our careers or return to civilian life, but for now, we all just wanted to disconnect—to try and reconnect with our past, our families, even old friends. To make sense of the horrible things we had seen, and to make peace with the things we had done. Hopefully, my thirty-day leave would be enough time.

While the others still needed to decide, I had already made up my mind. I would contact my career counsellor and see what was available. With my freshly polished Star of Military Valour, everyone wanted to be around me to talk about my experiences. I loved the attention and had found my niche. My home would continue to be the army, and the men I served with, my family. I would always remember that day out on that sandy hill when, with a simple click of a trigger, we sent shock waves through the terrorist community. I took pride in knowing I was partly responsible. Corporal Jones and Private Miller had gained a reputation abroad. Upon returning to the base, the duo received several invitations for demonstrations for the upper brass and dignitaries. Both were eager to accommodate. With his TAC-50, Jones was now one of the world's best snipers—an accolade of which he had previously only dreamt.

"One moment, please."

The familiar tap of knuckles on glass rattled down the corridor as Mom approached the door. Pulling the curtain aside, she gasped in astonishment. "Spencer, oh my God, you're home!"

I had not called ahead. I wanted to surprise her. The familiar smell of apple pie flooded my senses as I wrapped my arms around her. It had been an eternity since I had felt so secure, so safe.

"Why did you not tell me you were coming home?"

"What, and miss that look? Not a chance."

"Come, your dad will be glad to see you."

Not yet able to let go of me, she squeezed tightly onto my hand as she led me through the kitchen to the rear porch. "John, look, Spencer is home!"

This man in the wheelchair could not be my dad—so frail, so wasted away. Looking into the emptiness of those eyes, my heart broke once again.

"Hi Dad, I'm home."

I knelt, touching my father's hand as the tears welled up in my eyes. At that moment, as I caressed his motionless hand, I came to the realization that my job was not yet done. I not only wanted to move forward, I needed to. There was more I could do—more I must do.

The days and nights flew by as Mom shared her stories, re-acquainting me with the life I had once known. Hours would slip away as I listened to my Mom talk about the old hometown—who had married whom, who had divorced whom, who had died. I could not bring myself to talk about my experiences, and she never asked. Mom was a soldier's wife. She could sense I was a different person. Garnered from years of experience with Dad, she had learned that certain things were better left unsaid.

Stepping out of the shower today seemed like every other day since I had arrived home. Boredom and lack of purpose occupied my every thought. What would I do today? Something was eating away at me. I had to go north; I had to visit the family cottage. I needed to visit Wil's grave.

The sky was a bright blue, broken up by fluffy white clouds. A typical spring day with the exception that today I needed to visit Wil. The grave site was a three-hour drive northward to Huntsville. I had avoided this day for a long time.

The midday drive to Huntsville was relaxing and peaceful. Like the hundreds of other times, I had travelled this way. Trees with their newly erupting buds created a light green hue—not full enough to conceal the maze of twisted branches, but the buds were signs of the new life of spring. I loved the spring. It represented hope, belief that there was good in the world, and a reason to move forward. So much of my innocence had been lost over there. So much that I wished I could get back.

The family cottage lay west of Huntsville on peaceful Buck Lake. Wil and I had spent many days playing on the beach and fishing the lake. The closer I came to the lane, the more impatient I became, yet the more relaxed too.

Rounding the sharp S-curve, I could see the small local graveyard. Slowing as I passed by my eyes locked onto Wil's tombstone. Nestled among the tall white pines, it seemed so small and insignificant. Perched on top of the stone above Wil's name, a blue jay squawked as if calling out to me. Slowly turning my focus back to the road ahead, I tried to push the scene from my mind. Tomorrow I would visit Wil, but for now, I wanted only to reach the cottage and have a drink. I needed to build up my courage.

Crossing the small creek into the drive, I could see the little red cottage. The smell of the lake filled my senses, and all the old memories seeped back into my consciousness. The crunch of stones under the tires reminded me of the old, youthful enthusiasm. How I used to look forward to the weekends and summer vacations. I could not see a single tree or rock that did not hold a memory of Wil. Oh, how I missed my old friend.

Atop the rocky knoll, the cottage overlooked the peaceful little lake. Today it seemed especially so as the gulls drifted across the smooth silver surface, and the light breeze rustled the bushes along the incoming creek. Not much seemed to have changed since my last visit. That in itself was comforting.

Snapping the cap off a cold Budweiser, I listened. That fizz had become a familiar sound. I could remember a time when neither I nor Wil would consume alcohol of any kind. Since Wil's death, I could hardly remember a day without a drink. Some days I needed it to relax, wind down; others, I needed it to forget. Tonight, I would have only one bottle. Tonight, I wanted to remember; I needed to remember. Tomorrow, I would need to confess a secret. Even though Wil would not hear me, it had to be told.

The solitary echo of the loons drifted past the cabin as I doused the last flames of the evening campfire. Wisps of smoke and steam drifted away as I retired to the comfort of the double bed.

Light peeked past the curtains into my tiny room. Rolling to grasp the small alarm clock, I detected the faint aroma of bacon. The neighbours must be up having breakfast. Rolling over the side of the bed, I pulled my bathing suit on and shuffled toward the kitchen. The click of the doorknob alerted her to my presence. Fumbling with the cutlery, she turned toward the sound.

"Good morning, Spencer. Why don't you go see your father while I finish making breakfast? There is some fresh, hot coffee in the pot if you would like."

How could I resist? Mom always made the best coffee.

The clock on the counter showed ten-hundred hours.

"What time did you two arrive?" I asked.

"We got up about 6:00 a.m. Since you appeared rather agitated yesterday, we thought it would be a good idea to come and see how you were doing."

I had learned there was no we in any of her decisions, for Dad was incapable. Mom had to make all the decisions. Caressing my arm as we walked toward the porch door, she remarked, "It is so nice to have us all back up here together. I miss our weekends away. You sit with your father; I will only be a minute."

"How was your drive-up Dad?" I knelt and touched him on the shoulder. There would be no answer; I enjoyed asking anyway.

Rays of sunlight twinkled off the polished metallic flakes in Wil's headstone. Brushing away the fallen pine needles, I stared once again at his name.

WILLIAM WRIGHT

The silence at this moment seemed odd: not a sound, no birds chirping, no cars driving by. Looking down, I could see that the grave was rather neglected. The floral arrangement had wilted, and debris covered the ground. It had been so long since I had thought about visiting. Twinges of guilt again consumed me. My best friend lay beneath this ground and not once had I visited.

The silence buzzed in my ears; I would have to talk soon or risk going crazy.

Sitting on the small bench beside the grave, I welled up with remorse.

"Wil, I wanted to come and see you, but the time has just flown by." It was a lie. I had feared coming.

"Where do I start… Well, all the boys made it back alive. The team missed you…

"I cannot say you would have liked it because it was hell. Afghanistan was an eye-opener. We all came back with scars, mental and physical.

"Jones and Miller have become a real ticket, shooting up a storm wherever they go.

"The sergeant talks about you often. You do know, he liked you. Dunsmoore and James have not changed much. They kept us all sane once you left. Me, well, I am still as serious as ever.

"Wil…" I choked back the tears as I attempted to say what I had to say.

"Wil, I have to apologize. I am responsible for your death. I killed you that day, as sure as if I had shot you myself." The tears were now pouring down my cheeks, my heart pounding in my chest. Stuttering with broken words, I attempted to finish the sentence.

"I… I need to tell you that I altered one of your test scores. You should not have been on that final exercise. You should not have been anywhere near that bear. I am so sorry, my friend!"

I sobbed wildly as the sound of footsteps on crunching leaves approached. "Mom, I killed my best friend!"

Looking directly into my eyes, with both hands cupped around my cheeks, she tried to comfort me. "I knew you had something troubling you and now you have to let it go."

Holding on tight, cuddled in Mom's arms, I poured out all the anguish I had kept bottled up inside. All those years of guilt.

"Mom, I am not sure if I can continue, or if I even want to."

"Spencer, honey, you did no such thing, it is not your fault. It was an accident. It could have been any one of you. You know as well as I do that not being with you at graduation would have killed Wil. If he had failed or was forced to drop out, the result would have been the same. Wil loved you, and he loved the army as much as you do. You have done nothing wrong. Wil would understand.

"Come now, honey, let's go and see how your father is."

"Mom, I need just a couple more minutes."

"Spencer, honey, you take as much time as you need. I will be waiting by the gate."

I bowed my head, asking one more time for forgiveness—hoping I would hear Wil answer back with words of forgiveness, but nothing came. I rose and glanced one more time at the inscription.

WILLIAM WRIGHT
1975–2005

Our Pride and Joy. May you rest in peace.

Although emotionally drained, the walk back to the cabin somehow seemed uplifting. I could hear the birds singing and the laughter of the kids by the beach. I sensed deep down that nothing had changed, but I no longer had that heavy load. It was time now to move on.

"Mom, I believe I will find out what is available and try to get a posting close to home, but first I believe I will pay a visit to Wil's parents. It has been so long, and I would genuinely like to see them."

"You do as you must, but first you promised to paint the cottage. We can all use a little more quality time before you rush off again." Deep down, I knew work was her way to help cure my sorrow.

Billowing clouds of dust followed the old pickup as I sped down the freshly graded county road. Slowing as I entered the bumpy lane, my eyes focused to the hand-printed sign from so long ago.

"Caution—Speed Bump, Slow Down."

Flashbacks of Wil laughing as he described the horse owners rushing to leave the stables and, all too often, crashing into oncoming vehicles cresting the hill. The equestrian stables and barn still looked used, rented out possibly.

The old, green, two-storey farmhouse looked neglected, possibly for years. Layers of paint chips covering the porch crunched under my feet as I climbed the steps to the rear door. Now the old house looked cold—yet I remembered a day when it held such warmth.

Tap, tap of knuckles on the old wood echoed through the kitchen. Pushing the lacy curtains to the side, Mr. Wright peeked out. The paint-covered hinges squeaked as he flung the door open.

"Martha! Come quick it's Spencer Cook!"

Wide-eyed and smiling from ear to ear, Martha inched her way toward the door. It was obvious that time and Wil's death had taken their toll on both of his parents. I remembered those smiles. It hurt to see them so aged. These people had been like parents to me, and I loved them dearly.

"Come in, Spencer! Let's talk. My, oh my, how you have grown up. Such a handsome young man as well. Are you married yet?"

"No, ma'am, still single."

"Come sit, I just put on a pot of tea. How are your parents?"

"Mom is fine, and Dad's condition has not changed." Questions upon questions—it had been so long. We had so many things to talk about.

"I have been wanting to come and see you both, but I have been so busy." I hated to lie but telling them the truth about why I had not come would only have hurt them more.

"Spencer, do you still play baseball?"

"Yes, ma'am, I do. We have an officer's league at the base. We also have regular Tuesday night games against the town leagues."

"Spencer, I have something I think you should have."

Grasping me by the hand, she led me up the narrow attic stairs. As my head cleared the opening, I scanned the small, familiar room. The same old squeaky steps and a smell that only time can create.

Mementos of Wil lined the walls. In the middle of the room was a large eight-by-ten colour photo of Wil in his dress uniform, standing alone in the centre of a small hardwood table. A light layer of dust covered all but the oak rocking chair and the edge of the table. Signs indicated that this spot had been recently occupied. Cupping a slightly scuffed hardball, Wil's trapper rested against the narrow spindles of the rocker.

"Here, Spence. Wil would want you to have this."

Sliding my left hand into the mitt, I could feel Wil's presence, almost as if he were standing beside me. An eerie yet peaceful calm fell over me.

The onset of darkness had long passed as I turned right out of the driveway. Reaching over to stroke the lacing on the glove, I smiled, finally at peace. Nothing in our small town changed; life trudged on. Day after day, my urge to move, to do something with purpose increased. I could see with the passing of each day Mom was growing more tired. The house needed work and Dad was not getting any easier to manage. I did not want to leave but knew I must.

The end of my leave found me coming full circle. I had been ordered back to Meaford to meet with the commanding officer of training. Sitting across from the commanding officer, Lt. Colonel Sharpe, I wondered why Meaford.

"Lieutenant, welcome back. I figured you would find your way. I notice you are out of uniform. What have you got to say for yourself?"

I looked back at him in surprise. "Sir, I do not know what you mean!" Lt. Colonel Sharpe quickly slid two captain epaulettes across the table.

"This should make it right. Congratulations, Captain!" Lt. Colonel Sharpe smiled.

"The reason I have brought you here today is that we are about to commence a new training program. We have been watching your team for a while now. We see the strength and cohesiveness with which your team functions and have decided to model all our recruit groups in the same manner. I've been asked to coordinate that training and have decided you would be the best candidate for that leadership role.

"Unknown to you, Alpha Team was the first of its type. You had been so successful in picking the members that the upper brass wished to use it as a model for future recruits. Your job, for now, will be as training coordinator."

It did not seem that tough to me. Our team was more like brothers than soldiers; we were already close.

"The blue folder in front of you has the training outline. I will give you a couple of days to review it, then we can talk again. If you have no immediate questions, I will let you get to it."

I dove headfirst into my new assignment. Evaluating recruits and creating working teams required my complete attention. Instructing and teaching were my true calling—I genuinely enjoyed helping others.

Many returning soldiers who served in the Afghanistan battles, both as combatants and as peacekeepers, had been purposely stationed at the Meaford base. To pick the best of the best, I would be faced with the task of getting to know each and every soldier—their strengths, their weaknesses—then matching them up with other equally strong individuals.

Good teams do not always come from like-minded people or similar personalities, but rather from complementary personalities. I understood this and applied my skills, aligning the skill sets of each soldier to the needs of each team.

The administration building did not seem as large as it once did. Somehow, I remembered spacious rooms with large offices, but my new office was tiny. In the corner against the window sat my small desk, small file cabinet, and small high-back chair. Everything looked so small. I gave thanks to God, grateful that I was not claustrophobic.

Two large stacks of file folders sat on the corner of the desk. My job was clear. Rolling up my sleeves, I opened the first folder. From the flip of the first page, everything was right. Not as adrenalin-filled or exciting, but right. Rumours had been circulating at the base. A terrorist attack on a nuclear plant may be imminent—specifically the Bruce Nuclear Plant. Upper brass acted swiftly, pulling together counter-terrorism teams at all bases across Canada. Each team was to consist only of members who had served in Afghanistan or had recent, significant anti-terrorism experience.

Given the reputation we had gained in Afghanistan, Cook's Team, as we were dubbed, became the first team to be considered. We were the unanimous choice. Luckily, the whole team had survived and had re-enlisted. Now the task was to expand our combat experience to include the latest in techniques—counter-terrorism techniques.

Twelve weeks of training was laid out in the folder before me. But before I could start, I had to add one more person to my team. In Afghanistan, we had worked with a seven-man team. For logistical reasons, the team needed to consist of six members, including myself. We were currently one man short. We had no medic. I must find Lieutenant Renner's replacement.

Sitting on my desk were twelve folders, all potential candidates. I now had the onerous task of deciding who would be the newest team member. For the current dynamics of the team to remain unchanged, personality, experience, and ability would have to be paramount in my decision. I leafed through the folders; instantly, I was drawn to a folder marked "Sergeant Sally Cowalski."

Why did that name seem so familiar? I flipped to the attached photo, and it became clear. She was the medic that had treated Andrew James the night of the rattlesnake bite. That day seemed so long ago.

Reading further into her record I noticed she had been an ER nurse before enlisting. As well, she had served eighteen months in Kandahar as a field medic. Her academic ratings were at the top of her class, and she was extremely athletic. To her credit, she had competed in the Boston Marathon as well as world-class Ironman competitions. She had the potential to be a strong asset. As I read into her file further, I could see that she seemed perfect for the job.

I continued to review the other eleven folders. All candidates had good medical qualifications: some strong in weapons, others in communications, and others were just battle-tried, experienced soldiers. The strength of my team would be their ability to work under isolation and extreme conditions. Scribbling "arrange interview" onto the yellow Post-it Note, I stuck it to the folder.

PART SEVEN

NEW KID ON THE BLOCK

Mohammad Hassan had created quite a stir. Despite being a very new player in the world of terrorism, his name kept popping up. His organization had been rumoured to be involved in the street bombings in London as well as the dropping of the Asian airliner. He reportedly had his fingers in every kind of terrorist activity. With funding from radical Muslim organizations all over the world, Mohammad had pulled together considerable financial resources. His support network was spreading faster every day, including training camps around the globe. Wealthy individuals in all the Arab nations, West Africa, and Afghanistan started opening their wallets. Vast amounts of Arab oil money funded terrorism all over the world. Mohammad knew it and wanted his share. Worldwide anti-terrorism organizations could only watch and wait as signs of his organization popped up in every country in the free world.

Word had spread. Homegrown terrorists began pledging allegiance to his group. Mass rallies were being held in defiance of all attempts to stop them. Like a plague, they were spreading. Mohammad and his forces were becoming a growing concern.

Rumblings in the intelligence community indicated Mohammad Hassan was planning something big, and he intended to bring it to Canada. Canada had always been a tolerant peaceful place to live; however, our way of life would soon be tested. A country with numerous nuclear plants and thousands of miles of unprotected borders made it appealing. Mohammad Hassan saw Canada as an apple ready for picking and started concocting his next attack.

PART EIGHT

READY TO LEAVE—NORTHEAST AFRICA

Mohammad strolled back and forth across the hot desert sand. Soon he would be trading this barren wasteland of northeast Africa for the cooler climate of eastern Canada. Oblivious to the heat of the midday sun, he stopped. Deep in thought, he stared across the compound. This helter-skelter cluster of tents in the middle of the desert had been his home for the past two years. Born and raised in the desert, he did not find the stifling heat as unbearable as his comrades. Most of them had been raised in the much cooler climates of Russia and northern Europe.

Ruthless killers from varied backgrounds, people displaced by the fall of the Iron Curtain now lived in the many remote training camps of organizations such as Mohammad's. They were mercenaries with loyalty only to money. During the Cold War years, Russia and most the Middle Eastern countries had been havens for training terrorists—mostly ragtag groups, poorly organized with limited direction. Mohammad Hassan's organization was but one of them. It stood out.

At an early age, Mohammad became cold, detached. Amid constant violence, he grew up watching his friends and family killed. Now an adult, he held little regard for human life and wandered about the world, destroying whatever and whomever he wanted. He was described as a true sociopath—a person with deep personality disorders and antisocial attitudes. Mohammad's unpredictable behaviours manifested into hatred. He became a man lacking a conscience, often described as a poster child for the criminally insane. Mohammad survived using this same violence to his benefit. Having no regard for life of any kind, he would kill for fun. His network of camps and training locations extended from Sudan westward to Nigeria and down to

Angola, including the central parts of Africa. With little to no restrictions on land travel, his forces could move around freely, easily staying away from those who would like to see him stopped.

Having himself spent considerable time training in Afghanistan, Mohammad had grown to hate anyone or anything that represented freedom or the Western world. Having fought both the US and Canadian forces near Kandahar, he ranked his hatred for them high among his adversaries. The loss of many of his men to Canadian and US snipers fuelled his need for revenge.

PART NINE

CFB MEAFORD

The latest intel reports lay spread out across the large oak table. Alpha Team needed to understand our latest adversary. Mohammad Hassan was no ordinary enemy.

Intelligence Report—Nigeria

Today, I set aside six hours for Alpha Team to hash over the details listed in the latest reports. Mohammad Hassan was proving to be one interesting and complex individual. We hoped to better understand this new adversary and the security threat he posed.

"On your table is the latest status report. Please take a few minutes and read through it.

"Two weeks ago, satellite imagery had shown what appeared to be Hassan in Libya. Gentlemen, Mohammad Hassan's current location now appears to be in the wilderness of West Africa—Nigeria, to be specific."

The report went on to give a brief overview of the Indigenous people. The rural population were simple people—for the most part, poorly educated and willing to do just about anything for food or money. Their existence was purely day by day and hand-to-mouth.

"Gentlemen, upon landing in Abuja, Nigeria, Mohammad met with Desmond Atutu, one of his many personal guides."

Shifting position, I touched my wooden pointer onto the next photo. I continued, "Desmond Atutu is a native-born Black man from Abuja. He speaks all of the local dialects, as well as fluent English.

"Desmond escorted Mohammad by car to the Kaduna *province*. The Kaduna province is situated here, close to Abuja."

The tip of the wooden pointer moved westward on the map. "This area is scattered with poorly maintained roads, most of which lead to secluded camps, deep in the jungle.

"Nigeria is one of Mohammad Hassan's favourite training areas. Law enforcement in this country is nonexistent, so his people can train without the worry of being detected.

"The last report indicated that Desmond Atutu picked up Mohammad at the local airport, the drove him to a nearby camp.

"Satellite photos show this particular camp is situated on the southwest end of a small lake. The camp is well positioned: close to a water source with a rock wall on the west side providing a shield from attacks. The prevailing west winds blow all camp odours out and away from the camp. Their sleeping quarters have been positioned furthest from the compound entrance against the cliff. This area is hot, even at night.

"This small cluster of buildings on the east side of the camp are the latrines. The entire camp is surrounded by a ten-foot-high fence topped with razor wire; two six-foot lockable gates afford them minimal security, particularly at night. The camp is well laid out by someone who knows what he is doing—someone who has experience. Satellite photos show this individual at several different camps."

My pointer moved across the photo to stop on an image of what appeared to be a white male.

"We believe he has personally overseen all aspects of this camp's construction. As of now, we do not have his name.

"Inside information indicates that these camps are run very strictly—no disobedience is tolerated. I will give you one example of how ruthless they can be.

"Our source informed us that this subject, while surveying the compound last week, detected a young child hiding behind a pile of thatch. Somehow the child had managed to sneak into the compound, likely with the intent of stealing.

"Upon being detected, the unwelcome little intruder attempted to run away. The subject called to the child. As the child ran, he drew a pistol from his belt then squeezed the trigger. The bullet entered the back of the child's skull, spewing brain matter for ten feet in every direction. The child tumbled face-first into a pile of his own blood. Walking away, the assailant just laughed. This bastard—a cold-hearted killer.

"Promptly, two of the guards dragged the carcass through the gate, throwing his limp, lifeless body into a nearby pile of debris. No doubt the jackals ate well that night.

"You should by now have a mental image of the individual we will be dealing with."

I could see from the report that this individual was a force to be reckoned with. The report went on to describe Hassan.

SUBJECT

Suspected to be Mohammad Hassan
Identity—to be confirmed
Unpredictable, extremely dangerous
Source:
Paid informant—Desmond Atutu

The last item puzzled me. Mohammad Hassan was recently seen in Libya. Could Desmond Atutu be wrong?

PART Ten

SCHEMING

Mohammad lounged under the flap of the tent, pondering. He had numerous locations in mind that would be excellent for his next attack—Canada ranking foremost. Canada was going to know the anguish of war, war on their soil.

Plans were already underway. Mohammad had many allies within the USA and Canada, where he had no trouble recruiting someone to function as his eyes and ears. Transporting the required weaponry and explosives within Canada had already been arranged and awaited his direction. He could not believe how guileless these Canadians were. They accepted everything at face value, thinking there was good in everyone. He was about to prove them wrong—shatter their beliefs.

"I must prepare my checklist. Where is my pen? My notebook?"

Reaching into his tattered jacket, he extracted the tiny pad. He scribbled across the top of the page in Arabic, confirming tasks. Midway across the page, another column—tasks yet to be completed.

For two hours, he sat in the shade of his tent, writing. Roughly translated his list read:

- Acquire sample of explosive. Budget: one million dollars.

- Test sample. Use Angola as test site; brother Abid to oversee test.

- Transfer funds after successful test. Budget—eight million dollars should do.

- Ship explosives into Toronto. Need details.

- Warehousing of the explosives. Unresolved.

With much of the trucking industry already infiltrated by extremists, Mohammad could transport anything anywhere he needed, including hiding additional items within truckloads of products. Successful attempts had already proven it. Pickups were easily coordinated within the Toronto cell. Secure in this knowledge, he proceeded to list the remaining items. He could already envision success.

Years of mental torment in a war-torn country had moulded his personality. From a young age, death and destruction had been his norm. Violent and often paranoid, Mohammad lived in a world all his own. Both he and his younger brother suffered from the same affliction. Paranoid schizophrenia had been diagnosed early. Constant beating at the hands of their father only aggravated the condition.

Rambling on, Mohammad continued his list. "I am much smarter than them—powerful. Hah. They won't know what hit them."

- Pick my most loyal trucker. Needs to be resolved.

- Arrange vehicles to deliver explosives to the final location. Needs to be resolved.

"I must choose carefully. My bombers are most important. I must get them ready. They must be taught to hate; each must believe that it is Allah's will. I must convince them of the need to do his bidding. They must all want to do his bidding."

As the sun drifted across the sky, Mohammad passed in and out of consciousness. Unaware of the lost time, he would open his eyes only to resume writing. Unable to stop the voices in his head—they argued with each other—he pushed on.

- Pick suicide bombers. Unresolved.

- Complete radicalizing existing males. Unresolved.

- Radicalize new bombers. Unresolved.

"Unresolved, unresolved, unresolved! Why must I have to do everything?"

He screamed louder and louder as he became increasingly agitated. The whole camp became acutely aware of his state. All of them had seen it before. Soon he would get violent; soon someone would be beaten, even killed.

Since the capture of the Toronto 18 in 2006, his movement had slowed down. In this one incident, Mohammad had lost many of his most loyal followers. After 2006, recruiting for his cause had become harder. Many of the younger generations were now beginning to believe in the ways of the west, seeing the new way as a better way and no longer seeing the need for violence. RCMP and CSIS were also putting a tighter squeeze on Muslim businesses and community activities, watching the comings and goings of the known extremists within the community. The RCMP and local police forces had been able to see patterns and find ways to connect many of the dots. CSIS had even secured an Arab informant, an individual who had been influential in the capture of the Toronto 18.

Suspecting something was up, Mohammad had withdrawn further into himself and trusted fewer people. Times had changed; Mohammad realized these people were no longer like the people back home. In his homeland, constant war and violence supplied him with a steady flow of emotionally damaged people—people full of hatred, people whom he could easily sway. As his list of friends and loyal supporters dwindled, Mohammad became more secretive.

Mohammad had become an expert in manipulation, able to find and prey on people's weaknesses. Young Muslim males remained easiest to radicalize, especially when there had been a recent traumatic experience. An experience such as a death in the family or an unsettling event would make them question their values or beliefs, making them vulnerable. Mohammad remained confident that many of them could be swayed.

But could the new followers be manipulated enough to believe in his cause? Mohammad trusted that his compatriots would be able to complete the final act, the act of blowing themselves up—but could any of his westernized followers? This would all take time... time to do it right.

Further down his list, "BOMBS."

Bombs—how to accomplish? How to get enough raw materials to the warehouse—a secure place for assembly, ready for delivery?

Mounds of paper lay piled up in the corner of the tent. Mohammad had spent weeks gathering data on the CANDU reactor. Research indicated it to be the safest, most reliable nuclear reactor ever built. Still, it had to have some weaknesses. He needed to find just one, one where the C-4 explosives could do the job.

He did not have to destroy the plant or cause a nuclear explosion; he only needed to cause a large breach in the reactor wall. The radiation leak would do the rest. People would die, and thousands would be without power. He needed to plunge them into darkness, then, while chaos reigned, he prepared for the next phase of destruction. His plan seemed sound.

Across the Atlantic, informants were already busy gathering drawings, sketches, and details on each of the facilities. Mohammad smiled an evil grin. Just a little more information. Soon he would be able to formulate his final plans. Next to the actual explosion and subsequent deaths, scheming remained his favourite pastime.

Mohammad continued to connive. This endeavour would take months to plan and probably just as long to execute. He had the time and the resources. With determination, he would succeed. Right now, Mohammad needed rest. He would soon be leaving for Canada.

PART ELEVEN

NEW ORDERS—MEAFORD, ONTARIO

I had received our new orders—proceed immediately to Ottawa; report to the director of the Canadian Security Intelligence Service (CSIS).

Tomorrow our bus would take us to the new CSIS facility near Ottawa. Our orders required us to report to the director's office for a briefing of CSIS activities already in motion and the latest intel. Alpha Team would be spending weeks of intense training on the newest version of the Incident Software. Many years of development and testing had made this Canada's strongest tool in the fight against terrorism and organized crime.

I stood looking over my file of known terrorists, attempting to record them to memory. Individuals involved in attempting the attacks would more than likely be major players. I wanted to be able to spot and identify any of them instantly.

Mohammad would never conduct any of the work, I remained quite confident of that; rather, he would delegate his menial legwork to junior members. Only the important tasks would be managed by his senior people. Only by a freak chance of luck would CSIS or any of the local forces discover high-level tasks being overseen by the underlings.

Mulling over the files for hours upon hours, reviewing the files of the known associates, I hoped that I could find just a clue or two that may lead me up the ladder, hopefully to Mohammad Hassan himself.

Mounds of RCMP and military intelligence information lay on the table before me. Slowly, I started to assemble my terrorist wall. A corkboard stretching a full sixteen feet long by eight feet high currently stood empty before me. One by one, I filled the space with pictures of the known terrorists.

The information in each folder provided all known allegiances between the known cells and, most importantly, who was controlling them.

The photographs were up. Before each photo, a section for general information sat blank. Gradually, I filled in the blanks. As I cleaned out each folder and added more information into the data base, the program took over, systematically connecting all the dots. I began to see the common denominators, links between specific people and events—links, which would no doubt aid me in identifying the how, the when, and the where of the next attack.

I stepped back to survey my week's work. The electronic screen portrayed all past and current links to Mohammad. Pictures without enough information flashed red in the comment boxes, awaiting further data. Depicted high above the others, the black-and-white photo of Mohammad Hassan showed ties to all the cells and high-ranking individuals within his organization. Information had already started flowing in. I could see the program working. This new Incident Software updated faster than I could ever imagine.

No matter how small or seemingly insignificant the detail, the software revealed the association, correlating the ties between incidents and people. Information poured in from every agency. DMV, police reports, accident reports, credit card activity, even street corner traffic cameras supplied data. Any event with even the smallest trace of the person's profile was feeding directly into the database. This new software was being used by all major anti-terrorism organizations and governments. Work that would have taken me months, possibly years, updated by the minute. Upon entry, the data was analyzed, and tracking patterns were established. This new software had already been instrumental in compiling the movements of the Toronto 18, eventually leading to their capture. I hoped it would be as effective in finding and apprehending Mohammad Hassan.

With the use of wiretaps, video surveillance, and email monitoring, the RCMP, CSIS, and our team gradually pieced together an interpretation of the events to come.

One particularly troubling piece of information flashed across the screen:

"Serpent alive and well, expect venom to be extracted and delivered to doctor shortly. Will advise."

Judging by the source of the email, it could mean only one thing. The terrorists had found a source for the explosive they needed. Now, all they would need was for it to be delivered to the bomb maker.

Once again, I looked forward to getting down to some serious work. Day by day, the information piled up, filling in the gaps. Close to the action and able to make decisions that got results, I eagerly anticipated each new piece of information.

Sergeant Parker rounded the corner into my office. "Sir, I believe you will want to see the latest email transmission from Ireland."

The email read, "Venom purchased, due to arrive Cuangar, Angola in four weeks. Await destination coordinates. Will forward my banking info shortly."

Abid had just arrived from lunch; now he had to relieve himself before lying down for his afternoon siesta. He would have a brief two-hour snooze before returning to his scheming. As he entered the outdoor latrine, the stench filled his nostrils. Not one to be squeamish, he did not seem bothered by the odour. As he lowered himself to the wooden seat, the flies buzzed about his uncovered head. He took another deep breath, enjoying the stench.

Having emptied his bowels, he reached down with his bare hand and wiped away the remaining matter still clinging. With a flick, it flew down to rest on top of the revolting heap below. Removing a small rag from his pocket, he wiped his finger. With the rag folded, he placed it back into his pocket then retraced his steps across the compound to the cliff wall.

In the shade of the acacia trees, he flopped himself into the loose weave of a hammock slung from tree to tree. The breeze drifted over Abid. It took but a few moments before he fell into a restful sleep. Slowly, the steady drone of a bulldozer nudged Abid into consciousness. As the dust rose above the compound, Abid could see the makings of his new rifle range. Soon he would have the range completed. He could then teach his comrades to shoot and perfect their killing skills.

The workers and soldiers shuffled about the compound as usual, but the mood in the camp seemed a little different today. Although a few of the individuals had spent time together, no one in the camp had served with or spent time with Abid Hassan. All had been advised that he should be given a wide berth. He may employ them, but they should not believe him to be their friend.

PART TWELVE

THE PRODUCT—BELFAST, IRELAND

Encouraged by rumours of a new undetectable binary explosive, Mohammad Hassan contacted the Irish cell, wanting to see if they could supply a name or at least the contact info for the chemist responsible. Rumours began to circulate; someone had been looking for the unidentified chemist. Who he was, where he was, remained unknown. Rumblings of Mohammad's request circulated in Belfast. Surprisingly, it was not long before it reached Ralph.

Ralph sat all alone, squeezed into the corner booth at O'Reilly's bar. Ralph liked to be alone. The small pub had been a favourite meeting place for the local thugs and unsavoury characters. It was a dingy little hole in the wall, poorly lit and smelling like week-old beer.

At age fifty, Ralph had only one trusted friend. In this business, being anonymous was the only way of staying alive. Kind of a nerdy little man, Ralph had few friends; he preferred it that way. Always scribbling in his little book, most people viewed him as a little simple. He did not have a problem with this; it allowed him to go about his business unnoticed.

Ralph lifted his head as he heard a familiar voice: "Two pints of your best, Patty."

Jimmy O'Brien had grown up in this neighbourhood; he knew everyone. Strolling over to the little booth, Jimmy offered a glass to Ralph. Smiling, Ralph extended his hand to grasp the froth-covered glass.

"How be the wife and kids, Jimmy?"

"They be fine, thanks."

Lowering his voice, Jimmy leaned toward Ralph. "I suspect that you have heard the latest rumour about that mystery juice of yours."

Ralph took a sip of his beer. With the glass concealing his face, he acknowledged, "Yes, I have. You know, Jimmy, rumour also has it that this bloke is a whole lot more psycho than any of the others you have dealt with."

"Yeah, I know. The bigger bait usually brings out the bigger fish. Remember, Ralph, as soon as this sale goes down, you can retire to some southern island and watch the bikinis go by."

"Jimmy, I sent off a message last night. The response said I would receive eight million dollars. Half on order, a million after a successful test—the balance on delivery of the completed order.

"I replied that I would get a sample prepared, then we could arrange for delivery to a remote test site in Angola. Jimmy, I need you to take the sample to Angola. You know I do not feel comfortable meeting with the clients. If you go, I will split the money with you. Forty-sixty, plus all expenses, OK?"

"Ralph, I too received a message the other day. The bloke wanted to know if I had heard anything about the mystery chemist.

"I have been doing this for a long time. Never has a buyer come directly to me. The writing was very fragmented. I suspect whoever sent the email uses English as a second or third language. He said he got my name through a mutual acquaintance, that I have been mentioned often as a go-to guy. You had better be careful, Ralph."

Jimmy resisted the urge to show anything further. He did not want Ralph to know he, too, had been offered five hundred thousand dollars—a finder's fee to find the chemist.

"This bloke is determined to find you," he said. "He desires that mystery potion of yours.

"The buyer wants to proceed at once.

"Our mystery man disclosed that he has considerable funds and will pay whatever is needed. If we get the product through customs and the test goes over without a hitch, your DD90 is going to make you an extraordinarily rich man. But he wants a commitment that you will sell only to him. Ralph, this could be good for you. He does not want your DD90 to get snatched up by one of his competitors.

"He was very adamant and repeated several times that I must find the chemist for him.

"At the moment, Ralph, all I can go by is that he signed the email 'MH.'"

"You remember the incident back in 2009, the bloke the media dubbed the 'Underwear Bomber'?"

Ralph shook his head, not recalling the incident.

"Come on, you remember, the plane flying over Detroit?"

"Yeah, I remember now. The shit he was using is TATP, an organic peroxide and a primary high explosive. It is usually in the form of a white crystalline powder and has a bleach-like odour.

"It can be triggered by heat, friction, or even shock.

"His TATP sample proved to be unstable. The bomber had it sewn into his underwear.

"Tough stuff…! In that poor chump's case, the chemical reacted simply because of his body heat.

"You remember, it started burning his crotch before it could be detonated.

"It is not too surprising, there are many other chemists feverishly trying to correct the shortcomings of TATP."

Lowering his voice again, Ralph pointed toward himself and whispered, "I alone have dune it, Jimmy; my DD90 is totally stable, completely odourless."

"Ralph let's have another pint. I need to hear all about this stuff." Jimmy quickly waved the bartender over; Jimmy needed to keep Ralph talking.

"My new concoction, or as I have dubbed it, DD90, is stable. It will only detonate with extreme heat changes. Jimmy, I perfected the formula and a way to detonate it with a simple laser beam. I can prove how good it is with only an ounce.

"A small drop on this here table and the whole table disappears. Jimmy, I have just opened Pandora's box. Do you know what this means? It is the holy grail of explosives."

"OK, Ralph, here is what we have to do. First off, talk to no one. While this transaction is going down, we must not be seen together.

"If this leaks out, they be watching my every move.

"Eventually, we will be discovered. Once that happens, we are probably both dead… Quick dead, for sure.

"I will contact this MH guy to advise him that I have the sample and that I will personally arrange delivery to the test site. Get the vials ready; I will get back to you once the details are in place.

"Ralph, please stay off the internet, talk to no one. Am I clear?"

Ralph leaned against the back of the booth. Smiling, he nodded his agreement.

A short walk down the street Jimmy looked cautiously through the window, the internet café had only one patron. It should be safe to send his email tonight.

> MH,
>
> Venom purchased in Belfast, due to arrive Cuangar, Angola in four weeks. Await destination coordinates. Will forward my banking info shortly.
>
> Jimmy

Re-reading the email, Jimmy quickly removed the words, "in Belfast." The word trust was not in his vocabulary, and he did not know this person.

The return email flashed onto Jimmy's computer screen.

> Jimmy,
>
> Deliver venom Cuangar Camp, four weeks, large snake, require three vials. Location and timing to follow.
>
> MH

"Acknowledged," appeared briefly onto the monitor.

Then Jimmy clicked "send."

All Jimmy needed to do now was lie low and hope Ralph could keep quiet. This DD90 had to remain a secret. Should the chemical be as good and undetectable as promised, Jimmy O'Brien would be able to carry it through customs at both Belfast and Huambo without detection.

With the explosive supplier secured, Mohammad could make travelling arrangements for Abid. To avoid authorities and arrive at the same time, Abid would have to leave soon. A flight from Nigeria to Angola, then the last leg of his trip by river and dirt roads. Mohammad loved how unrestricted travel allowed him to do whatever he wanted. Unlike the rest of the world, moving about in Africa, although slow, was unhindered. Mohammad loved how, with enough money, you could go anywhere or buy anything. Once verification of the DD90's destructibility was received, he would purchase enough explosives to complete his final plans. All he had to do now was to keep all the authorities confused.

"Bouncing a few more emails off foreign servers should help the cause. They should still believe I, Mohammad Hassan, am still in Africa. Briefly, at the least, it should keep them confused. Just long enough to finalize my plans," Mohammad mumbled.

PART THIRTEEN

RCMP, CSIS DIVISION—CANADA

DD90
URGENT—TOP-SECRET

Recent email activity to and from Jimmy O'Brien (Undercover agent - Ireland) leads us to believe that he has arranged a buyer for the new explosive DD90. Routing of the email puts the buyer in Nigeria. Based on previous correspondence, we also believe the DD90 will show up shortly near Cuangar, Angola.

Correspondence from Ireland's Directorate of Military Intelligence and Britain's MI6 has also confirmed the existence of the DD90 explosive. DD90 is rumoured to be twice as destructive as the standard TATP explosive and can be transported in liquid form. The explosive is also rumoured to be stable, triggered only by intense heat changes. We already know a laser beam is used as the trigger device.

We have ascertained the identity of the chemist and placed a twenty-four-hour surveillance team on him. As well, we are monitoring the chemist to study all his contacts.

Your team is to be deployment-ready in two days. Details to follow at zero-nine-hundred tomorrow.

Director Sharpe

Director, Canadian Security Intelligence Service (CSIS)

I re-read the email then hustled my way down the hall to the doorway of the Director's office. "Permission to enter, sir."

"Come in, Captain. This is something you will want to read."

With a flip of my right hand, I handed the email to the director. "I was wondering if you have seen this, Sir."

"Yes, I have, Captain. We will be briefing you and your team tomorrow morning. The Brits advised us a buyer's meeting has been set up. The threat appears to be real. Tell your team to get their game faces on. We cannot afford to miss this opportunity."

Saluting, I dismissed myself. Back in my office, I quickly forwarded an email to each of my team: **"Special Meeting Called. Your presence is requested for zero-nine-hundred tomorrow, Meeting Room #1."**

PART FOURTEEN

DECEPTION IN NIGERIA

The new rifle range neared completion as the bulldozer pushed the last pile of earth into place. Off to the side, Abid answered his satellite phone, "*Na'am.*" An indiscernible voice started talking in Arabic. Without revealing any of the dialogue, Abid stepped away from the surrounding individuals. Covering the mouthpiece, he continued with the conversation.

As the others continued discussing the recent work, Abid ran his fingers through his ragged beard, absorbing the directions issued from the other end of the phone. Just as quickly as the conversation started, Abid clicked his phone off. Turning, he rushed toward his sleeping quarters. Emerging shortly after, he signalled the others to stand around the table. Slowly, he unrolled the tattered set of maps onto the discoloured square of wood. Staring intently, he slowly moved the lead of his pencil across the outstretched map.

"Tomorrow I will leave. This is my travel route to Cuangar."

Abid continued. "To avoid authorities, we will fly our private plane from Kaduna above the Benue River to our airstrip at the junction of the Benue and Gongola rivers. We fly at night and rest during the daylight hours. Once we are refuelled, we procced down to the Sanaga-Lom camp in Cameroon.

"I need not remind you that our Cameroon camp is by far the most dangerous of all our camps. There is excessive poverty, jobs are scarce, and rival tribes control much of the area."

Abid glanced toward Desmond. "It would be best to get in and out of this particular airport as quickly as possible. Plan to only have a four-hour layover, you will refuel while the pilot and I rest. The warlords there would love nothing better than to get a free plane. Someone must always stand guard.

"Once this most dangerous part of our trip is over, we will start to relax our pace. When we reach Angola, we will stay one night to catch up on rest."

Desmond and the other help had never travelled far beyond their villages, let alone flown. Supervising them would be a full-time job. It had been a customary practice for Desmond to have a woman in every city.

"Desmond, need I remind you that on our last trip, your men were constantly trying to sneak away to taste the local wares, as they say, *to get their backs straightened.*"

Abid knew it would be a challenge to keep them focused on the security of the plane and the contents. Trying to scare them, he looked each man square in the eyes. "There are plenty of whores there, but with that comes alcohol, disease, and the possibility that I will shoot you if you leave camp.

"I remind you again: you are not to leave the airstrip. At least one is to stay with the plane at all times." Their disappointment was obvious, but Abid couldn't care less.

In detail, Abid explained the last leg of their trip through Angola. Though Angola was no longer tied up in civil war, rural bands of marauding thieves moved about the countryside, robbing from whomever they pleased.

Only two stops would be required in Angola. The last leg of the trip from Barragem do Gove would be by car to Caiundo, then by boat to Cuangar. With the tip of his finger, Abid followed the route of the Cubango River southeastward toward Namibia and the Caprivi Strip, stopping at the Okavango River.

Abid continued, "Travelling with the current should speed up this part of the trip, but it will still take us about two days to get there."

With the amount of local river traffic, Abid felt confident that the authorities would not detect them. Abid knew travelling by river would take much longer than flying but landing a plane at any city or town near the Namibian border would be too risky. Abid completed describing the details of his plan, then folded the maps.

Satisfied they all understood, Abid clicked away on his laptop as the group readied for the three-week expedition.

"Prepared, leaving soon. Will contact you upon arrival," was all Abid's email read.

PART FIFTEEN

MISSION PLAN—OTTAWA, ONTARIO

At zero-nine-hundred, I, along with Alpha Team, awaited the arrival of Director Sharpe and the advisors.

Proceeding to the front of the room, the director introduced himself and the other advisory staff. "Captain Cook, please introduce your team so we can get started."

"Yes, sir." I introduced the team: Sergeant Michael Parker Private Richie Miller, spotter. Corporal Robert Jones, sniper; Private Andrew James, armaments; Private David Dunsmoore, communications—radio operator; and Sergeant Sally Cowalski, medic.

With each of the names, I gave a brief narrative of the members' experience, responsibilities, and attributes. Each member of the team stood to attention as their name was spoken. For the benefit of the other dignitaries, Director Sharpe noted that the sniper team of Corporal Jones and Private Miller were now recognized as having made the longest confirmed sniper kill during their service in the war in Afghanistan and held the sniper team championship record.

Perfunctory applause was issued as Director Sharpe opened his red case folder to the first page. "We calculate that our best opportunity to eradicate Mohammad Hassan and acquire the sample of the explosive will be when Jimmy O'Brien arrives at Cuangar to meet him. Jimmy is scheduled to contact us as soon as he arrives in Cuangar.

"Namibia is agreeing to allow us to land a plane, with your team, in the capital city of Windhoek."

A large map appeared on the wall behind Director Sharpe. The bright red laser dot pointed first onto the city of Cuangar in Angola, then down to the country immediately below.

Circling the red pointer, Director Sharpe outlined a brief history of the area. "Namibia, to the south of Angola, became a separate country in 1990 when South Africa gave up control of the colony. They have remained a friendly government with little tolerance for terrorism."

Extending his laser pointer toward the right side of the screen, he circled the words Kalahari Desert. "Namibia, as you may know, is classified as a semi-arid zone. You will be travelling through the desert with dunes as you leave Windhoek, then bushveld like the rolling terrain of Southern Ontario as you approach Otjiwarongo."

Slowly moving his laser along the route, he described the details of their operation. "Then, as you move northward, you will approach Angola, where the bush gets thicker, the hills get higher—similar to northern Ontario—except no desert.

"You have been trained in similar environments, so other than the danger from wild animals, you should be prepared for the terrain. Sergeant Cowalski, ensure you are versed on the hazards of the area before shipping out.

"As per our usual practice, you will arrive near the destination, a few weeks early. You will be travelling as a group in three minivans towing two small pull-behind trailers and one larger storage trailer. To maintain the security of your equipment, we have arranged for you to stay at local farms near Otjiwarongo and Grootfontein. Travelling casually as tourists should allow you to stay undetected. Previous civil unrest and guerrilla activity have led to a ban on military camo, so on this mission, you will be allowed to wear casual clothes, but no camo clothing. Even with casual clothing, they frown on the use of camo patterns. Only after you have established contact and have moved to the outlying bushveld will you switch to your mission clothing.

"The main northbound road from Grootfontein will take you to Rundu, a small town adjacent to the Angolan border. Close by and across the border is the village of Cuangar. We have an operative on route to Rundu as we speak. He will contact you at the town market three weeks from today. The tiny airstrip where Mohammad Hassan and Jimmy O'Brien are expected to meet is located approximately forty kilometres from Cuangar. It appears to have easy access.

"The objective of this mission is to acquire a sample of DD90 with the detonator. If Mohammad or Abid Hassan is there, terminate them."

Director Sharpe looked over the room and asked, "Any questions?"

Private James piped up "Can you give us some of the characteristics of this explosive, sir, like how is it detonated? Is it a stable element? What level of power does this explosive have?"

Director Sharpe frowned, replying, "Well, just let me say that it is considerably more powerful than any C-4 you've ever used.

"It is rumoured that it is stable from plus fifty degrees Celsius to minus thirty degrees Celsius. Outside of those parameters, it is unclear how it will react, and I would not want to be near it to find out.

"And one last thing. The explosive is liquid, crystal clear, and will probably be transported in a sealed plastic bottle. We expect the detonator will be a laser, so look for a small object such as a pen or laser gun.

"The liquid could be labelled as shampoo or liquid soap in a dark or black coloured container. Gentlemen, and lady, your plane will leave in two days.

"Dismissed."

Upon dismissal, I requested the team stay back for further briefing. Addressing them informally, I reiterated the importance of the upcoming mission, informing them that we would assemble in the War Room the following morning at zero-six-thirty hours.

PART SIXTEEN

DEPARTURE—NIGERIA

Awakening early to the sound of a squawking rooster, Abid gathered up his sleeping bag and pillow then headed for the plane. To keep the men busy and away from the lure of local women the night before, Abid directed them to pack up all the personal gear, weapons, and food for the first leg of the trip.

Skipping down the dirt runway, the plane gathered speed. The noise of the tires on the runway ceased as the pilot pulled steadily back on the yoke. The plane eased upward toward the clouds, both engines giving off a steady hum as they spun endlessly. Departing to the east, "Circle the camp," Abid instructed the pilot. "I need to overlook the progress of the labourers from the last few days."

The long, open rifle range stood in contrast to the dense bush surrounding the camp, the now completed grenade and rocket launching area buzzing with activity. Visible from above, the trail of a rocket launched from a distant launcher, shot across the ground, culminating in the explosion of a small shack. This was satisfying to Abid since only a few short days ago this same group of individuals had no idea which end of the launcher meant business.

Teams of men could be seen rappelling down the cliff face then crawling through the muddy obstacle course. Numerous small buildings were cropping up, some for supplies, others for training; all seemed well. With pride, he smiled inwardly—his efforts were starting to show results. Soon he and Mohammad would be acknowledged by the world. They would be number one in terrorism.

Planning to be away for an extended period, Abid made it quite clear what work needed to be performed. His instructions were to be followed to the letter, or else. These men could only manage simple instructions; long lists were of little use. Upon arriving at his destination, Abid would again contact them. Further directions would then follow. For now, Abid could not be bothered with camp details; he had to focus on his present task.

144

All this time, during months of preparation and communications, no one had even suspected that he, not Mohammad, resided in Nigeria. This secret must be protected. For their plan to work, everyone must believe he is Mohammad. Abid smiled. Their ruse was working. In fact, Mohammad had left Sudan and was already in Canada preparing for the attack.

Just as a precaution, Abid instructed the pilot to fly low and stay between the hilltops—maybe an overreaction, maybe paranoia, but better safe than sorry. You never knew who was watching.

High above, he could make out the savannah grasslands, tropical forests, mountain plateaus, and the mangrove swamps scattered on the landscape below. Such a diverse land, full of peaceful existence in one second, then displays of savage survival in the next.

On the grassland below, a sample played out in Technicolor. A warthog scurried across the savannah, darting left, then right under trees and over grassy knolls, racing toward the safety of a tight thicket of pencil thorns. Right behind it, a cheetah in majestic all-out flight followed the pig's every move. With one long leap, then a swat to the rump, the cheetah rolled the warthog, end over end. The chase ended as quickly as it has started.

Although the sounds could not be heard from above, squeals of distress broke the silence. Overhead, the observers watched as the warthog fell to the ground. The cheetah flung its total weight onto the prey, clamping its pearly white incisors solidly into the neck. The pig would squeal no more. The cheetah, with her young, would eat today and the circle of life would go on. The brutal savagery sent a tingle up Abid's spine; he was as excited as if he had done the killing himself.

As the plane dashed from one white fluffy cloud to another, a multitude of birds in flight traversed the landscape, carrying on with their simple existence. The constant drone of the engines soon numbing his senses, Abid faded off, dead to the world. Slowly closing his eyes, he became oblivious to the wild yet beautiful land below.

PART Seventeen

TEAM BRIEFING—OTTAWA, ONTARIO

At zero-six-hundred the following morning, I sat patiently awaiting the arrival of Alpha Team. One by one, the team arrived, claiming their seats.

"OK, let's get started. Corporal Jones, Private Miller, you are Team One. Your objective is to assume a position on the ridge, southeast side of the airfield.

"You should be approximately five hundred yards from the exchange point. When Mohammad and/or Abid Hassan present a shot, you will terminate them. You're to also provide cover for Team Two and Three. Please remember, if at all possible, we must seize the explosive and the detonator intact.

"Sergeant Parker, you and Private James will be Team Two. You will proceed to the east side of the runway adjacent to the two old service buildings. Once there, you will set explosive charges on the fuel tanks and surrounding vehicles. We should expect that we will require fifteen charges total. As well, you are to take ten grenades per man/woman. Prepare five hundred rounds of ammo each and individual sidearms. Due to the arid temperature, rain gear is not needed; medium green camo should suffice. Angola is currently in the middle of a severe drought; the smaller riverbeds will be dry.

"Private James, you will be responsible for assembling and verifying each man's pack supplies.

"Sergeant, you and Private James will be located closest to the action and anticipate that location will provide the best chance to commandeer the explosive. Intel has confirmed an old tank is to be used for the test. I believe we can assume once the explosive is set in place, Mohammad Hassan and Jimmy O'Brien will want to be the furthest from the tank.

"Sergeant, you will stay at the far end of the runway closest to the explosive. Remember, the incendiary is extremely powerful; stay well concealed from the blast path.

"Private Dunsmoore, you're to ensure no one goes near or touches the explosive until the detonator is secured and disabled. Your job, as usual, is communications. Please requisition the required headsets and radio packs.

"Sergeant Cowalski, requisition the medical supplies today and distribute them to the men.

"We will be posing as tourists, so we will be making the usual stops at game farms with a short stop into Etosha National Park. To maintain our cover, a personal camera is permitted, and photos will also be allowed during this part of the operation."

Standing, I took one step backward and, with a crooked smile, announced, "Since we will be in Namibia three weeks early, I believe this will be our first sightseeing trip together. Personal gear should include three changes of clothing and a good pair of hiking boots. Khaki and browns will be good; leave the blue jeans at home.

"Sergeant Cowalski, please get acquainted with the local hazards and be prepared to discuss them with me at zero-nine-hundred tomorrow. Everyone else, you know what to do.

"We leave at seventeen-hundred hours on Wednesday, so we only have forty-eight hours to get ready.

"The plane will be noisy and most uncomfortable, so get a good night's sleep."

With all the necessary equipment lists prepared and submitted, the team settled in for their last night in a Canadian barracks. The first leg of the flight would be to Frankfurt, Germany, for refuelling, then down to Windhoek, Namibia. The total flight time without layover time: seventeen hours.

At zero-nine-hundred hours, Sergeant Cowalski tapped firmly on the small pane of glass adjacent to the door and awaited a response. Hurriedly, I arranged paperwork on my desk, then stepped forward to greet her.

"Come in," I said, smiling as she opened the door. "Please take a seat, Sergeant."

Stepping past her, I detected a faint whiff of perfume in the air. Casually I noticed how the camouflage clothing accentuated her waist and her small but shapely breasts. Everything was perfect right down to the shine of her boots. My mind drifted off for a second… Just as quickly, I regained focus and stepped behind my desk.

"Good morning, Sergeant. What are your findings and what should we be prepared for?"

"Firstly, sir, the men will be required to update all their booster shots, typhoid, hepatitis, and rabies boosters—required. I have arranged appointments with the base doctor for later today. Your appointment, sir, is at fourteen-hundred hours.

"Malarone for malaria must be started today; as well, we will need a supply of Aquatabs for each team member. I have been advised that the water within Namibia is acceptable, but I would recommend bottled water as long as we can get it.

"Animal threats are very real possibilities.

"We will be near the Caprivi Strip and the waters surrounding the Zambezi River. Hostile animal encounters could be expected. Hippopotamus attacks near water may occur. They are very territorial and extremely protective of their young. The next serious threat is the Nile crocodile, the largest of the crocs. It can grow to twenty feet in length and can eat its body weight in one sitting. You do not want to fall into the water when they are around!

"I am not sure of the Cape buffalo population around Cuangar Camp, but, if threatened, they are said to be one of the most revered and dangerous animals alive. Apparently, if startled or wounded, they have been known to hunt the hunter. We should give that animal space.

"As you are aware from Private James's issue with the rattlesnake, venomous snake bites can be deadly. Primarily, the puff adder and the Cape cobra are a big concern. I have requisitioned anti-venom for both. Hopefully, their use will not be required. The Namibian government will have it waiting for us when we touch down."

I hesitated as I looked at the sergeant. "The only thing that I can think of that you have missed is the human factor.

"Most of the locals in Angola have been raised amongst civil unrest, so they will kill without remorse. Raised in poverty, they will steal anything left out. Although they are not always a physical threat, we must be always mindful of this."

"I have advised the team that later this morning you will be giving them a medical briefing of what we have just discussed.

"If that is all, Sergeant, I must excuse you, I have much to get ready before tomorrow. Oh! Sergeant, once the mission starts, the luxury of perfume, is not an option—lovely, but not in the bush."

I stood sharply, saluted, then dismissed her. As she exited the doorway, I could not prevent myself from glancing in her direction. I may be an officer, but I still appreciate beauty when I see it. After all, a little eye candy never hurt anyone.

Slight twinges ran up my spine as she disappeared around the corner. I could not help but think she certainly has a way of bringing out the animal urges in me. Looking away, I shook it off, returning to the mound of unfinished paperwork still sitting on the corner of my desk.

PART EIGHTEEN

THE INTRUDER—CUANGO, ANGOLA

Lightly dropping onto the bumpy airstrip, Abid and his entourage exited the plane. After the long flight, everyone needed to stretch their cramped legs. It felt good to be back on solid ground. Facing east, all knelt onto the ground, bowing their heads, thanking Allah for the blessing of still being alive—the plane had not fallen from the sky, as each had feared.

Abid watched as they raised themselves from the ground. "See, I told you everything would be fine. In time, you must learn to trust me."

As the lackeys unloaded the plane, Desmond rushed into town to arrange accommodation. Glancing at his watch, Abid noticed the round trip had taken him less than an hour.

In Arabic, Abid announced, "Sir, the only rooms available are in a shoddy hotel. I have been assured that the rooms will be cleaned and ready by the time we get there—Cuango is not a place with luxury hotels."

"We will make do. Our schedule allows us only one night's stay."

The rooms were on the second floor of the three-storey hotel. Paper-thin walls and no glass in the windows allowed every sound from the street and the adjacent rooms to permeate their little ten-by-ten domiciles.

Through the hazy bug net canopy, a tiny bedraggled single bed dominated the room. A dresser and rickety old nightstand did nothing to add appeal. The *drip, drip, drip* of a tap drew his attention to the water-soaked floor across the room. Someone had recently filled the large white pitcher and placed a bar of soap in a tiny white bowl. A quick wash and rinse in the round porcelain basin, and Abid was now ready for dinner. Roused by the smell of freshly cooked fish, he hurried out the door and down the hall.

"Come, let's go, I am hungry!" echoed down the hall, in passing he knocked on each of their doors.

Sitting at a small table in the corner of the café, Abid was quick to order. "I will have the funge with fish."

Funge was his favourite Portuguese dish, especially when served with fish or chicken. Abid had become accustomed to eating this dish while serving time in the training camps of Angola. He looked forward to having a meal of it whenever he could.

Although typically a dish of the poorer people, Abid had learned to enjoy it. Tonight, he would have it with fish. On the menu, he noticed the option to have pork as the meat, but that was out of the question. For a beverage, he would have boiled water. He did not wish to experience the ravages of drinking local unfiltered water. His funge tasted especially good tonight. Three days of eating dry bread and biltong had intensified his desires.

Raised on the streets, mostly in slums, Abid remained watchful of his surroundings. Throughout the evening, he had sensed that he too was being watched. Something was making him uneasy, a bit paranoid. It might be danger, but maybe not. Eventually, he relaxed, dismissing it as just being overly cautious.

The evening passed quickly. Exhausted, they all retired. Their flight had been tiring. Combined with their full bellies, the desire for sleep became overwhelming. Not sure if the lackeys could be trusted to stay in their rooms, Abid lay listening for telltale sounds in the hallway—any indications that his men were trying to sneak out to grab a little female companionship. Not a sound was heard from any of the rooms.

"Ha. I must have really scared them." The whispered words broke the silence of his room. Abid had picked up the habit of talking aloud to himself from his brother Mohammad.

11:00 p.m., exhausted, all the lackeys seemed to be down for the night. The darkness of his room soon wrapped around him. He too was tired from their long day. Sounds and smells from the street below drifted into his tiny room as the pitter-patter of raindrops lulled him into sleep.

The clink of metal roused Abid. Slowly, he opened one eye. Adjusting to the darkness, he strained to focus. Standing beside the chair where he had left his money belt stood the back of a rather large black man.

Confused, Abid struggled with what his next move would be. He realized he had placed his dagger below his pillow. The cool sensation of metal heightened his awareness as he gripped the handle. Abid jumped out of bed. Focusing on the intruder's form, he lunged forward. Oblivious to the fact that Abid had swiftly narrowed the gap between them, the thief stood opening the zipper to remove the cash. Suddenly he became aware of movement. As the intruder turned, Abid forced the tip of his dagger below the ear, just above his collar bone. The cold metal of the dagger met bone as coins clanged to the floor. The large black form dropped to his knees. Although conscious, the intruder knelt motionless, unable to utter a sound. The point had found its mark.

Staring into the thief's fear-stricken eyes, Abid could see the intruder was not dead, just unable to move or speak. Abid sat cross-legged, enjoying himself, smiling, having fun. He had killed many people but had never been able to study them as they drifted away to wherever it is that dead people go.

"Come now, my dear man, surely you can help me here. You know, and I know, that you are going to die. The only question is when."

Abid realized at that moment that the thief was aware of his predicament, as he widened both eyes with fear. Staring into the man's eyes, Abid wanted, no, needed to see if he could analyze the exact emotions. No longer in pain, the thief lay motionless, gazing toward the ceiling.

"You infidel! Can I make you afraid? Can I make you experience pain? When will you be ready to face Allah?"

Abid kept whispering as he looked into the eyes of the deplorable man. "What does death look like?" Abid hungered to experience every new emotion.

Looking downward, he realized he was becoming aroused, sexually aroused. He had never experienced this kind of stimulation. Each time the thief would look like he were about to pass out, Abid would lightly twist the knife, bringing him back. Each time, Abid's arousal increased. Never had he enjoyed himself this much; he wanted it to continue... A slight breeze flipped the curtain, forcing a realization: the sun was coming up. He had been torturing this pathetic creature for three hours.

"Surely the hotel owners will associate me with the corpse. What to do with him—I must decide," Abid mumbled incoherently as he paced the floor. "Wait, wait, he is going to die. I have one more thing to do."

Looking into his victim's eyes, he could see the last sparks of life draining from the immobilized body. Reaching down, he looked, absorbing the moment as he shoved the blade further up and into the skull. The warmth of blood ran over his hand as the blade scraped against bone.

"My, what a rush. I must do this again."

Looking about, Abid noticed his window led to a small roof ledge, probably where the thief had entered. Grabbing the corpse, Abid lifted the lifeless weight, shoving it out the window onto the roof. Twenty feet away, a small parapet wall rose upward—not a large wall, but it would be enough to conceal the body.

"Ha. Good a place for Allah's gift. It will be at least a few hours before it will be discovered. By that time, I will be on my way to Cuangar.

"That was exhilarating. If only Mohammad had been here to experience it. When we meet next, I must tell him all I have seen, all I have experienced."

His mumbling ceased as Abid exited the room. Now he must get the others and leave.

PART NINETEEN

OFF THE GROUND—CFB TRENTON

Staring across the tarmac at the CC-177 Globemaster III cargo plane, I looked in awe, not able to get over the sheer size of the plane. The thought that it could even get off the ground, let alone fly, amazed me. There were larger planes, but this one was huge. Ground crews merely dropped the rear loading ramp and drove our fully loaded vehicles and trailers inside the plane's belly.

For the first time in years, I was bursting with anticipation. The importance of the mission, the responsibility it held—it excited me. A brief respite in a country heralded as one of the most scenic in the world… what more could a soldier want?

Enthusiasm bubbled from every pore as we approached the main door on the port side of the plane. Short and stubby, the plane looked like a sausage on wheels. The belly of the plane sat only a few feet off the runway. I had seen plenty of these planes while in Trenton but had yet to ride in one. It seemed hard to understand how a plane of this size could operate with only a crew of three. Our gear looked so tiny in comparison to a space designed to carry 102 troops and three CH-146 Griffon helicopters, complete with refuelling tanks. There would be plenty of room to move about on this flight and I would not have to worry about reserving a seat.

Secured to the floor of the plane, our vehicles with the trailers almost looked ridiculous. Today, the flight would carry no additional troops. Our mission objectives held far too much importance.

Slowly, the thrust of the engines increased, pushing us faster toward the runway. The sensation of rubber moving on asphalt increased as the CC-177 headed along the east–west runway. Moments later, CFB Trenton disappeared. With tipped wings, the plane banked to the right until we were heading east. Below, the Bay of Quinte sparkled as we climbed to thirty thousand feet. Frankfurt, Germany, would be our next stop. At a cruising speed of 520 mph, it would be roughly the same duration as a commercial flight, putting us into Germany the next morning. After a quick refuelling, we would then be southbound to Windhoek, Namibia.

Joking and kibitzing as most soldiers do, we settled onto lighter topics—discussions of where each team member had vacationed, or where they had visited during their last time off. All of the team members had been raised in rural Ontario, hunting and fishing were normal everyday occurrences in their lives. Corporal Jones loved to talk about steelhead fishing: how it kicked off at the end of April with the spring run; riverbanks filled with anglers, waist-deep in the rapid current; the thrill of that first fish as it snatched up his roe bag, looking for a tasty meal only to find the sting of a hook.

After the lockdown period of basic training, the team would often see Jones sneak away in the evenings. With fly rod in hand, he would be gone until dark, only to return with his limit of rainbow trout or steelhead salmon. He would traipse over to the kitchen to hand over his prize to the chef.

Playfully, Andrew James looked over at Sally. "Sally, have you ever fished?"

Halfway through Sally's reply, he announced, "The Canadian Fisheries Department have just bred a new species of fish. They crossed a coho, walleye, and muskie. They named it a cowalski. All they have to do now is to teach the dumb sucker how to swim!"

A huge uproar rang out from the team.

Sergeant Cowalski took it all in stride. "James, they have snakes in Namibia. You do remember snakes, don't you, Private James?"

Sergeant Parker snapped back, "Touché!"

Cowalski smiled, everyone knowing she had won that joust. Private James went quiet. He still had very vivid memories of his rattlesnake incident, an event he endured during basic training and one he was not about to forget. Sergeant Cowalski seemed to be just as sensitive about her heritage as Private James was about snakes.

All the while, everyone avoided discussing Afghanistan. That place had only bad memories.

The mood on this flight was different from that of our trip to Afghanistan. In Afghanistan, there was no adjustment time before the battle. You landed and immediately you fought.

Three weeks lead time would allow the team to settle in, to prepare. We all knew the time for tension and stress would arrive soon—far too soon.

Twenty-four hours later, our oversize chariot touched down in Windhoek. The amber lights flashed on the roof of the security car as airport police drove to meet us. At the furthest end of the runway, our wheels taxied to a stop. The CC-177 stood alone at the remote hangar, far away from the main terminal. Slowly, the rear tailgate dropped, exposing the interior darkness to the bright morning sunlight. Awaiting approval to disembark, we watched as the load captain quickly disconnected the vehicle straps.

Stepping into the bright sunlight, I commented, "Shortly, our equipment will be offloaded. We will clear customs, then wait for our contact to arrive."

As I stepped out of the plane, the heat hit me. It had to be at least forty degrees. A momentary feeling of suffocation grasped me like a plastic bag placed over my head. All air movement ceased; my lungs were forced to draw in harder.

"Gentlemen and lady, we are now at approximately 1,700 meters above sea level. Breathing will be slightly more difficult, and yes, it is hot out there."

Clearing customs would just be a formality; the Namibian agents already knew this plane carried military personnel. The purpose of our visit could not or would not be disclosed. A quick check of our ID against the manifest, and the agent handed back our passports.

I could see all the tourists exiting the Air Namibia planes, anxious to start their vacations. Even after their long flights, their moods remained relaxed and jovial. I, however, felt exhausted.

"Sergeant Parker, please escort the team to the money exchange wickets so they can convert their Canadian currency into Namibian dollars."

The sergeant promptly replied, "Hey, Lieutenant, did you see the sign? Nine-point-five Namibian dollars for each Canadian dollar. That seems like a fair trade."

Stepping out of the terminal, I glanced to my left toward a group of waiting vehicles. The morning sun shone a bright gold as far as the eye could see.

"Sergeant Cowalski, would you not agree—that has to be the most beautiful sunrise you have ever seen?" She smiled back at me. Staring, we absorbed the beauty of the moment.

Tourists rushed about collecting their baggage. All around them, a plethora of outfitters and tourist representatives were holding up signs.

Hunters claiming their guns hustled back and forth across the large, spacious arrivals floor. The world at this moment seemed safe.

PART TWENTY

HASTY DEPARTURE—CUANGO, ANGOLA

Abid, knowing he had better get as far away as possible, decided to add one more flight. Hasty instructions directed Desmond to immediately leave and get the plane fuelled and ready for immediate departure. As the sun peeked above the buildings, Abid finished the tasteless breakfast of stale bread and cassava porridge. Dull, but it would have to do.

Their departure had to be fast. With the sun still hidden behind the eastern horizon, the plane should be in the air long before the hordes of townspeople started moving about. A half-hour drive to the airstrip put Abid at the tiny field just as Desmond completed the pre-flight preparations. Abid grabbed the soiled grip of his radio, attempting to reach the pilot, but he received no answer. Again, he tried. No reply.

Fearing something had gone wrong with the plane, he pressed the accelerator closer and closer to the floor. With every bend in the road, the balding rear tires cast clouds of dust and debris into the air. Speeding down the sun-dried path, Abid grew more and more agitated. Approaching the runway, Abid was relieved to see the plane still on the ground, and still in one piece.

Jumping from the vehicle, he ran toward the sentry, "What has happened to the pilot?"

Hesitantly, the guard pointed toward the small cluster of circular buildings. "There. In the centre hut, sir."

Abid waved Desmond toward the little shack. "Why is our pilot not at the plane?"

Furious, Abid pushed open the door. To his dismay, the sorry-ass excuse for a pilot lay wrapped around a rather plump Black female. Rushing over to the bed, he slid his fingers around a handful of hair, jerking the pilot's head upward toward the end of Abid's waiting revolver. Alarmed and still suffering from the effects of the previous night, the pilot opened his eyes to stare straight down the stubby end of the barrel.

"Why could I not reach you? You worthless piece of shit!"

With wide eyes and a stammering voice, the pilot replied, "I did not expect you for another day. I… did not want to run down the batteries!"

Shoving the barrel of his pistol into the pilot's face, Abid sternly proclaimed, "If I did not still need you, I would blow your brains all over this harlot! Get dressed and get to that plane! You… you waste of a man."

Releasing the fistful of hair, Abid hustled out of the hut toward the vehicle.

Downcast and still weary from the night before, the pilot ran to the plane. First the right, then the left engine revved. A constant drone meant only one thing: they were ready to depart. Five minutes short of ninety was far too long. Abid hoped the body had not been found, but there was no doubt the vultures would soon disclose the corpse's whereabouts. The little escapade with the pilot had cost him at least an hour, an hour of valuable time. Time meant distance, and distance meant security. The plane had to get off the ground, now.

PART TWENTY-ONE

ON THE GROUND—NAMIBIA

I pulled, adjusting the grey shoulder strap. Tension pressed across my chest as I nestled into the front left seat of the lead Toyota, adjacent to our military guide, Reinhart. Private Miller and Corporal Jones occupied the rear seats. All members, except myself, would rotate riding up front in the lead vehicle. This permitted each the opportunity for updates as the trip progressed.

Ever watchful, I scanned the roadway as we sped along one of the many exit ramps. The *click, click, click* of the turn signal pointed us toward a huge sign up ahead: Otjiwarongo. Curving left, we manoeuvred our way out of the airport, eventually leaving the maze of roads and bridges and moving onto the main highway. In only a short time, we would be at the first of our scheduled stops.

On the edge of the Kalahari, the intensity of the midday sun cast wavy rays of heat skyward from the searing hot pavement. Sand was in every direction—everywhere different shades of red. I could not help but wonder, even though it was pleasing now, would I enjoy this as much if I had to live here, or would it become bothersome? Would this constant level of sun and heat become an annoyance?

We departed Windhoek. Our first layover would be at a small ranch near Otjiwarongo, approximately two-and-a-half hours north of our current location: 20.4545° S, 16.6645° E, elevation 4,790 feet above sea level.

Trotting leisurely along the sides of the highway, a small horse-and-donkey-drawn carriage inched toward town with passengers cuddled together, seemingly too many for the small animals to pull. The occupants, all smiles, waved as our vehicles whizzed by. Green stems of vegetables and wares for sale hung over the side rails. In each little village, small children scampered about the schoolyards kicking soccer balls, jostling each other around, oblivious to the world around them, presumably without care. Everywhere heat, dryness and a constant reminder of the lack of water.

No running rivers or lakes made Corporal Jones uneasy. With such a passion for fishing and any activity around water, he frequently commented, "I do not believe I could enjoy living here."

Reinhart noted that with three hundred days of sunshine per year, Namibia was truly a hot place. Knowledgeable, he jumped at every chance to share the local customs and culture.

The needle on the fuel gauge sat almost empty as Reinhart pulled toward a cluster of buildings surrounding the small petrol station.

"Tourist shopping in rural Namibia is a unique experience as we were soon to find out. Why don't you all do it a little shopping while I fill up the vehicle? Stretch your legs and visit some of the small establishments across the road."

I collected the team members at the rear of my Toyota, suggesting it best that we now refer to each other by names rather than rank. I did not want to inadvertently draw attention from bystanders—especially as we drew closer to the Angolan border.

Entering the small roadside store, Robert Jones proceeded toward the rear wall where an array of leather belts hung. Leafing through them for his size, he found one with the name NAMIBIA etched in bold letters.

In his usual good-humoured manner, Richie Miller walked over to Robert, uttering, "I think this one suits me. What do you think?"

"Well, Richie, it may suit you, but it will be hard for you to keep your pants up without a buckle. But then, from what I have heard, you don't have much to worry about."

Smiling, Richie investigated the glass-covered counter. "Mr. Jones, I have the perfect buckle." Reaching into the cabinet, Richie pulled out a buckle with a spent rifle cartridge. An H&H .375 cartridge was secured across the face of the pewter buckle.

"Perfect," Richie uttered as he reached for his wallet.

Directly ahead and just down the street, Reinhart pointed toward a small group of local vendors. Standing by their ramshackle huts, they waited for oncoming tourists.

"There you go. You will find lots of local artisans with souvenirs over there."

As Sally and I approached the group of vendors, it was like a feeding frenzy at the zoo—not at all like the stores we had just left. Vendors emerged from their little sales areas and hovered around prospective clients.

"Hey, mister. Come see my store. I have very, very good stuff… Special prices just for you today."

Past several doorways, I spied a small young Black girl shyly watching. She was a complete contrast to the other pushy vendors; it was almost as if she feared approaching us.

Bypassing the other vendors, I approached the young lady. "Is this your store?" I queried.

"Yes," came the reply as she stepped back to allow me in.

A narrow aisle stretched between two rows of tables. Sixteen feet of tables on each side were lined with wood carvings of all sizes and shapes. Animals, birds, and human busts, all carved in exquisite detail. Everywhere there were human forms, all with an erect penis. I could not help but notice, they were everywhere.

As I moved into the booth, I detected a follower, a male from another cubicle. While not alarmed, I became uneasy. Approaching the centre of the row, the male tugged on my clothing, trying to pull me away from the young lady. Out of annoyance I grabbed a statue of carved animals and inquired, "How much?"

"Three hundred dollars."

I did a quick conversion and came up with thirty dollars Canadian. All that time, the male vendor kept tugging on my shirt. This pushy little creep had begun to piss me off.

Just as I was reaching for my wallet, Sally barked out, "Go away! Stop touching me!"

I watched as she accelerated her pace, quickly crossing the road to the waiting vehicles. Annoyed at what had just happened, I quickly opened my wallet, paid for my purchase, and departed the stall, all the time very aware of the eye and body movements of the other vendors. I was almost sure I was going to get my pocket picked. The vendors reminded me of a pack of vultures over a kill: all wanting to take their piece, all eyeing the contents of my wallet.

Souvenir wrapped and bagged, I hustled out of the maze and back to safety across the road, away from the vultures. Once I had stashed away the carving, I approached Sally, inquiring what had transpired.

In a surprising, rare expression of emotion, she exclaimed, "I detest people touching me or pawing at me! When I shop, I want to be left alone, period!"

"Years ago, I travelled to Jamaica with my parents. This similar type of harassment was commonplace around all their little shops. It bothered me equally, though I did try to understand the culture…" My account did not soothe Sally's frustration.

Like a football coach, Reinhart swiftly huddled us into a circle.

"The remaining portion of our trip to Otjiwarongo should take about one hour.

"Once we reach Otjiwarongo, we should have only a thirty-minute drive to the first of three layover farms.

"I expect we should arrive just before the dinner hour. That will give you all time enough to settle in before getting cleaned up for dinner. Hustle up now, I would hate to be late for dinner."

Travelling through the countryside, I could see the changes in terrain from Windhoek, with the countryside full of sparsely covered, soft rolling dunes: varied grasses, scrub bush, thorn trees—and lots of sand. Everywhere impala, springbok, and blesbok pranced across open grassy dunes as they moved to safer ground. The southern deserts stood in sharp contrast to the thicker bushveld of Otjiwarongo, where you could only see about one hundred yards into the bush.

I found it very difficult to take a picture without animals in it. Oryx, blue wildebeest, hartebeest, all standing proud against the deep red sands. In the north, the kudu, warthog, and jackal showed their presence. Everywhere, animals—scurrying about, ripping up the ground, or barking as they searched for food. Sally found the kudu to be the most amazing. How an animal that big could just walk into the bush, stop, and disappear was beyond her. Each member of the team seemed to be attracted to a different animal—some for their size, others awed by beauty or grace.

Exiting the main road, our small caravan wound its way up the narrow lane between two strips of freshly cut hay fields, the sweet smell capturing the attention of the warthogs darting amid the stubble and keeping a wary eye on our approaching vehicles. With childlike abandonment, they playfully tossed the hay skyward with their snouts. With each short thrust of their tiny tusks, dirt flew, exposing the tender roots.

Robert casually raised his arms as though holding his rifle and announced, "Boom!"

With the image of the crosshairs etched solidly in his mind, he pictured how easy it would be to take down some fresh pork for dinner.

Rounding the corner to the yard, Sally commented on how hardy these people had to be with very little water, regular drought, being far from town, far from what westerners considered the necessities.

PART TWENTY-TWO

THE GETAWAY—CUANGO, ANGOLA

"Load up!" The lackeys jumped into the plane, slowly shuffling into the dinky seats. "We must get out of here, now! You will fly me to Caiundo!"

The rather blurry-eyed pilot turned, heading for the weed-infested runway. All the while, Abid gestured for him to get going, frantically needing him to get off the ground.

With a look of bewilderment, the pilot reminded Abid, "Sir, the Caiundo airstrip is not far from the Namibian border. Highly populated. Many people, sir."

The dust curled behind the wings as the plane skipped along the narrow runway. Only when the last bumps of the rubber tires ceased did Abid's nervousness dissipate. Peering downward through the tiny window, he could see deeper into the bush—farther and farther in as the plane cleared the tops of the trees.

Abid motioned. "Circle the airstrip."

Abid was too close to their goal to have it ruined now. He needed to know if the local police were onto him. He needed to see if he was being pursued. From high above, Abid could see only an empty road with no lights approaching the airstrip. He had eluded them. Feelings of excitement overcame him—tingling feelings. The same sensation he had felt when the big Black man had drifted away into the afterlife.

Southward, small villages speckled the earth below. Like flashlight beams in the darkness of night, specks of light shone upward. A new day was peeking over the horizon. Flying the new course, more villages appeared— more people. Abid became nervous, agitated—he despised people, hated the towns, the cities. All those strangers, too close, no space. He needed to avoid them. Sternly, he directed the pilot to head east toward Luena.

Flying this route would take them longer, but at that moment Abid did not care; they were already ahead of schedule; that was all that mattered.

PART TWENTY-THREE

OTJIWARONGO—NAMIBIA

Pulling up to the farmhouse, Reinhart exited the lead Toyota, into a cloud of billowing dust. In turn, each vehicle stopped. Travel-weary bodies stepped out, all needing to stretch their muscles.

Reinhart collected the group. "This is the home and game ranch of Uta and Frederick Linger. I must remind you that the Lingers are not aware of your group's status. I contacted them earlier, presenting myself as a travel agent, and you as a group of tourists. The Lingers are not to be informed otherwise."

Just as he finished his instructions, the rear door to the kitchen opened, and Uta and Frederick emerged—Frederick in his work clothes, Uta in her dress and apron. Flour dust clung to her apron; she had been cooking. It looked like the evening meal may soon be on the table.

Reinhart made his perfunctory introductions, noting where they had been and how the group looked forward to continuing their photo safari on this interesting piece of property. Frederick, jumping at the opportunity to talk about his home, decided to take the group on a quick tour of the main yard.

"The property has been in my family for four generations. To your right is our home, where you will be served your meals. Our original old farmhouse was constructed by my great-great-grandfather and still has the original ornate fascia and trims. Lodging for our guests is to your left in that smaller farmhouse. Ahead are two large implement sheds full of tools and equipment. The farthest building is the skinning and butchering building. As you can see, we are almost totally self-reliant."

As we passed the implement shed, the aroma of death drifted our way—the familiar smell of a butcher shop. All along the front wall, sun-bleached skulls with horns still attached lay leaning against the wall. I wondered at the significance. Frederick indicated that there was a strain of kudu rabies that occurred every few years. These were skulls and horns from various animals that had died recently on his ranch.

All the time we were walking about, I was reminded of my grandfather's little farm in Palmerston. My grandfather, also of German ancestry, had a small plot of land along the railway tracks. In summer, my brother and I would be sent off to see Grandpa and Grandma for a vacation. I fondly remembered how much I missed those times. Grandpa was a kind, gentle soul, always making me feel special. Every day at Grandpa's was a new adventure, much like this trip,

Returning to the guest house, I broke the team into pairs. "Richie and Robert in the ground floor front, Andrew and David behind them with Michael, and Reinhart on the ground floor rear."

Each room contained two single beds and a common washroom. On the second floor were two spacious bedrooms, each opening to a common washroom.

"Ms. Cowalski and I will take the upper two rooms."

All the rooms looked much more comfortable, cozier than the barracks we were used to.

Before supper, everyone gathered around the firepit for appetizers and beer. Lifting his glass of wine, Frederick offered a toast: "To our new guests and future friends, may you enjoy your stay at our home and in our beautiful country."

Gathering before the meal became a daily ritual; each person would discuss the highlights of their day. Supper each evening was cooked over the braai—steaks of kudu meat, fried green asparagus, and an egg with vegetable dish. Dessert was German fruitcake. The meal was hot, tasty, and plentiful.

Hosts Frederick and Uta aimed to please, displaying pride in both their home and country. Frederick especially enjoyed pulling anyone aside to discuss his family history. "My family lived here through the First and Second World Wars. My Namibia is a never-changing world, both politically and environmentally."

Hanging about the campfire with a beer after dark seemed different to the team. No studying, no drills, no exercising—a man could soon learn to enjoy this life. Pulling our chairs up close to the firepit, legs extended, the warmth from the open flame encircled our tired feet. The warmth gradually travelling upward, drawing us toward slumber. Exhausted from the day's events, the team readied for a good night's sleep. Bellies full of food and beer, two by two we meandered back to our rooms.

PART TWENTY-FOUR

ARRIVAL—CUANGAR, ANGOLA

Abid adjusted his position as the plane banked to the right, levelling out for the approach into the tiny airstrip. As they passed over the Cubango River, he could see fishermen casting out their nets with hopes of catching their evening meal. Lone females washed their clothing on the rocks, peering up at the plane as it passed overhead.

Like a silver moth, it gradually descended into the horizon, dropping lower and lower until obscured by the trees. Below, Abid could see people milling about, waiting for them to land. Out of the plane Abid lifted his sat phone, dialing a number.

"*Na'am*" came over the phone. Abid commented, "Doctor early, will wait for patient at Cuangar—appointment unchanged."

The receiver clicked silent as Abid returned to the plane. "Desmond, go secure a taxi, then go into town and arrange accommodations for the next six nights."

It would be about a three-day boat ride down the Cubango River to the town of Cuangar. Quickly calculating for his early arrival, Abid would now have seven days to kill.

As the pilot circled, he received his final instructions. "You will need to arrange security for the plane. Should I return early, you are to be available for immediate departure. Make sure the plane is fuelled and ready to go. At all times, understood? I trust I do not need to explain the consequences."

By his tone, the pilot knew exactly what he meant—what would happen if he did not comply.

Desmond rushed away, now, he would have his first opportunity to call his contact in Angola. Opening the seam along the bottom of his shirt, he removed a small piece of paper. Scribbled in black ink, the phone number for his contact appeared. Content, he shoved the small note deep into his breast pocket.

Departing with the rental car, Desmond searched for a phone, a place safely away from the ears of Abid. He had to make sure there was no way anyone in his group could see him making this call. Confident no one was watching, Desmond extracted the small piece of paper from his breast pocket. Punching in the numbers, he waited for the phone to ring.

Speaking Afrikaans, Desmond uttered, "We are on schedule, we will arrive on schedule in Cuangar.

"I will make contact upon docking at the local pier. We will be arriving on a commercial fishing boat—bright red and black with the Angola flag emblem painted on the bow. I will be wearing a shirt with the colours of the Nigerian flag, green/white/green, and a black knitted toque."

Hanging up the phone, he smiled. He had just earned one thousand dollars US. He earned that same sum every time he reported in with new information. Life was good. Soon he would be able to buy another wife. He already had three, but not one had produced a son.

Finally, they would sleep in a comfortable bed, if only for a few nights.

The evening entertainment had been arranged, as Abid had requested. Hoping this would please Abid, Desmond scooted away in the shiny new car, heading toward the best hotel in town.

One hour later, Desmond Atutu approached the airfield in the now, dust-covered rental car.

The midday sun rested high in the sky as they entered the main lobby. The ceramic floors glistened as the sun's rays sparkled off all they touched.

The openness of the foyer permitted the breezes to flow unobstructed in and around the tall pillars, gently moving the suspended chandeliers. As cool as air conditioning, the welcome breeze drifted across their hot, exhausted bodies.

Lowering themselves onto the rattan chairs, they sat enjoying the relaxation the chairs provided. Abid, for the first time since they had left Nigeria, did not have to hurry. Days ahead of schedule, he could relax, taking time for himself.

PART TWENTY-FIVE

REVISITING THE PLAN—
TORONTO, ONTARIO

Mohammad clicked off his sat phone. Abid seemed to have everything organized in Africa. His younger brother had grown to be a very organized and powerful ally. Now, if he could keep his temper and perverted desires intact, all would end as it should.

Mohammad had spent the last year analyzing the nuclear-generating facilities, identifying all the roads, in and out. He was sure he could deliver the explosives into the facility; even with all the security measures There seemed to be only one problem. With the CANDU reactor design, an explosion would have to be significant, directed either at the heavy-water cooling heat transport system or at the steam generators. New information showed the concrete walls of the reactor building to be eight feet thick and heavily reinforced. Any explosion there would need to be enormous, or it would have little or no effect.

The latest information had indicated that the heavy-water cooling system had eight-inch-thick steel piping. He could see no place where he could contain the explosion. A blast without containment would cause insignificant damage.

"Where can I create enough damage to knock out the plant?"

Reviewing the turbine and generator buildings, he discovered any explosion at this facility would result in minimum devastation—this was not his goal.

Although not confirmed, rumours indicated since 9/11 there had been measures put in place to prevent any air attacks on the plants: fifty-calibre machine guns set up on the roofs, and a greater air force presence. He was sensing that an attack at the plants would prove to be fruitless. He sat, annoyed at himself. He had just spent a year compiling the information for what he thought was such a great plan, only to find out it was trash. Recruiting, structuring the trucking details, planning for how to get the product into the facility, five hundred and fifty thousand dollars spent, and now, in the eleventh hour, to find out his information was flawed—someone was going to pay. He would not—could not—accept such incompetence in the people he trusted.

Staring out the window across the evening skyline, he looked eastward toward downtown. All those buildings, all those infidels. Staring at the high-rise buildings and the CN Tower, he pondered. Dropping the CN Tower onto the capitalist landscape of Bay Street... Yes, yes... arousal crept in... the devastation...

His rage grew gradually; unaware, he started talking aloud, arguing with himself, pacing the floor. "Yes. Yes. That could create serious long-lasting damage.

"No... no... no. They will be watching, expecting that. The statement has to be big, brash. I need it to be something that they are not going to expect.

"The test in Angola is scheduled in only two weeks... then the required production lag... I still have time to plan something. I must start now. This time, I will do all the planning. It is obvious; no one else can manage the task."

Mohammad's mind kept drifting back to the power distribution grid. "If I can upset the power grid, then I could have a chance to succeed. I need to know how powerful this new explosive is.

"If I could knock out the lines from each of the nuclear plants, and the lines from Niagara Falls, it would only leave the Quebec transmission lines. All I would need is four or five coordinated explosions.

"Ah, yes, yes. This too could create considerable damage.

"I can destroy both lines, leaving the Bruce Nuclear Plant and the Pickering plant at the same time. Oh... there will be such chaos directed toward the north that the Niagara Falls lines will be easy pickings."

Deep in thought, Mohammad analyzed every little detail. "Trucking, no problem. The minions, and their trucks are engaged. Yes!

"All the towers are rural, unprotected—easy.

"The arrival of the product, if undetectable, will also be no problem. But the product, how can I package the product?"

His devious mind shifted from topic to topic. Grabbing a pen, Mohammad frantically started writing the who, what, where, when, and why of every detail. His mental and physical being was aroused, stirring to a frenzy…

"Hundreds of miles of unprotected transmission lines. Just a matter of finding the most secluded sections, then planting charges.

"Something is not right, what am I missing? This is wrong, it will not kill, or cause misery, only inconvenience. I must find something else."

Then it came to him. The new UP Express, the fast rail transit system from Union Station to Pearson International Airport. There would be constant human traffic, and bombs could be easily placed on the trains and at the stations. His excitement and fervour heightened. This was even a better target. More people, more carnage… Yes, yes, this is the carnage, the terror, the goal…

"To take down the trains, I need one bomber on each train and one for each station. I must understand the design strengths, the weaknesses of the trains, the stations. I need drawings."

"I have contacts in the rail—need people to stake out the stations. Need to analyze all the weaknesses. Why, why, why must I do everything?"

Mohammad rambled, growing more exuberant. "These dumb Canadians, they welcome us in, then give us all the jobs in the places where we can do them the most harm. Hah!"

His previous havoc and death plans in the financial sector had been thwarted.

His rage grew more uncontrolled. Mohammad yelled, "Plan must succeed!"

Pacing the floor, he conjured up images of mass damage, death, and confusion. He remembered 9/11; he wanted the same thing to happen here.

"People will remember my name, Blessed be Allah. I will show them." Yelling even louder, he started shaking his fists in the air. His eyes grew red as he spat with every word.

"It may not be permanent, but I will send a message—a message that they have no business being in my country, my part of the world!"

For hours, he continued his rampage, knocking over furniture, stamping his feet. Finally exhausted, he sat, knowing now that he had much work to do. The deadline of only two weeks sparked a new drive within him—the needed incentive to get started.

Tired, he needed to relax. Reaching into the cabinet drawer, he pulled out a videocassette. Inserting the tape, he sat back to watch. It seemed so long ago since he had recorded it. Two years since his last torturing session. He loved to watch his tortures. They made him aroused, powerful. He felt good when others suffered the same way he had suffered.

PART TWENTY-SIX

EARLY TO RISE—OTJIWARONGO, NAMIBIA

The ring of the alarm came as no surprise. I had been lying awake for some time. With a big stretch and yawn, I rolled over to silence the annoying buzz. Zero-five-thirty had been the agreed-upon wake-up. I knew I had better get moving; I never liked to be last up. I had no desire to be viewed as the group slacker. "Lead by example, Spencer." I could hear my dad's voice again. I seemed to be hearing him a lot more recently.

Out of habit, I started making my bed. Suddenly I remembered, Reinhart had informed us the camp staff took care of all the household chores, like bed making and daily laundry. Not wanting to upset the apple cart, I ceased. I needed a quick shower to wash away that sleepy morning look. With a sharp right turn, I headed to the lavatory. Garbed in only my boxer shorts, I opened the door. Lowering my briefs to the floor and with one foot in the shower, I looked up as the door reopened. Standing in her bathrobe, Sally, although surprised, made no attempt to rush away—definitely, she was not embarrassed.

Feeling no desire to cover myself, I calmly asked, "Is there anything that I can do for you?"

With a smile and a longing glance, she stepped backward, closing the door. "Not at the moment, sir."

Well, that was fun. Perhaps tomorrow I had better lock the door, raced through *my mind.*

The sun seemed suspended on the horizon, peeking through the distant clouds as I completed shaving. I had always loved this time of day. Today was no exception.

Dressed, I headed down the old wooden stairs to the front porch. Staring out across the parched savannah, my senses filled with the smell of the air, the chirps of the birds. Everything was new; everything fresh. Most of all, I could not believe the beauty. Everything was in Technicolor. Bright, vivid colours everywhere. Every sunrise and sunset, different from the day before. Possibly it was the purity of the air or the angle of the earth; I was not sure. I could not remember seeing such consistent beauty back home.

Just when I thought it could get no better, the sweet smell of coffee caught my attention. FOOD!

Breakfast today started with brewed coffee and rusks. Dipping the dried bread into my coffee, I could see why it was considered the snack for rumbling tummies. The unique taste made it ideal for early morning—fast and filling. Alongside the rusks sat a platter of cold meats with cheeses.

Today I wanted some bacon with eggs. Uta nodded, in a couple of minutes, the plate slid across the huge colonial table. It was easy to see that the homes and everything in them were designed around large families: big rooms, big tables, and plenty of chairs.

"What would you like to do today?" Frederick inquired. "Is it your desire to take a game drive, or just tour around to see some of the local sites? Both can be managed if you wish to split up into smaller groups."

I chuckled, remembering back to the story of Aladdin, "*Your wish is my command.*"

Nodding, we all seemed in agreement—a game drive it would be. The team would split up into two groups. A driver for each group, would mean four in one vehicle, five in the other. The vehicles had plenty of room up back, so that seemed perfect. The Toyota trucks were equipped with a bench seat, or seats elevated above the box, a storage rack above the cab, and a gun rack behind the cab's rear window. For those on a hunting excursion, there was a winch assembly in the box below the passenger platform. Very functional, as most things here seemed to be.

Michael, Andrew, Robert, and Richie would ride in the lead vehicle with Frederick as their driver. I always liked to have Robert and Richie together. Sniper teams needed to think and operate as one— constant interaction.

Sergeant in one vehicle and myself in the other, I could be assured the discussions did not get off track, and someone inadvertently disclose mission information to the outfitters or their drivers. Reinhart, David, Sally, and I would ride the rear vehicle.

Once we had climbed up the side ladders and seated ourselves, the vehicles inched away down the narrow path behind the skinning shed. I managed to secure the seat next to Sally. I wanted time to get to know her. As we rounded the shed, the savannah spread out wide in front of us, scatterings of thorn trees and low bushes dotted the land. Everywhere you could see mounds of rocks—broken granite and boulders weighing tons piled upward toward the sky.

"Look, it is almost as if God had placed the rocks one by one." I exclaimed.

It was hard to conceive that these pyramid-shaped piles were a natural occurrence. Reinhart explained that they were called kopje—derived from the Afrikaans language for small rock hill.

Reinhart slowed the vehicle to a stop beside a huge kopje. Gesturing for us to follow, he headed up the rocky mound. In turn, we weaved and circled the large boulders, climbing until we were standing on the summit. We could see for miles. Slowly, Reinhart pointed downward to a cluster of trees about two hundred yards out. Barely discernible to the naked eye, Reinhart gestured, pointing out the legs. A group of zebras meandered lazily below the trees. Perfectly concealed—blending into the shadows. Peering through the binoculars, I could see not only the zebra herd but groups of oryx and other animals. Two, three, four hundred yards away—I watched as they grazed in the shade of the trees.

Casually I glanced over at Robert; I could see his mind working, estimating the distance, marking the target. Any one of the shots would be easy pickings for him. In a few short days, Robert would need to demonstrate this skill once again. Deep down, I hoped Mohammad Hassan would be the target.

Descending the kopje proved a little more treacherous than going up. More than once, a foot would slip, then the unsuspecting climber would fall ass-first into a crevice between two boulders—feet and hands pointing toward the sky. There he or she would sit helplessly until someone could pull them out.

Midday, while we stopped to eat our box lunches, Robert approached me. "Sir, would it be OK for me to take the following day for hunting? I have not practised for the last week; I may be getting rusty!"

We were not authorized to arrive at Rundu any earlier than scheduled, I did not see any harm with the request, and Robert was probably right.

"Maybe you should take Richie along with you." Robert nodded his agreement. Whispering I asked, "What about a rifle? You cannot use your fifty-cal."

"Well, sir, Frederick had commented that they have guns that we can rent on a per diem."

"You do realize that any trophy fees or other costs will be yours to absorb?"

Smiling like a kid with a new toy, Robert swiftly turned, "No problem, boss. My plastic works everywhere."

Feelings of pleasure exuded from me as I watched Robert return to give Richie the good news. My team gave so much while asking so little. Although a small gesture, this would be remembered long after the mission ended.

Back at camp that afternoon, Robert approached Frederick eager to discuss the rifle options. Robert wanted to see the weapons available. Frederick returned with three: a Ruger 30-06, H&H .375, and a Remington 7mm Mag. Robert thought for a second; he would opt for the 7mm Mag. The 30-06 was not as good at longer distances, while the .375 was more of a close-range, heavy knockdown weapon. The 7mm was a good, flat shooting, longer-range rifle with plenty of punch. Frederick promptly insisted that they fire a few rounds to make sure that the gun and the shooter could hit the target. With three boxes of shells and some clean targets, the trio headed out to the makeshift range.

Frederick peered through his range finder and confirmed the distances: one hundred and two hundred yards, respectively. Trying not to look too proficient, Robert inserted the first-round while Richie watched with the binoculars. With the crack of the shell, Richie announced three inches high and four inches right. Robert looked at Frederick. Taking a second shot verified his suspicion that the scope was off. "With your permission Frederick, I would like to adjust the scope." Robert commented.

"Looks like this gun has not been sighted in for a while. Would you like it set for one hundred or two hundred?"

"Two hundred will be just fine," replied Frederick.

Sixteen clicks left would be the only adjustment for the next shot. Three inches high at one hundred yards, although a bit higher than usual, it would be a good starting point. Robert chambered another round. Waiting a while for the barrel to cool, Robert relaxed.

Letting out a light sigh, gently he squeezed the trigger. Richie smiled. Left-right good, three inches high at one hundred. Another shell clicked into the chamber as Robert announced the two-hundred-yard target. Richie already pictured where the shell would hit—the same place it always did, in the centre of the bull's eye.

Fredrick smiled. "I think you are ready for tomorrow. That rifle has never shot so well. Maybe you should sight in my other guns."

As they rounded the huge baobab tree, small globes of light shone like moons in the sky, illuminating our path. I especially loved this time of day, watching the shadows slowly creep across the savannah, wrapping a blanket of darkness over all living things... Like a sentry, the ancient tree stood proud beside the lane, as if welcoming us home.

In the warmth of the fire, with a couple of Windhoek lagers down, I relaxed. From across the fire, I stood alone, sipping on my ice-cold beer. William, as usual, exhibited his protective skills. Like a well-trained sheep-dog, he was constantly watching and drawing any solitary individuals back into the circle—constantly encouraging all to take part and share their stories of the day. I could feel his eyes observing me.

"Spencer."

I nodded, "Just a few more moments."

Gradually, Robert and Richie moved their chairs toward Frederick. I could not hear the conversation, but I was confident it involved tomorrow and their upcoming hunt. Although rusty, all Robert would need was a target—something to shoot at. A day of hunting would be the ideal way for him to relax and reclaim his edge.

Against the counter, Sally stood with Uta as she arranged the table for the evening meal. Sally glanced toward me. Her gentle smile met with a nod and a tip of my bottle. For a moment, I forgot our reason for being here and closed my eyes. The point in time seemed so surreal; it was like Frederick and Uta had known us a lifetime as if we too belonged here.

Morning arrived all too soon. Everyone was scurrying around preparing for the day. David, Andrew, and Michael decided to go into the local town of Outjo for a little sightseeing. Richie and Robert were going on a hunt. Discreetly, I informed the team that I would not be accompanying them. I needed to check in with Command. I would not be leaving the ranch today. Grabbing my satellite phone, I scurried off to make the required calls. Command would have our update on the events of the preceding days.

Sally, not feeling well, opted for a day of rest.

PART TWENTY-SEVEN

INTO THE DARKNESS—
CUANGAR, ANGOLA

Abid stood in the lobby of the hotel pondering what he should do. He did not want to stay in his room, but he needed some seclusion and time for himself. He attracted the attention of the hotel bellhop and inquired as to the best halal places.

The voice in his head said, "You must practise halal. You must." But the other voice pushed him forward toward the haram, the unlawful.

The bellhop directed him toward the local park. "You should find plenty of nature there."

Rambling among the trees and flowerbeds, he felt different, calmer. For a few hours, Abid managed to get away from his conscious world—a world where thoughts of any kind of fun are haram.

Walking along the narrow aisles of the market, Abid could feel he was changing. The sights and sounds of the halal animals being slaughtered awakened something within him. He watched as the razor-sharp knife sliced down into the meat of the neck, severing the trachea, esophagus, and both jugular veins in one sweeping motion.

With every slice of the knife, the slaughterer's voice rang out, "*Bismillah Allahu Akbar!*"

"Halal, it must be halal if you are to eat it." Abid could hear his father's voice echoing over the sounds of the market. "That man; that mean, cruel man."

The smells of the market—blood, fresh meat, and fish—stimulated his senses.

Haram, haram, haram, rang through his brain as he stood watching the young females.

Even though they were walking ever so lightly, their adornments jiggled. He could still see them, round, plump, moving beneath the black dreary fabric, their *alsudur* bare to the clothing above. Abid silently mused, *After all, I am a young man, a virile man, and I need excitement, passion. I need a break; nobody can pray all day.*

Halal, halal, halal. Abid fought with the tormentor as the darkness swept steadily over him.

Go to the beach, you coward. Don't listen to Abid; he is a gutless coward.

The voice of the darkness got louder and louder until he could no longer hear himself think. Abid was now so far away, locked inside the darkness that moved him toward the unlawful. The dark one was taking over; Abid was now powerless to stop it.

Peering forward into the crowd with eyes like an infrared camera, he could sense the heat of their bodies, their hot spots, their cooler spots. His excitement rose.

PART TWENTY-EIGHT

REPORTING IN—
OTJIWARONGO, NAMIBIA

Grabbing a Windhoek lager from the fridge, I popped the cap and took a big, long swig—cold; it tasted so good. Although the housekeeping staff had already made the beds and collected the laundry, I needed to be sure that no one would hear. Before punching in the numbers to CSIS's secure line, I glanced down the hall toward the stairs. I could see that Sally's door was slightly open, and the hall was empty.

Propped against the headboard, I could keep an eye on the hall. Should anyone come in the foyer door, or come up the stairs, I would know. With my laptop booted up, I sat, reviewing the mission file. The encrypted file had been updated within the last twelve hours. Updates now showed a photo of Mohammad and the last photo taken of his brother, Abid Hassan. It was amazing how much they looked alike.

The satellite phone rang. "Captain Cook here."

Director Sharpe's voice came over the line. "Good news. All plans are progressing as expected.

"Our intel indicates Mohammad has left Nigeria and appears to be in Angola. We have a watch on him, we will advise when he starts to move. It appears that Mohammad has grown a beard since the last picture on file. An updated photo is in your folio brief.

"Jimmy O'Brien is still in Ireland. It appears he is not stepping up his departure and should be on track for your arrival in Cuangar as planned.

"How is the team?"

Anticipating a transmission lag, I waited before replying. "Well. The team is getting a little lax. They are like schoolkids on vacation.

"Corporal Jones and Private Miller are currently out getting some small-calibre practice.

"Sergeant Parker has taken some of the team to check out the small town of Outjo."

Director Sharpe looked down at his watch. "At twelve-hundred hours today, I am expecting a call from our agent Jimmy O'Brien in Ireland. Hopefully, more bomb and detonator specifics will be provided.

"It would appear they intend to use the explosive on a tank currently sitting abandoned on the old airstrip. Satellite imagery shows its location at the north end of the landing area in an isolated valley outside of Cuangar. The airstrip is quite secluded.

"Due to the remoteness, we are hoping the test will go unnoticed. We're a little baffled at the lack of internet traffic, especially from Abid Hassan. He's been constantly corresponding with his brother, but over the last couple of weeks, silence.

"Keep an eye out for him when you get to Cuangar. He may just show up. Check back with me tomorrow, twelve-hundred hours. I will have an update for you then. Director Sharpe out."

I continued reading the file while sipping my second Windhoek lager. Not the best beer I've ever consumed, but far from the worst. A little groggy from the beer and the reading, I shut down the computer link and rolled over for what I was hoping would be a few minutes of undisturbed rest.

Frederick drove the Toyota slowly upward onto the large kopje. With each bump in the road, the vehicle would squeak, creaking like the bones of an age-weary soldier. Slowly, the truck pulled to a stop behind a small clump of trees, just far enough away that they should not alert prey on the other side of the hill. Signalling for Richie and Robert to get down, Frederick gently closed the cab door. Robert grabbed the 7mm rifle from the rear gun rack and promptly chambered a round. Nearing the summit of the kopje, Frederick signalled for them to come forward, beside him. He had spotted a small group of Hartmann's mountain zebra. The knurled wheel turned slowly, bringing their binoculars into focus. Frederick pointed to the lead animal, "that one in the lead, he is a shootable stallion. Unaware, the striped targets meandered behind a cluster of small thorn bushes.

Frederick once again reminded Richie, "Stay close in behind me. Zebra are nervous animals. The slightest movement or shift in wind direction will most definitely spoil our stalk.

"Richie, you stay behind with Davvi our tracker; too many stalkers are not good." Being left behind felt odd. For years, Robert and he had been inseparable.

Richie and Davvi sat motionless, surrounded by huge boulders, waiting, watching. Like pieces on a giant chessboard, the zebras would move, then the hunters would counter. The stalk had already taken them around the kopje and across a dried-up riverbed. Downwind, concealed behind a small kopje, they gradually approached the unsuspecting animals.

Just as quickly as it had started, Davvi's radio went silent. A solitary kopje was all that stood between the hunter and his quarry. Robert lowered the rifle from his shoulder as the large stallion meandered away from the hunters. In a single motion, Robert could be seen flipping off the safety and raising the rifle onto the shooting sticks.

The stallion guardedly advanced the small herd into the wind. The animals grazing from bush to bush unknowingly presented the hunters with an opportunity. Then, just as quickly, the stallion turned, taking it away.

The bush was just thick enough to create uncertainty. Robert wished he had his fifty-calibre; the small branches would not have any influence on the bullet's flight. With only a 7mm, branches could easily deflect the small projectile. He did not want to be chasing a wounded animal.

He needed more elevation, needed to climb higher. Up to the top, up and around, he climbed until finally, he had an unobstructed vantage point directly above the herd. The stallion stepped slowly past a small pencil thorn bush toward a small opening. Robert checked his range finder; it showed 280 yards. Three inches high would be all he needed. The downward angle would put the bullet directly through the front shoulder to rest in the heart. Death would be almost instantaneous.

"Aim for the chevron on the front leg."

Broadside, 280, no wind. It should be a breeze. Peering over the boulder, clicking the safety off, he lowered the crosshair slowly down onto the chevron.

Raising the crosshair slightly onto the next black line on the shoulder would be the only adjustment needed.

Breathing slowly, a calm came over him as he squeezed the trigger. As if in slow motion, he could see the skin of the shoulder move and a small spot of blood appear. Robert chambered another round, waiting to see what the stallion would do.

Jones was confident… he could take the stallion on the run, but he preferred not to demonstrate that ability in front of Frederick, so he waited. In a customary manner, Frederick elevated his open hand; Robert knew all too well what the gesture meant.

"Well done! We can now retrieve your first trophy."

Fifty yards from where the stallion experienced the sting of the 180-grain bullet, he lay motionless among the thorn bushes. Robert approached the now still figure. Although he was trained to detach himself from the killing, he still felt a twinge of remorse. Breaking off a small twig covered with leaves he placed it gently into the mouth of the zebra. His token of respect paid to the now departed spirit, the hunter's ritual was complete.

Davvi and Richie sat glued to their binoculars like it was a night at a drive-in theatre, watching as the scene unravelled. With a single crack of the 7mm, the story ended. Climbing into the Toyota, they weaved their way through the thick brush and down to the waiting hunters.

Since the beginning of time, it had been survival of the fittest. This same situation, of man against prey, had played out thousands of times on this harsh and rugged land. And so, the cycle of life continued.

Richie focused the camera while Robert posed, kneeling behind the stallion, smiling, confident in knowing that this was just a prelude to the days to come.

PART TWENTY-NINE

RETURN TO THE LIGHT—
CUANGAR, ANGOLA

Walking along the narrow streets with the darkness still pushing him on, Abid felt helpless, out of control. He was unable to overcome the grasp that the darkness still held over him. Tasting the bitterness of the alcohol he had consumed nauseated him, combined with the stink of rotting fish carcasses at the ocean's shore. Abid bent over the pier railing and purged his stomach bare.

He had been wandering without purpose through the tattered shanty-town, staggering past the whores and filthy children not knowing why or where he headed, or even where he had been. It had been six days since he'd had a bath, six full days since he could remember sleeping in a clean bed—he stank. Trying to regain control, he thought of pleasant things, things that could push the darkness away.

Reaching back to his childhood, he dragged up enjoyable times when he and his brother would talk, play, and hug their mother. As quickly as Abid could draw up a pleasant memory, the darkness would counter with something bad, something that would destroy the pleasurable feeling.

Abid could feel his consciousness returning; quickly, he switched to thoughts of his mother. She was good and loving—*no, not my father.* Images appeared of his mother, of times when she was being punched and kicked—bad images rushing back into his consciousness.

His father—how he hated his father.

Flashing back, he remembered when the darkness started. That terrifying day by the river. His father beating him across the head with a stick—that day, his first known experience of the intense pleasure of hurting someone, when he had first experienced the darkness.

212

The adrenalin rushed through every inch of his body, he remembered seizing the rock, lashing out, smashing his father's skull, time, and time again.

Abid remembered. Each crack of the rock against that ever-softening skull—his father would not beat them anymore.

"No one will ever beat me again," echoed down the vacant shoreline that dreadful day, when he made that promise to himself.

The stink of the river and the sweetness of his father's blood all came back to him. How he had pulled his dagger from beneath his robe and hacked that vile creature into pieces—limb-sized pieces, pieces that the crocodiles would enjoy.

For hours he faded in and out of consciousness, his mind drifted as he wandered aimlessly. In the distance, the sound of birds, the children playing—Abid reached out. *If only I can hold onto these thoughts, I can win, I can push the darkness away.*

A heavy fog surrounded him, making him unable to see all but the immediate area, only a few feet around him—a protective fog. This had never happened before; it was so surreal, as if no one else existed in this world but him. Slowly, the pleasant thoughts stayed, lingering longer. Abid emerged from the fog. He had returned to the park, again able to see beyond himself. He stood alone, alone in the same park where he had gone to find peace.

Groggy, unaware of the date or time, he hurried back up the street to the hotel and toward the security of his room. He had to be somewhere, but first, he needed to remember where and why.

Approaching his room, Desmond rushed toward him. "Where have you been? We were worried. We thought you might have been killed.

"I have secured the boat and captain. We must leave tomorrow at 8:00 a.m."

Abid strained to recall where he must be, just a small mental glimpse of the where; he also needed to know the why… It was coming back, slowly, just a little more time…

"Desmond, go get me some dinner, anything but fish."

Entering his room, he disrobed, stepping into the tiny shower. With all the lights on, the sun shining through the windows, he felt secure again—away from the darkness.

PART THIRTY

A PAINFUL LESSON—
OTJIWARONGO, NAMIBIA

Robert and Richie bumped along in the back of the hunting Buckie, chatting. Both experiencing the peacefulness that only time in the wild can deliver. Rounding a corner in the narrow lane, Davvi tapped on the roof of the cab. Frederick stepped out of the cab as Davvi whispered in Afrikaans, "there is an animal along the bush line. Unaware, Robert gestured for Richie to go. This time, he would be behind the scope. Richie slipped over the side of the truck as Robert handed him the 7mm. Richie stepped in tight behind Davvi, ready for the signal that the animal was still there. Davvi stopped and set up the shooting sticks. Seventy yards ahead stood a beautiful warthog with four big warts and twelve-inch tusks. A nice male.

Covered in dust with wet stains below his eyes, the large boar stood motionless. Richie froze, staring straight at the boar, slowly setting the 7mm onto the sticks and picking the perfect spot—square on the front shoulder. He could not miss at this distance, or so he thought.

The metallic click of the rifle hammer broke the silence of the afternoon air. Where was the boom? He gazed at the pig, then back to the rifle. In the haste of getting off the vehicle, he had forgotten to chamber a round.

In total bewilderment, he looked at Davvi. "I cannot believe I just did that."

In a split second, the warthog was gone. All that was left were the little puffs of dust as his hoofs propelled him forward, away from danger. Richie smiled inwardly; *that is why I am the spotter, not the sniper*. Sluggishly, they trudged back to the truck, everyone wondering what had happened. Richie said nothing as Davvi maintained a huge smile.

The hot afternoon sun beamed down, radiating heat onto the hunters. Creeping along the dry riverbed, Robert hoped to catch a glimpse of a mature kudu bull. As the riverbed wound first to the right, then left, Robert noticed the padded footprints of a leopard and her kit. Robert was intrigued by what he was seeing.

Sniper training taught him to use cover and concealment to the fullest. The way the leopard was walking along the riverbed was very interesting: prowling the water-void stream, always staying on the inside curve of the river's edge, quietly slinking up to the next bend in the river, peeking around the corner. Once sure that there was no prey, she had walked to the opposite side, then repeated her silent stalk, again. She performed this same technique over and over. I had been told animals do not think with structured logic—this observation proved otherwise. How efficient this method of hunting must be was soon to be discovered. A mile or so up the river, a young kudu bull lay dead in the dry sand, the meat still red with dripping blood. Parts were torn away—a recent meal.

Frederick patted Robert on the shoulder. "Do not worry, my friend. I will find you a mature bull, a much bigger bull."

Two hours into the morning, I clicked off the sat phone, my required duties completed. Cool air swept across my hand as I grasped a bottle of Windhoek lager, my first of the day. The old wicker chair awaited me in the main foyer—I could relax.

Sally slowly staggered down the stairs, plunking herself onto the empty lounge chair beside me.

With a smile, I lifted my face from the book I was reading. Marking the spot, I queried, "How was your sleep?"

With a yawn and an arms-wide stretch, she responded, "Great, it was just what I needed."

"I hope I did not wake you. Your door was ajar when I came down." My eyes met hers, not sure if I should say anything. "I noticed you lying on top of the covers."

Sally thought for a second, then smiled. Her room had been very hot. She remembered the cool feeling of her naked flesh against the satin sheets. Quick to change the subject, Sally redirected the conversation away from her previous thoughts to a new topic.

Embarrassed and stumbling for words, she inquired, "Any word from the rest of the team?"

"Well, the sergeant, David, and Andrew have not reported back yet."

Jokingly, I commented, "Maybe they have all gone AWOL. Maybe they are now full-time tourists.

"As far as Robert and Richie… I heard six shots from outback. I suspect that they will have a truckload of animals when they return. You know how Robert loves to shoot and he loves hunting even more."

I proceeded to give Sally a brief overview of the command communication of earlier in the day. It seemed odd, calling each other by our first names. Years of military life had conditioned us to refer by rank first, then surname.

Even though I had received the names of the informant and CSIS contact that we were to meet in Cuangar, I decided not to divulge it to Sally or the others, at least not yet.

Gazing across the yard, I could see Uta walking briskly toward us. I could not help but think how slender and attractive she had managed to stay. Apparently in her forties, of sturdy stock, she remained very vibrant. The fact that she was a diligent worker only added to her appeal. Out here you had to be tough. It looked like she had a mission; she was in a hurry, possibly heading out somewhere.

Uta approached brandishing her usual broad smile. "How has your stay been so far? I am heading to town. Is there anything I can get for you?"

"Something chocolate would be amazing!" were the first words out of Sally's mouth.

Smiling, Uta commented, "We do not serve many sweets here, so I will have to see what I can find. The refrigerator is full. If you would like a snack, there are plenty of sandwiches ready as well."

As she turned to leave, I inquired, "Will they have any black licorice? I love black licorice."

"I will see what I can find," was all I heard as she sped away in the dusty old Land Cruiser.

A big cloud of dust followed her down the lane as she disappeared around the bend, lingering curls rising upward, following her effortlessly in the still afternoon air.

"I think it is going to be a hot afternoon," I expressed while eying the billowing clouds of dust.

As the dust cleared, their old dog meandered around the front of the house, sniffing every bush and rock, protectively checking out his dogdom, as Dad used to say. We sat quietly, gazing around, occasionally glancing at each other. Both Sally and I tried not to focus on each other, for we both sensed what was happening. Sally slowly and gently reached her hand across to caress my wrist. Butterflies raced through my stomach. I sensed where this may lead. It seemed I was helpless to stop it. I should stop it, but I was not sure I wanted to. I fought with my urges, all the time wanting to continue. It would not be seen as appropriate by my men or my superiors. It may even damage my career. Most of all, I did not want my first encounter to be cheapened in any way.

Memories of the last words from my mother when she had left me at the start of basic training flashed through my mind. "Remember your religious teachings, resist the devil's temptations." Sally was not the devil, but this could not continue. At least not now...

I paused to collect my words. "Sally, it is not that I do not want to continue, because I do. You mean much more than this, and I would want it to be special, not just an afternoon fling."

Sally smiled, reluctantly withdrawing her hand. These few moments of tenderness slipped away as the old guard dog barked. Grinding and squeaking sounds of the hunting vehicle could be heard approaching the skinning shed. I gazed at Sally gently, caressing her shoulder as I quickly headed upstairs. I would need a few minutes before my excitement subsided and the evidence of my arousal was gone.

Sally left the foyer, heading out toward the skinning shed. Confusion on here face, she stared at me, unsure, had she made a mistake—had she destroyed her opportunity to show how much she cared?

Hesitantly, she uttered, "It would have been special."

The hunting vehicle creaked under the load. Between the two hunters, they had harvested six animals. Now the work of gutting, skinning, and butchering became the focus of the camp staff. Frederick recorded the mounting wishes of the hunters, then let the skinner take over. Lifting the animals by the rear legs, he would take the skins off in minutes, always mindful of how the cuts should be made.

With three of the animals skinned and, in the cooler, Davvi, winched the zebra off the floor. Not sure about the position of the animal, he decided to pull it over on the hook. With no warning, his hand was drawn into the pulley. Instantly, he stood, right arm raised, hand firmly seized in the pulley.

Sally witnessed what had transpired immediately rushed to assist. She was too late. Davvi, now in extreme pain, panicked, yanking his hand free. The load shifted, ripping open the hand. The palm of his hand dangled freely, exposing the muscles and bone, blood poured down his arm, drenching the floor below. Grabbing Davvi, Sally spun him around, sitting him on the tailgate of the truck. From that point she took control.

"Richie, the bag. Davvi. Look at me. I need you to stay calm. Everything will be fine, but I need you to lie still while I deal with your hand."

In what seemed to be only a matter of seconds, Richie crossed the yard, returning with her field bag. Opening the bag, he stood, awaiting direction. Saline splashed against the open wound, washing the blood and dirt onto the tailgate, quickly disappearing as it blended with the already present animal fluids.

Sally whispered, "Hand me that blue syringe. The morphine."

Bypassing the urge to cleanse the wound, she hurried to get the morphine administered. Slowly, the contents of the syringe disappeared into Davvi's shoulder. The injured tracker would soon relax, and she could now worry about the wound.

"Antiseptic. Gauze. Now press here."

The instructions were fast and furious as Sally cleansed the wound. Her many years of ER training showed as she skillfully calmed Davvi. "Lay your head down; the pain will be gone in a few seconds."

As predicted, Davvi's head rolled to the side as his eyes closed. The morphine taking effect, Davvi now lay motionless across the tailgate. Hopefully, the risk of shock had been abated.

All the while, Frederick watched intently. Discussing the chain of events, I tried to keep him distracted. Morphine in a tourist's first aid kit—this would be a tough one. I had no time or desire to try and explain.

"Richie, hold his arm still. I need to stitch up his hand."

Again, flushing the wound with saline, then drenching the palm with antiseptic, Sally made one last check. "Doesn't appear to be any nerve damage. I believe that we can close. Richie, I can close now."

Slowly, Richie refocused, releasing the pressure on the gauze. It was immediately apparent that there was still a problem as blood spurted from the wound. With each pulse of Davvi's heart, small spurts of blood trickled from the still-open wound.

"We must have a bleeder."

Gently lifting the flap of skin, Sally peered into the wound. "There it is. I will need to tie off the vessel before closing or the hand will have to be reopened.

"Richie, take the tweezers. Grab that vessel."

Gently squeezing the tweezers, Richie pulled the vessel outward. With the ease of a surgeon, Sally tied the vessel off—seconds later, the bleeding ceased.

"OK, let's close."

Richie replaced the gauze then applied pressure to the flap of skin as Sally started closing the wound. Stitch by stitch, she moved around the swollen palm.

"Infection is a possibility, so I will leave a small piece of surgical tubing hanging out of the wound." Blood-stained fingers opened the sealed bag, extracting a small coil of sterile tubing. "There, that should keep it drained."

With a steady hand, Richie padded the gauze around the wound, soaking up the blood as it seeped outward from the stitches. The sight of blood did not bother him, in Afghanistan he had witnessed horrific scenes: men with limbs completely blown off, head wounds that seemingly bled forever.

Richie, watching intently as Sally inserted the needle and tied off each stitch, quietly remarked, "I wager his hand will hurt tomorrow…"

Reinhart patiently stood by, trying to reassure the watching workers that these minor kinds of slip-ups happen and Davvi would be back to work in no time. Sally knew different. That hand would be out of commission for weeks, maybe even months. Thirty-six stitches later, his hand bandaged,

Davvi rested comfortably. Frederick could not help but notice how proficient Sally performed the task.

"Uta usually looks after first aid, but I am sure glad we had you here, Sally, I am not sure that Uta could have handled this one."

Cleaning up the area, I glanced at Sally. Smiling, I gave a nod. "Very good work, Sally. Very good."

Dinner that evening was subdued. Although Robert and Richie had a very successful day with plenty of stories, the incident with Davvi left a grey cloud hanging over their moods. Before long, they swallowed down the remnants of their last beer and trudged off to bed.

PART THIRTY-ONE

MOVING ON—NAMIBIA

Time was running out at the ranch. The team would be moving on shortly. The chit-chat at the fire was no longer centred around their daily activities, but rather the next destination and what they should expect.

Reinhart sat discussing the next day's plan and the five-hour trip up through Grootfontein to Rundu. With approximately five days before the contact with the Cuangar agent, we could make tomorrow a slow, pleasurable drive with a one-night stopover in the park.

Richie and I stood observing the huge map of Etosha National Park. To our left, the whitewashed walls of the historic Namutoni fortress stood in contrast to the green of the palm trees and the rich blue of the sky. It was an ancient place whose only inhabitants now were a family of grey meerkat.

Scampering along the base of the wall, showing little regard for the human intruders. Watching like a sphinx, then raising themselves onto their hind legs— studying the newest group of tourists wandering by.

Momentarily separated from the others, Sally and I studied the little family of rodents. Hesitant for a second, I then insisted on a photo. Just in case another opportunity did not occur, I wanted a special memento of our time here, our momentary togetherness.

Everywhere there were sun-bleached elephant skulls.

"Sally, those skulls would take a cool picture. How about you and me?"

Standing with one foot on an elephant skull, Sally snuggled in close while an obliging tourist captured the moment.

Arrival at the resort had been well coordinated. We would meet in the main dining room at seventeen-hundred hours. The mood had changed. We all knew this would be our last leisurely meal, the last evening before going back to work—back to the mission, back to cold rations and sleeping on the hard ground under the stars. The agreed-upon time would leave us only one hour for a relaxing shower and a change of clothes.

The hotel had a quaint open-air lobby, decorated with intricate wood carvings and flowering plants. The pathways of red cobblestone wandered from cottage to cottage, short, narrow paths illuminated only by small moon-shaped globes of light. Everywhere house cleaners and groundskeepers smiled pleasantly as we wandered by.

A far cry from our usual dorms, the spacious, beautifully decorated rooms was yet another reminder of the life at risk. The comfort and luxury had its appeal, something I could easily get used to. The reality was that we would be back in the bush soon, and all this would be just a memory. I wondered if these people even knew what was happening throughout the world. Possibly not, and for now, I wished I too could forget.

The bellhop courteously escorted Andrew and David to their room, opened the door, and ushered them in. A room with one king-size bed, lace and frilly pillows. Andrew looked at David.

"I don't think so," he announced.

"Captain, they have the wrong idea about David and me. We have one king-size bed in a honeymoon cabin," Andrew jokingly commented again. "I do not believe this will work, Sir. I'd like to cuddle, but not with him."

Seeing the humour in the situation, I promptly noted, "But I always thought you two looked so good together.

"I have a solution for you: why don't we go see if Sally will switch with you?"

Knocking gently on the cabin door, I awaited an answer. "One moment," was the reply from behind the door.

Scanning the room to make sure there was indeed only one bed, I inquired, "Sally, we were wondering if you would be willing to switch rooms with Andrew and David? Apparently, Andrew has a headache tonight and doesn't want to waste the honeymoon suite."

Sally, quick to grasp the opportunity for some girly luxury, answered with a resounding, "Yes, most certainly. I don't have a headache!"

"Andrew, since you are getting a deal here, I am sure you would not mind helping doc move her stuff. I will advise David that the two of you have been relocated.

"See you all in the dining room at seventeen-hundred hours."

Content that the problem had been resolved, I double-timed it back to my room. I was expected shortly to check in with HQ—Director Sharpe would be awaiting our arrival update. I did not wish to be late.

"Director Sharpe here," sounded through the receiver.

"Captain Cook, sir."

"Captain, I have received news that the target will be a couple of days early at Cuangar.

"The product is now scheduled to leave Ireland early as well, so we will have to advance your arrival time."

"Roger that, Sir. We are ready to move. We will have no trouble leaving early for Rundu. We can be ready and on the road by zero-eight-hundred hours tomorrow morning.

"As soon as we arrive at Rundu, I will go into town to check things out. I will coordinate the meet with the contact and report back, Sir.

"The team will stay back at the rendezvous point to assemble our equipment. We should be ready to cross the river by tomorrow evening."

"Captain, you and Reinhart will report into Rundu daily until contact is made with the informant.

"The Irish intelligence will have an agent following Jimmy O'Brien. The agent will be carrying a sign marked, 'COOK PARTY.' You are to initiate contact. He will brief you with the most current updates."

"Roger that, Sir."

"Oh, one more thing, Captain. We are not to terminate Mohammad Hassan, or Desmond Atutu. We need them all alive and well for interrogation.

"I have not informed anyone else of their names for fear of a leak, but you are to be read in; Jimmy O'Brien is our Irish under-cover agent, and Desmond Atutu is a paid informant.

"These three individuals are to be brought back alive. Any other insurgents should be terminated. No loose ends.

"Good luck. Safe hunting. Director out."

PART THIRTY-TWO

CHANGE OF PLANS—NAMIBIA

Immediately after dinner, I ushered the team toward a secluded table away from staff and tourists. The team needed some privacy.

"First off, we have just received new orders.

"Boots on the ground at zero-eight-hundred tomorrow to resume our mission. This order accelerates our planned departure to Rundu by several days.

"We are to meet with our contact in Rundu by eighteen-hundred hours. Also, as of tomorrow morning, we will address each other appropriately, and we will conduct ourselves as soldiers. Gentlemen, and lady, the vacation is over.

"We will be taken to a staging area where we will wait until contact has been made with Desmond Atutu, our informant.

"Once we are sure of their arrival and plans, we will be taken upriver by barge to a suitable drop point on the Angola side of the river. The contact has chosen a location for us to set up and to deploy.

"Unless an emergency arises, we will maintain radio silence until we are safely back in Namibia.

"When we reach the staging area on the Angola side, we will resume wearing our military attire, and prepare for our insertion into the old airstrip.

"Our present orders are to secure the explosive and the detonator. Mohammad Hassan, Jimmy O'Brien, and Desmond Atutu are to be captured. Not killed, I repeat, NOT KILLED.

"Any other non-essential parties or witnesses are to be terminated, and their bodies disposed of.

I snickered, "With the crocodile population as high as it is, we should have no problem disposing of any bodies."

"Tomorrow we will drop any unnecessary equipment to make room for the additional packages. We will then return by barge to Rundu, on the Namibia side.

"Tomorrow afternoon at the rendezvous point, we will assemble our gear and perform our weapons checks.

"Understood?" Each member in turn acknowledged.

Raising my glass, I proposed a toast to the mission. "There is no joking tonight; our brief period of relaxation has ended. We all know what tomorrow will bring. May we be successful and all return home safely."

In the distance, the sun sparkled off the water of the tiny watering holes. Animals of every species took their turn approaching to drink, ever wary of the dangers lurking in the grass. Elevated high above the park floor, I watched as predators and prey tap-danced around each other. Shadows of evening crept slowly across the sun-dried salt pan, gradually obscuring the events below.

Although distant, the ever-evaporating water's edge of the Etosha Pan glistened, lions could be heard bellowing out their low, guttural sounds as they stalked their way through the tall grasses. With each loud grunt of the lion, goosebumps ran up and down the spines of the listeners. The big cats were on a mission of their own—to kill, to eat, and to survive another day. I understood the lions, for we too were on a potential mission of death.

The moon shone brightly as we separated for the walk back to our cabins. Scattered loosely around the winding pathways, small dome lights stood like sentries against the wooden stake fence. Small moon-like spheres shining their meagre amounts of light onto the cobblestone walkways, creating a relaxed and romantic atmosphere.

Sally and I talked casually as we meandered along the narrow trails back to our cabins. Shuffling our feet, kicking up small clouds of dust, neither of us wanted to say good night. Rounding the walkway into the shadows, Sally glanced up, looking toward the moon. A mere four inches taller than she, I glanced down into her eyes.

Quickly looking around, softly, I pulled Sally close to me, bending down to place my lips close to her ear. Caressing her tiny lobes, I whispered, "Would you care to spend the night with me?"

Her arms were quickly wrapped around me as she rotated her head toward my waiting lips. "Yes, very much. But… what about the other day?"

"I have had some time to think; now the time is right. This place, this night—most of all, this room. Everything is perfect." I whispered.

She opened the cabin door, leading me across the threshold. Moonlight from the doorway threw shadows across the dimly lit room, accenting the hanging curtains draped daintily across the canopy bed. Leading me by the hand, she stopped beside the bed.

Slowly, I lowered my eyes to meet hers. "I haven't done this before."

Sally unbuttoned my shirt, running her slender fingers through the tight curls on my chest. I could not believe how easily she could arouse me. Wanting to touch her, needing to touch her, I gently slid my fingertips downward, first across her breasts, then slowly around and down the small of her back.

With every inch I moved, Sally sighed, pressing in tighter. Goosebumps rose on her skin as I lightly caressed the small of her back. I sensed this aroused her. The sounds of the night came drifting through the open window as one by one the tiny buttons of her blouse gave way.

Outside, the low guttural sound of a roaming lion echoed in the darkness, almost as though it could sense the moment.

Sally sighed softly as she lowered herself to the bed. Gently, my hands caressed her stomach upward to each of her waiting nipples. Moans of pleasure gently mixed with the sounds of the night as my tongue followed the route of my hands, first to the left and then to the right.

I wondered, where was all this coming from? I had no previous experience, yet it seemed natural. Lowering my half-naked body, I pressed myself firmly between her now wide-spread legs. The firmness of her pelvis sent waves of pleasure up the entire length of my now erect penis.

Standing between her legs I slowly removed my shorts, letting them fall to the floor. Once again, I pressed my bare self against her. Gradually, I found myself on my knees, caressing my face against the warmth of her stomach. Grasping the zipper, I gently pulled down, exposing the delicate skin below. Beneath the pink of the delicate lace, I could see the dark firm curls of her mound.

I leaned in, inhaling the sweet aroma, as I lowered her panties to the floor.

Sally grabbed my much larger hand and slid it firmly between her thighs.

Outside, the lion continued his rhythmic serenade.

With tender, steady hands, Sally grabbed me by the hips, pulling me close, gently guiding me into her waiting warmth. Inside, I caressed every nerve, sending spikes of pleasure with every thrust. The gentle gliding movements of her pelvis emulated the steady rhythmic sounds of the African night. Her soft, gentle moans filled the silence of the room, our primal passion peaking until the only sounds were hers. Like an awaiting audience, the night went silent, as if anticipating, waiting patiently for that special moment, the moment when we both became one.

Hours passed before I glanced toward the nightstand. Zero-four-hundred; it was late. Soon we would need to get up. I did not want the night to end. I wanted to hold onto the moment, needing the security of her arms. Tomorrow; it could all end.

As the moon descended toward the distant horizon, Sally escorted me to the door. She whispered in my ear, "Spencer, I have loved you for a long time."

A lingering kiss faded to a smile as I turned and disappeared, not wanting to think about the coming days.

PART THIRTY-THREE

TO RUNDU—NAMIBIA

Southeast from the park heading toward Tsumeb, the bushveld started its conversion to more open savannah—miles and miles of sand mixed with a multitude of thorn trees. Casually, I commented to Reinhart that in all the bushes I had seen, there were only three that did not have thorns.

Reinhart corrected me: "Then you were not looking close enough."

Hours slipped by as the team gazed out the van windows. Birds chirped, flitting from tree to tree, as oryx meandered freely among the sparse vegetation. For them, it was just another day.

Nearing Rundu, the yellow grasses of the savannah stood in contrast to the dark green leaves of the thorn trees. In the distance, the snake-like bends of the Okavango River wove back and forth across the horizon. Small shantytowns scattered randomly along the roadside announced our approach. Native women, adorned in their brightly coloured dresses, attended their open market shops. It seemed so peaceful here. I found it hard to believe this serene town was just across the river from the war-torn villages of Angola.

Reinhart flipped the left signal on as we approached a small cluster of shops. Only one hour out of our destination, it would be a good spot to stretch our legs and grab some lunch. The restaurant smelled good; however, the menu proved to be of no help. Written in Afrikaans, it was just lots of words that had no meaning to us non-native travellers.

Huddled around the small wooden table, Reinhart recommended the Mahangu flatbread with ground nuts and stewed meat. Rumbling bellies prompted all to accept.

Sergeant Cowalski took out a small bottle of pills, handing one to each of the team. "We are going into a malaria zone tomorrow. You will need to take one Malarone pill each day while we are here, then one pill each day for seven days after we leave the zone."

Outside, the open market bustled like a beehive—vendors trading and selling their goods, tourists strolling from booth to booth. This market was nothing like the one in Otjiwarongo. No one appeared to be getting harassed as they shopped.

"Captain, do you mind if I take a look to see if I can find a souvenir?" uttered Cowalski.

"OK but hustle it up. I want you back in fifteen."

A short time later, Cowalski returned to the restaurant.

With a smile of success, she announced, "I found one! African blackwood is absolutely beautiful, don't you think? Look at this carving."

The blackness of the wood sparkled as rays of sun bounced off the native girl's face.

"It will look great on my nightstand."

All the men rolled their eyes, but I saw it—the two entwined native figures, wrapped in each other's arms. As I gazed at it in the early morning light, there seemed to be something sensual about it, or was it just the memories of last night?

PART THIRTY-FOUR

THE MEETING—RUNDU, NAMIBIA

Abid stood on the bow of the fishing boat, staring down the Okavango. Only a few more days and he would be in Cuangar. Eagerly anticipating a free meal, crocodiles scurried into the water at the first sight of the boat.

Abid admired these neolithic creatures—such efficient killers. Dragging their prey beneath the surface, rolling it over until it drowned, then quickly jamming it under a log, storing it there to tenderize. Deadly predators able to kill in a matter of seconds, he admired them.

With his back pressed tight to the galley door, Abid fantasized. *I wonder if any of the crew would miss one of my lackeys; I would enjoy watching it.* He closed his eyes; he could see it. *I could wait until everyone was down below, then I could shove my dagger under his ribs, slide him overboard, and no one would know. I could stand and watch as the crocodiles snatched him from the surface. Maybe tomorrow.*

Stepping closer to the railing, Abid could feel the butterflies in his stomach. Oh, how he anticipated stepping ashore; he did not like the water, he even hated taking a bath, ever since that day as a toddler when Mohammad held Abid's head below the shallow surface of his bathwater.

His thoughts tormenting him again and again, Abid pushed them aside. He could not risk being drawn into the darkness, not here, not now. He needed to focus on his mission; he needed to stay alert.

The explosive would be on its way; the test day was drawing near... absorbed in thought, he rocked with the rhythm of the waves... Eagerly waiting to test the explosive, he relished the thought of blowing something up.

Desmond leaned tight to the railing, rocking back and forth, ready to toss the bow line ashore. Abid, on the other hand, stayed well back from the edge as the boat coasted toward the dock. Abid shivered; there was no way he could do that. As the lines were pulled up tight, the boat lightly bumped the dock. Scurrying across the narrow gangplank, Abid planted his feet firmly on solid ground, well back from the water's edge.

The boat had docked facing downstream—ideal, his contact could easily identify the boat by name and confirm their arrival. Time was of the essence; he would need to rush. Desmond would have little time to pick up his rental car and rendezvous with his contact before leaving with Abid. Desmond would need to convince Abid to stay by the docks so he could make his calls. He would need to call the car rental depot, then reach out to his contact.

Nearing the lunch hour, Desmond politely directed Abid toward a local vendor. "I trust you are hungry. I will run to get our vehicle while you eat. The help will stay with you to carry your bags. I should be back shortly."

Before rushing into the street, Desmond ordered the lackeys to wait with Abid, then disappeared into the crowd.

Abid pondered; this seemed a bit odd. They had travelled before, and never once had Desmond offered to go off on his own to get the vehicle. Signalling the lackeys to come to the table, Abid asked them to sit and ordered their lunch.

"I must go do something, you two stay here, and watch our luggage. Your lunch will be here shortly."

Quickly paying the waiter, he turned and disappeared into the crowd.

Abid pushed his way through the crowd, trying to catch up.

Desmond fumbled with a scrap of paper; lifting the receiver, he dialled the first number. Abid watched with curiosity as Desmond spoke; he could not hear what was being said, but he knew it was about the boat since Desmond kept glancing back toward the dock and nodding his head. Abid watched as Desmond placed the paper back into his pocket then proceeded to dial another number.

Concluding the second call, he proceeded to dial the third number. Abid was puzzled; he should only have had to dial one number. Who were the second and third calls to?

PART THIRTY-FIVE

NAMIBIAN CONTACT

Reinhart eased the Toyota around the sharp bend in the road, heading up the steep grade toward a distant house. I instructed the team to stay at the vehicles as Reinhart and I approached the side door. A mature bearded man opened the door wielding a rifle.

"This is not a campground, so you had best be on your way."

Stepping forward, Reinhart started speaking Afrikaans. Gradually, the barrel of the rifle dropped, and both men stepped toward me.

The tension subsided as we shook hands, turned, and walked back toward the vehicles. It was easy to tell that this individual did not like unwelcome guests but was nevertheless prepared to deal with them.

Their light lunch finished, the team with their vehicles were ushered behind the house into a large storage shed. Closing the sliding doors, I directed the team to ready the equipment. The only small ferry on the river had been arranged; unfortunately, it would not carry all our gear. Crossing the Okavango River was risky enough, a second crossing was out of the question.

"We will need to downsize. All non-essential equipment and supplies will have to remain in the barn until we return."

Inside the barn, Corporal Jones assembled his TAC-50 and pulled ten rounds for testing. Private Miller meticulously laid out all the clothing and backpacks. Removing the footlockers from the storage trailer Private James set out the armaments, organizing them into seven equal piles beside each soldier's pack. Once issued the necessary gear, each soldier then became responsible for assembling their pack. Rifles and ammunition lay neatly piled beside each person's CADPAT AR clothing.

"There will be no room for helmets on this crossing, we will be taking only our Boonie hats.

"Private Dunsmoore, the light assault radios and headsets only. We will have only two days in the bush; there would be no need for the extra batteries or chargers." I ordered.

"The radios are at full charge, sir."

Sergeant Cowalski opened her medical chest—wound seal kits, morphine, bandages, and stitching needles with thread. Each man would have a basic kit. She would carry a more comprehensive kit just in case they encountered more resistance than expected. Anti-venom, antiseptic, and malaria pills completed her supplies.

"Medical supplies ready, sir."

The camping trailers, although very typical looking, had been re-modelled for this special mission. To accommodate our equipment, all the interior panels had been made removable, creating numerous locations to stow gear. The ceiling of the hardtop campers had drop-down panels for the rifles, while the propane tanks were hollowed out to store ammunition and explosives. Director Sharpe had also ordered the pull-out beds to be altered to store human passengers—ample room for Abid Hassan, O'Brien, and Atutu. Removing the trailer front and rear walls, each soldier neatly stowed their gear.

"Private Miller, Corporal Jones, there is a small valley to the rear of the building. Take your TAC-50 and confirm you are still sighted in.

"Reinhart and I will head into town to meet with our contact.

"The remainder of you, sit tight until we return." I ordered.

Ranged in at six hundred metres, the TAC-50 shot dead-on. The abandoned airfield to be used for the DD90 test was approximated at seven hundred metres. The small valley available behind our shed could only provide a six-hundred-metre shot. An additional one hundred metres for the TAC-50 would have no significant effect on the impact point. All was ready, and the team settled in, awaiting the return of Reinhart and me.

Downtown, Reinhart led the way through the streets toward the docks. I watched for the boat with the flag while Reinhart kept an eye out for Desmond Atutu in his multi-coloured shirt.

Proceeding down opposite sides of the street, we scanned oncoming traffic, alert for anyone who may be watching or who appeared out of place.

Reinhart stopped by a fish vendor to answer his phone. Across the street, he could see someone talking on a payphone, near the docks.

"Hello." Desmond hesitated momentarily. "We have arrived. Are you in town?"

"Yes," replied Reinhart. "We are ready to go. Has the third party arrived yet?"

"Not yet, but you should cross the river tonight. We will be there tomorrow, early in the morning."

Desmond clicked the receiver down. He had arranged the vehicle rental; now he must hurry back to the restaurant before Abid became suspicious.

Concealed behind a small hut, Abid watched as Desmond approached the rental shop. He had to get back to the restaurant before Desmond. Cautiously, he retreated into the crowd. Always suspicious, never trusting, Abid found this chain of events intriguing, and he was determined to find out what Desmond was up to.

Abid slid into his chair and started hastily eating he needed Desmond to believe that he had remained in the tiny restaurant. Only half completing the meal, he shoved the plate to the centre of the table. Speaking softly toward the two lackeys, Abid slid two, one-hundred-dollar bills in their direction. "Tomorrow I may need you to perform a little favour for me. Can I trust you to remain silent about this until I advise you?"

Both nodded yes, quickly stashing the money into their pockets. Neither would ask what or why. For that amount of money, either one would kill, if asked. Both knew, to say no to Abid would mean a permanent burial place in Angola.

Desmond honked the horn of the Toyota Land Cruiser, the two lackeys dragged the luggage toward the open trunk. Abid excused himself and went to the restroom; he needed to get away so he could make a quick phone call. He needed to make contingency plans.

Propped backside against the car door, Desmond awaited Abid's return. Abid approached the door; grasping the handle, he swiftly placed himself in the rear seat, behind Desmond; he no longer trusted him. He needed to stay behind Desmond, just in case.

A block away, Reinhart and I watched, with our intel complete, we turned and headed back to the storage shed.

I slid open the large double doors. "There has been a change of plans; we will be crossing the river tonight. We depart in fifteen minutes. Hustle, hustle."

PART THIRTY-SIX

THE EXPLOSION—ANGOLA

"Private James, did you pack my gear as I requested?"

"Yes, sir," replied the private. "Complete, sir."

"There is a small barge concealed just upriver from Rundu that we will use to cross over. Once on the Angola side, we then double-time it to the target location.

"Reinhart will accompany us as far as the demarcation point on the Angola side. There, he will cam-up the vehicles and wait for our return.

"Once we have seized the packages, we will head back to the river and await the barge. The whole operation will take place during daylight hours tomorrow. I have directed the barge captain to pick us up at dark. Remember, we want the three of them alive.

"Any questions?"

Each soldier knew what they had to do; like a well-oiled machine, they jumped into action.

I inched the truck and trailer slowly onto the barge, it was a perfect overcast evening. In total darkness, the barge moved slowly out into the current of the river. Little traffic moved along the dirt-stained waterway tonight. Purely as a precaution, lights out and silent running would be maintained. Slipping in and out of the small coves on the Namibian shoreline, the barge surged northward until in line with our destination across the river. Turning ninety degrees, the boat headed east across the river, navigating through the narrow channel and dropping out of sight.

The tiny inlet was a perfect spot, concealing the barge completely. It was clear that the skipper had done this before. Up onto the bank with barely a bump, the barge ran aground. Dropping the ramp, the offload took only five minutes.

Travelling southward for thirty minutes, the tiny caravan arrived at the demarcation site. If luck were on our side, we would arrive at our hooch long before sunup. Disguising the vehicles well off the road, the team scurried about, readying themselves for the long hike to the opposite end of the airfield. Eventually, silence returned, leaving only Reinhart as he swept away the vehicle tracks. Huddled down beside a small creek, we made one last review.

"Sergeant Parker, once we arrive at the valley, you will take your team along the base of the west ridge and set up in thick cover as close to the south end of the runway as possible.

"There you will await sunup.

"From your position, you will be able to see where they intend to plant the explosive, and from where the detonation will occur.

"Corporal Jones and Private Miller, you will head upward onto the southeast end of the ridgeline and find a suitable set-up point.

"As much as possible, maintain radio silence. Clear as mud, Miller?"

The blank expression showed Miller was not fully understanding the order. "Sir, at what party are we shooting?"

"I would suggest, it should be anyone other than our team or the three people we are to take hostage. Understood?

"Was I not clear before, or are you just having a brain fart? Focus, Private."

"Aye, sir, won't happen again."

Isolated neatly between two large hills, the airstrip was invisible to the local traffic. Along the east ridge, a faint game trail wove its way upward, making the trek easier. Slightly overgrown, the lush bush easily concealed our entry.

"Private, you need to be able to see the complete valley."

I pointed. "There, see that ledge, it looks suitable. Assemble some debris and branches around the ledge face and behind so you are not silhouetted."

Corporal Jones pushed his way through the dense underbrush, then upward along the ridge until he reached the small plateau. Well above the valley floor, the spot would supply a perfect view of the valley. Jones lowered himself into the prone shooting position awaiting sunup, and their subject's arrival. From above, he could see the narrow roadway as it wound around the hill, eventually entering the old, slightly overgrown runway. From any other location, it would be barely visible. While the rising sun would illuminate the opposite ridge, anyone on the western ridge would be blinded if looking their way. With the ghillie suits pulled up over their heads, both lay motionless, watching and waiting. In the darkness, Corporal Jones dialled in the range to the tank while Private Miller confirmed the distance and checked windage.

Private Miller nudged Jones. "Sir, movement across the field—halfway up the other ridge. We have company moving southward, above the sergeant's location."

PART THIRTY-SEVEN

DECEPTION—TEST SITE, ANGOLA

Abid stood talking in Arabic, holding the sat phone tight to his mouth, occasionally nodding while glancing at Desmond. Gesturing for Jimmy to come over, Abid insisted Desmond go with Jimmy to place the explosive. Setting the explosive below the tread of the tank, Jimmy peered over his shoulder. Abid stood fumbling around in the carry-on, obviously looking for the detonator. Jimmy's first suspicions were confirmed. Abid could not be trusted.

Glancing toward Abid, Jimmy confirmed he had a direct line of sight from the location to the DD90. Carefully, Jimmy slid open the carry-on zipper, exposing the three small bottles. Jimmy promptly removed one bottle, his sample. Abid had something up his sleeve; but so did he, guardedly Jimmy inserted the vial into a black cloth pouch, then into his jacket pocket.

The Land Cruiser dragged a cloud of dust behind as it sped away from the tank, back toward the opposite end of the runway. Jimmy slowed as he passed Abid. Jimmy as instructed would need to lead Abid closer to the marker, closer to where we lay waiting. Near the tree line, concealed in the tall grass, Sergeant Cowalski and I lay in wait. Jimmy could see the marker—just off the edge of the runway an old, tattered piece of red cloth hung in a tree next to the rusty vehicle. Approaching the marker, Jimmy turned the wheels left, across the runway.

Hopping out, Jimmy yelled to Abid, "Yee had better get farther away; over here, boys!"

Signalling for them to come over, Jimmy set the trap. Extending his arm to grasp the detonator bag, Jimmy could see the aggravation in Abid's eyes. Abid's plan was foiled—Abid was outraged. Seeing his fury, Jimmy knew that Abid planned to end him at some point.

Standing behind the Land Cruiser, Jimmy inserted the power pack lead into the detonator. Squeezing the small pocket clip on the detonator, he showed the intensity of the beam, burning a dung beetle in half. The beam was indeed powerful. At this distance, it would be hard to focus the beam on such a small target; Jimmy would need to steady the light. Assembled, the miniature tripod and laser rested on the vehicle hood. Slowly Jimmy focused the beam above the tank track.

"Gentlemen, yee will need to use binoculars if yee wish to see the laser dot at the tank."

Steadying themselves against the vehicle, both watched as Jimmy focused the laser downward onto the tank track. Just above the small carry-on, the bright red dot moved across the tank body, settling above the bag.

Gesturing toward himself, Jimmy suggested, "yee may want to step behind the car."

With a childish smile, directing a nod at Abid, Jimmy commented, "Yee are going to love this."

The rising sun had slowly cleared the predawn shadows, illuminating all as it moved downward toward the valley floor. Adjusting his binoculars, Miller zoomed in on the activity. "Someone has approached and set up directly behind the sergeant and Private James. It could not be our team; they would not expose their position like that. Besides, it was a white-beam flashlight; all our lights had red beams."

Whispering into his mouthpiece, Private Miller called across. "Sarge, Miller here. We have spotted activity directly above and due west of your position. Looks like two individuals and what appears to be a twenty-five-calibre machine gun. Can you see them?"

Covering the microphone, the sergeant whispered, "Roger. We saw them move in. When the shit goes down, you need to take one of them out."

Corporal Jones cut in. "Roger that, Sarge. We've got your six."

"Miller, I will take out the gunner if you can take out the one in the black toque.

"Wait for the blast of the explosion before you shoot."

"Roger that."

At twenty-three-fifty-six the preceding evening, Jimmy O'Brien had just arrived at Rundu airport. As the plane jolted to a stop, Desmond hopped out of the Land Cruiser to greet him. Reaching to aid him with his bags, Jimmy grasped the smaller black carry-on, commanding Desmond to take the others. Desmond sensed by Jimmy's actions that there was something of value in those two bags; he wondered what?

Abid stood waiting, anxious to finally meet Jimmy—Jimmy the mystery man. The Land Cruiser turned in toward the hotel lobby. It was late, but Abid was curious; he wanted to know more about this new man. Jimmy, on the other hand, was tired. It had been a long flight. They would sleep here for the night. Arrival at the abandoned airstrip was scheduled for the following morning.

Abid promptly led Jimmy across the lobby to the elevator.

Without a second thought, Jimmy extended his right hand toward Abid.

"I am sorry, we do not shake hands. However, we have much to talk about, my friend. Is that the sample?" Abid inquired.

Jimmy gave him a slight nod as he tugged on the zipper. "Sensitive to light, you know."

Throughout the evening, Jimmy sipped on cups of tea while he and Abid exchanged viewpoints—how to pick targets, the degrees of carnage with various bomb types. Abid showed a special interest in the ways Jimmy avoided detection by the authorities and how Jimmy planned his car bombings. Abid expressed special interest in his favourite places to attack, such as highly populated places, sports events, and election campaigns—places guaranteeing destruction and carnage. Jimmy, however, liked to send political messages. Getting his bombs past security had recently proven to be exceedingly difficult, thus he chose pipe and car bombs loaded with nails, detonating explosions at the entrances and exits.

Smiling, he added, "Not to destroy the buildings, but rather to kill and maim as many people as possible."

Abid especially liked Jimmy's latest idea of disguising the bombers as Santa Claus at Christmas—Abid liked the irony. Jimmy kept asking questions, all the while gaining an insight into the Hassan's operation. Abid was eager to talk. Into the wee hours of the morning, the dialogue continued. Jimmy began to see how dangerous the Hassan brothers were. Abid took immense pride in announcing to Jimmy that America, the United Kingdom, and France were the top three countries in the list of targets—Canada and other crusader countries were next in line.

The blackness of the night had long since crept through the small window when Jimmy finally announced, "It's been a long day; tomorrow will probably be the same. Best yee get some sleep."

Sunrise came quickly. Tired and yawning, Jimmy stood beside Abid on the deck of the small boat. The water was choppy today. Small waves rolled over, making a slapping sound as they beat against the side of the barge. On the short ride across the Okavango, Jimmy explained the process that was to be used today and what Abid should expect to see. The bomb consisted of only three six-ounce bottles of DD90, and it was to be placed below the tank next to the tank track. After placing the charge, Jimmy would drive back to the southern end of the runway, where Abid and Desmond would be waiting. Abid eagerly suggested that Jimmy take Desmond with him to place the bomb.

Jimmy pulled the handheld laser from the side pocket of the smaller black carry-on. Abid was surprised at the size; it was no larger than an oversized pocket pen. The power pack was the size of a small GPS with a short cable for attaching it to the detonator.

"Very small, very compact. Jimmy, I am impressed." Abid noted.

Jimmy now had to get Abid into a position where he could be subdued—to where the soldiers waited. Scanning the far end of the valley, he could see the marker: an old rusted-out truck. That was the spot where he must lure Abid. By this time, Jimmy knew he could not trust Abid. He would need to keep the detonator and cable; he could not distance himself from them—not even for a second. Turning his back to Abid, Jimmy bent down to tie his shoelace while stashing the items into his coat pocket. Abid and Desmond circled the end of the car.

"O'er here, lads. Yee view will be unobstructed."

Pulling down the rusted hood, Jimmy waited, then steadied the laser at the black bag. All sound ceased as we waited for the explosion. Seconds passed like an hour, then the sky erupted into a large ball of fire. Everywhere, wildlife scattered.

Almost imperceptibly, the first of two shots rang out. Abid turned, looking up the ridge like he had expected to hear the shots. Twenty-four hours earlier, Abid had asked his lackeys to perform a future deed. The lackeys had no idea it would be dying on a remote hillside.

The hillside erupted with birds scurrying as Jones placed the first of the shots centre-mass on the armed hillside intruder; his weapon flew back against his now limp body. The sergeant instantly rose and place a shot behind the ear of the second assailant as he turned to flee. Abid's plan to sabotage the test had been thwarted; the two ambushers lay dead on the ridge, his two lackeys would not be going home.

Behind the rusted auto, Abid turned and shoved his knife into Desmond's chest. With each breath, blood sprayed from the open wound. Desmond fell limp to the ground.

"You treacherous snake, this is what you get for betraying me."

Abid instantly rose, looking about as both Sergeant Cowalski and I lunged forward. Abid fell backward, turning his dagger. Cowalski was first to reach Abid as the silver tip lunged forward, striking flesh. Her shriek of pain rang out as I tackled Abid to the ground. Unable to strike a second blow, Abid fell backward into the dirt, clumsily dropping his knife.

Tackled, Abid lay facedown in the dirt. Straddling his back, I secured his hands. Jimmy turned rushing toward us.

"Your plan is fubar big time, you asshole." I had to say something. It was either that or pull out my sidearm and execute him. That I could not do.

By this time, Jimmy was at my side, pressing his knee firmly into Abid's back. "Have you got him?"

"Aye, I do."

Only feet away, Sally lay moaning, grasping her chest in pain. I had to get to her—help her. The need overwhelmed me. I had seen more than my share of injured soldiers, but this was different. A feeling of doom swept over me as she lay across my lap. She could not die, not now.

"Miller, hand me the T3 bandage and antiseptic! Sally, you will have to lie still. I will get you fixed up." Lowering her to the ground, I pulled the material up and away from the wound. A steady stream of blood flowed from her left breast. No frothing or squirting blood. Great: the diaphragm and lungs had not been punctured.

For a moment, I feared Sally had bought the farm. The jagged incision from Mohammad's knife had run up her rib cage, struck the underwire of her bra, and luckily deflected outward into her breast.

"Sally, you have been stabbed," I calmly commented as I applied pressure over the gauze.

"No kidding, Captain," she replied.

"Thankfully, your diaphragm was not punctured. For now, all I can do is clean it and apply a compress. We must evac this area at once! Do you understand?"

Sally nodded.

Quickly, I bandaged her wound and applied a temporary sling. "OK. Let's move!"

Two added bodies and one wounded member in tow, we headed out. One hell of a ruckus had been created. Hopefully, we had not been heard.

Patiently waiting for us to return Reinhart sat with his rifle drawn. Concealed behind the small storage trailer, he waved as we approached. It would have been hard for him not to hear us coming. Noise had not been my primary concern. Scrambling around, we loaded up and headed for the river.

"Sergeant, when we reach the barge, bag all the extra gear and drop it into the river. We need to make room in the trailers for the prisoner. When we get to the river's edge, sedate Abid, then stuff him in the compartment below the fold-away beds. We will deal with him on the other side. Sergeant, take a photo of him and send it off to command before you stash him away. They wanted to see him." Moments later the sat phone wrang.

"Yes," I answered.

Captain Cook, we ran his photo, that is not Mohammad Hassan as we had believed, it is Abid Hassan repeat you have Abid Hassan."

"Acknowledged, I replied. "We will bring him back for interrogation.

Since there were no stops by the border guards on the first crossing, Jimmy would be able to stay up top with us. "You do have your papers, don't you Jimmy?"

"Aye, I do." Jimmy replied.

"Doc, I am not going to be able to give you any painkillers. We need you coherent in case we get stopped on the river. I will take better care of you once we're back on Namibian soil. OK?" Cowalski nodded, yes.

Quickly, we boarded the tiny barge and pushed away from shore. No lights on the water was a good sign. Slowly, the captain inched his way into the current.

High winds slapped waves against the bow, tossing us off course and slowing our crossing. I eagerly awaited reaching the other side. I'd had enough excitement for one day. What I wanted was to hold and take care of Sally, but I could not show any special attention. I hated the feeling of helplessness.

Cross-current, our tiny barge drift over the Namibian-Angolan border,— soon we would be home free.

"Sergeant, you stay with Cowalski and make sure she stays comfortable. I will take her vitals and check on her bandage at the barn."

"Roger that, sir," he replied.

"Alpha Team, after we are packed up at the barn, we will be heading straight back to Windhoek and catching our plane back home.

"Sergeant, radio ahead to the military hospital in Windhoek. We will need medical attention for Sergeant Cowalski as soon as we get there.

"Roger that, sir."

"Any questions?"

No one responded, Alpha Team had all been through this scenario before.

Director Sharpe had given explicit orders that Abid was to be brought back alive—any added prisoners were to be handed over to the Namibian military for interrogation. What happened to them after that was not to be my concern. With Desmond dead, we no longer had to worry about additional prisoners.

"Reinhart, as soon as we reach shore, we will give Abid another dose of morphine. That should keep him quiet."

In his very distinct accent, Reinhart replied, "That should be fine, Captain."

"Jimmy, we will be parting ways when we reach Rundu. It would be best if you gave me the extra vial of DD90 now."

"Aye, I can do that. Here also is the detonator. Best be careful; keep them separated.

"Captain, it has indeed been a pleasure. If you are ever in Ireland, drop by for a pint."

"Well done, Jimmy." I commented.

Sergeant Cowalski did not fare as well as the rest of us. The Namibian military surgeons, although disapproving of her release, allowed her to board our plane and depart for home. This home-bound flight would hold few memories for her; sedated and lying flat on a gurney, her time would fly by. This time, the Trenton base medical team would be rushing to take her off the plane; rehab would be lengthy.

PART THIRTY-EIGHT

HOME SWEET HOME—CSIS, CANADA

At CSIS, things were heating up. The sample and detonators had been analyzed and their chemical composition proven. It was indeed far more powerful than expected. In Ireland, the chemist would be awaiting approval to continue with the shipment for Canada. Thanks to Jimmy O'Brien's intel, CSIS would now be able to track the shipments bound for Canada. Safe handling procedures had been established; it was now a waiting game until the shipment's arrival.

Slumped head down on a wobbly metal chair, Abid awoke. His head was banging with pain. Six straight days of interrogation. He had given them nothing—well, at least nothing he could remember. Another pail of chilly water splashed against his face. Gasping for breath, he yelled, "Stop, no more."

Disoriented, freezing cold, not sure he could hold out any longer, Abid could feel his darkness returning. The heavy cotton bag was pulled off his head, blackness suddenly replaced by a blinding white light. Daggers of pain shot through his eyes as he turned, trying to shield his them.

A single white male sat in the corner uttering monotone instructions and clicking the recorder on and off, over and over. Invisible in the dark, he repeated his demands. "Abid, you will record the message, or we will start all over again. You must hurry, your brother Mohammad is waiting. Do you want the icy water? Do you want the electricity?"

Sparks bounced from the battery cable, giving off that awful hissing sound. Touching them repeatedly, the stranger grinned. Touching the leads to Abid's legs, he asked again, "Will you send the message?"

"Please, no more!" Abid screamed.

"Abid, you smell like a sewer, would you like a bath?"

On and on the stranger persisted, uttering only a few words at a time. Reluctantly, Abid gave in; unable to take any more, he agreed. "I will do as you wish. You must stop—please, please stop."

"Abid, we need you to complete the whole message—read from the page." He sat—shaken, exhausted, tired, cold, a broken man.

Time after time I sat with our team of translators listening intently to the message, trying to find even the smallest mistake. Abid's piecemeal messages, now spliced together from hours of coerced recordings, were convincing. Mohammad would believe Abid was still alive and well. Director Sharpe knew as soon as CSIS released this message, Mohammad would no longer have the upper hand.

Director Sharpe read the final message aloud—from brother to brother, it translated as, "Brother, the test went well. You can expect much destruction, much death. Proceed as planned; buy the whole shipment. I will head back into Nigeria and contact you when the camp is complete. Praise be to Allah."

Satisfied the message sounded authentic, Director Sharpe released it to the airways. Status report—waiting for Mohammad to take the bait.

Abid lay naked on the floor, pale white, covered in his own excrement, no vital signs, no longer tormented.

The next morning, Director Sharpe issued the CODE RED to all Canadian military Services, CSIS, RCMP, Canadian Police Service departments, and all global intelligence agencies. The directive read:

ATTENTION—CODE RED ALERT—CSIS, Canadian Border Services, RCMP, Police Services

Shipment is expected to arrive in Toronto. All ports of entry have been alerted and advised to be on the watch for inbound shipments from Ireland or West Africa.

The liquid chemical is DD90, a very stable but deadly explosive. This chemical must be kept in the dark, out of direct sunlight or bright light. At present, no further special handling requirements are known.

Once the DD90 explosive arrives, it will be switched with a near-harmless incendiary chemical. Within one day of notification, the replacement chemical will be delivered to the designated location. As soon as we hear from our source in Ireland, I will confirm the delivery site.

Canadian Border Security Agency will conduct full detailed inspections of all shipments. Once the suspected shipment(s) arrive, the crates are to be quarantined. The shipments will remain in quarantine until tracers are affixed to each package. Our intent is to follow the packages, then identify and capture as many of their people as possible. All shipping manifests are to be sent to me and cc'd to Captain Cook. Captain Cook will oversee the tracking of packages once released to the consignee. As of today, the target is unknown, though suspected to be a Metropolitan Toronto location.

CODE RED surveillance of all passenger and freight arrival points has been requested of the Greater Toronto Airport Authority security forces.

*NOTE: The number of shipments is unconfirmed. We are currently awaiting a communiqué from our Ireland contact.

*ADDITIONAL NOTE: Due to the risk potential for a leak within the Toronto freight terminals, no other parties are to be involved at this time.

CODE RED authorized.

Director Theodore Sharpe

Canadian Armed Forces

PART THIRTY-NINE

ANALYZING THE ROUTE— TORONTO, CANADA

Mohammad re-read Jimmy O'Brien's email.

Venom packaged.

Ready to ship.

Doctor requires final payment.

The explosive would be here soon; no time to waste. Smiling, he reached for his computer. The cost of the explosive he was buying would deplete the organization's reserve cash. Eight million dollars—worth every penny—five containers weighing one kilogram each plus five detonators.

Swiss Bank account number 236-546150 keyed in, Mohammad scanned the on-screen file for accuracy, then pressed "Send."

The transfer file number blinked once before the computer acknowledged the transfer. In a flash of the cursor, his money was gone. Soon he would have the explosive, and soon money would flow again. Soon he would be known as the terrorist "go-to man."

Bing. The familiar chime of an incoming email brought Mohammad back to his computer; the chemist had received the payment and the explosive would be in production tomorrow, ready for shipment within two weeks.

Only two weeks left—ample time.

Scribbling notes into his small black note pad, he wandered from room to room, trying not to miss even the smallest of details. Muttering aloud, he paced from room to room.

"Praise be to Allah… Praise be to Allah… Praise be to Allah…

"This time I will have no mistakes…

"I have eight million dollars invested…

"I must personally check all details."

Shaving off his beard, he stood admiring his features: dark olive skin, midnight black hair. "I think I will leave my mustache; I like the look."

Changing from his traditional attire into casual street clothes, Mohammad headed for his grey cargo van. Dressed in blue jeans and a bright yellow shirt, he felt like a new man. He would blend in—he was confident no one could recognize him.

Mumbling to himself, Mohammad shuffled into the driver's seat. "September 10: today I will see how well they are prepared. I will have my dummy bomb left at the CNE GO Train station. This will tell me how much time I will have to place the package, set it up, and detonate before the package is noticed and their security imbeciles are alerted."

Pulling into the GO Train parking lot, Mohammad gave the final instructions to his waiting accomplice. "It is now 2:00 p.m. You will take this box and a small carry-on suitcase to the station.

"There you will find an out-of-the-way location to sit down. You will tuck the small box under your seat. Then you will depart on the next westbound train.

"When the train arrives, you will get up, leave the box under the seat, and leave on the train. Two stations west, you will exit the train and wait in the parking lot. "I will pick you up in the parking lot at exactly 3:15. I will stay behind at this station to evaluate the response time."

With the box in hand, the young male extended the handle on the suitcase, then turned and headed toward the station. From the parking lot, Mohammad could see the train approaching, punctual as usual. Travellers moved forward like cattle waiting for the doors to open. Last to get up, the young man departed, leaving the small suitcase behind.

Ten minutes passed before the station became a beehive of activity, with sirens wailing and the public scurrying from the station. Hah! They had discovered the box. Ten minutes would be ample time; one more question was answered, ticked off his list.

Mohammad smiled. *The emergency response teams will be of no use when the real time comes. There will be no wait time needed; my bomb will explode almost instantaneously. All I need to do is have my people in the right place at the right time.* Content, heading westward out of the parking lot, Mohammad chauffeured leisurely to retrieve his awaiting accomplice.

Awaking at 6:00 a.m., Mohammad's mind went directly back to where he had left off. *Today I must investigate the shipping and the pickup.* A quick breakfast was all the time he could afford. He wanted to find his way around the airport shipping terminals. Exiting the 407, he headed south. From the off-ramp, he could see the familiar shape of the air traffic control tower. The shape always reminded him of the flower on the top of the wild thistle. A unique shape.

Airport Road was congested as usual—cars, trucks, tractor-trailers, cube vans, every kind of transport vehicle imaginable. From a block away, he could see the freight carrier terminal buildings. Constructed in a horseshoe shape, large letters from A to H highlighted the buildings. Overhead, carrier signs depicted the various airlines using their services. Like a beehive, trucks and people were everywhere.

Mohammad could see no problems with the pickup of his crates. Not yet aware of which airline would be carrying his shipment, he now knew where his people would need to come to pick it up.

Building D housed the CBSA Customs Clearance Office. Thirty-four steps upward led Mohammad to Suite 245: bright red and white lettering alerted Mohammad to the door. This neat, tidy government office stood in contrast to the dirty, dingy counters of the freight carriers' offices, where it appeared they never cleaned.

Mohammad's mind jumped from thought to thought. "*If I am to have problems, this is where it will happen. I will need to send one of my more experienced people to oversee the clearance. These border agents ask too many questions. If at all concerned, they may stop my shipment. I cannot afford that.*" He continued to mutter in a soft, indiscernible voice as he left the freight warehouse. Rounding the bend, he headed toward the nearby stoplight.

PART FORTY

ALPHA TEAM—TORONTO, CANADA

"Gentlemen, today we received information from the FBI that the terrorist attempt is imminent.

"We have not yet ascertained the target, but the Greater Toronto Area is the anticipated location.

"For over two years, the FBI, the RCMP, and local police forces have been following Aaron Q. Master, a Canadian-born citizen. He had been posting numerous terrorist-related blogs on local social media sites—he is considered unstable and a serious threat to both Canada and the United States.

"Master's was quoted as boldly stating he was looking for a highly populated area where he could explode his bomb. Only twenty-five, Master has a lengthy arrest record and will re-offend if given the chance. A federal peace bond for threatening terrorist acts was exercised against him, directing him to have no communication with known terrorist extremist organizations, nor use of the internet.

"Master's is currently living in the Brampton area. Before his arrest, he had associations with numerous Muslim extremists, all known to reside in the same area.

"Master's was ordered to stay in the city and to wear an ankle bracelet. Even with a 9:00 p.m. curfew and firearms restrictions he continued to be an extremely dangerous threat.

"The two-year period for his peace bond has now lapsed, and Master is again instigating chatter and posting to blogs, praising the efforts of Muslims worldwide for their attacks against what he calls 'foreign aggressors,' Canada in particular.

"All RCMP and local police services have been upgraded to a medium alert status. As well, all associated emergency medical services will be contacted today, and their alert status upgraded.

"Similarly, the GTAA police and our Elite Task Force personnel are upgraded to 'CODE RED' status.

"Though still unconfirmed, Union Station and Pearson International are considered probable targets."

With the briefing concluded, I pulled my team aside. "We will meet back here at thirteen-hundred hours, you will then receive your assignments."

Gobbling down my lunch, I hurried back to prepare for the afternoon session. Loading the last of my presentation onto the large monitors, I awaited the arrival of Alpha Team. I was anxious. Today's meeting seemed different from all our previous meetings. A sense of doom permeated the room. Like no other time, I felt his presence—like a wolf hiding in the bushes. Mohammad was close; I could feel him.

"OK. Let's get started.

"Recent internet activity has led CSIS to believe that the terrorist attacks will occur downtown in heavily populated areas. Our team, gentlemen, is assigned to Union Station and the UP Express corridor.

"Union Station is the hub of Toronto's pedestrian movement—upward of two hundred thousand people a day pass through those doors. That building handles pedestrian movement for travel throughout the Greater Toronto area.. And it is extremely vulnerable to attacks.

"Likewise, the UP Express system operates nineteen-and-one-half hours a day, shuffling travellers between Union Station and Pearson International Airport.

"All security services are compelled to work fourteen-hour shifts or longer until the CODE RED alert is lifted.

"Authorities anticipate the terrorist's goal is to cause considerable loss of life and inflict many casualties; property destruction is not their focus. It has been concluded only three of the seven stations along the UP Express route are valued targets."

The red dot of my laser streaked across the screen, stopping on Union Station. "The highest density of travellers will be during peak a.m. and p.m. rush hours, in particular the stations closest Union Station and Pearson International.

"Although the Viscount and Terminal 3 stops are the farthest stops at the airport, it has been determined that the Terminal 1 Station will more likely be the target of choice as it has considerably more pedestrian movement, and thus is suspected to be a more valued target.

"Sergeant Parker and I will each take a spot at the extreme ends of these routes. The remainder of the team will be posing as TTC employees.

"I will be positioned at Union Station, Sergeant Parker at Terminal 1.

"Security forces will attempt to identify any known threats as they board the trains. By the way, Interpol and MI6 facial recognition software has been loaded on your handhelds.

"Cameras have been installed in all train cars and at loading platforms, this will provide 'real-time eyes on' at all locations..

"Each UP Express consists of only three cars. There should be ample time for our agents to casually walk through the stationary cars, scan the passengers, and assess threat potential before the train departs. If a threat is identified, additional security agents will be ready and in position to enter the trains at any station along the route—Pearson to Union Station.

"The plan appears solid, but if you see any holes in the logic, please review it with me ASAP. Dismissed."

PART FORTY-ONE

STUDYING THE UP EXPRESS— TORONTO, CANADA

The van tires squealed as Mohammad rounded the curve to the Terminal 1 parking garage. Starting his analysis of the UP Express on September 11 was no mistake; security would be at its peak, and any weaknesses would be evident. Increased activity on the internet had CSIS and global security agencies on high alert. Everyone expected an attack soon—really soon. Mohammad planned it differently; it would not happen September 11 this year, but it would be another equally important day.

Backing into the Level 7, D44 parking space, Mohammad gathered up his black notepad, then headed for the train loading platforms located on Level 5.

Mohammad jotted down notes as he gazed about the small passenger boarding area: terrazzo floors, steel structure, arched roof, lots of glass, great for spreading the blast and deflecting the shrapnel. Good.

Outside the window, roadways of asphalt and concrete crisscrossed in and out of the terminal. Below, concrete statues dotted the sidewalks, welcoming arrival and departure guests. What opulence, what waste—no purpose, no function. Waste, always waste...

He watched as a male and female passenger laden down with backpacks and a kayak entered his commuter car. *Tourists,* he thought. *Now this has potential.* An opportunity appeared plain as day; with no checking of bags or objects, this would indeed provide easy opportunity to transport explosive packages to any point desired, with no worry of inspections. His plan was coming together.

September 11 was a grey day. Fingers of sunlight shining through the overcast sky bounced off the cold, dreary galvanized steel along the train platform. Mohammad could feel no warmth, no reason for compassion or kindness. These people needed to be hurt; they needed to feel his pain.

Once more, he glanced around, looking toward the air traffic control tower. He noticed what appeared to be a machine gun turret hovering above Terminal 3, attached to the roof of the round structure. He remembered back to 9/11 when rumours circulated that fifty-calibre machine guns had been placed at key-value targets: airports, nuclear-generating stations, and valuable landmarks. He was not in a good location to tell if this was indeed a gun; however, on the return trip, he would have a better angle and opportunity to confirm his suspicions.

As the train pulled away from the station, he pointed his pen to the bottom of the first page and scribbled a brief note: "Check potential turret above tower at T3."

Mohammad continued with his notes. Moving down on his page, he stopped at "departing time" and inked in "10:00 a.m." Each station in sequence was listed on the page. He must detail the time intervals between each station and the overall trip. Nothing could be left to chance.

Watching the young couple adjusting the position of their kayak, it was at that moment he noticed the overhead storage compartments. Quickly he decided the compartments would not be usable. The light beam needed to shine on the explosive. However, the open storage areas below the seats would do the job nicely. He could strap down the carry-on packages there and leave the bag slightly open, providing the ability to activate the bomb from the seat across the aisle. Once the trains were full, then, he could detonate. The train would be cast off the tracks as the explosion ripped the grey-green seats from their moorings. Like ping-pong balls, they would bounce them around inside the cars. He smiled, picturing everyone within the car, and the surrounding station perishing.

The calling from Allah, at last, avenged. Praise be to Allah!

Timing of this suicide trip: crucial. Only his most loyal follower would be picked to celebrate—praise to Allah!

Part Forty-One

Mohammad was pulled back to reality as the PA system announced the train's approach to Union Station. He jotted down 10:25 a.m.—exactly twenty-five minutes; exactly what the advertising literature stated.

PART FORTY-TWO

WATCHFUL EYES—UNION STATION, TORONTO, CANADA

Atop the overpass at Bay Street, I waited, watching. A middle-aged male exited the centre car. Turning right, he stopped at the café. At first, I thought nothing of it—a male Caucasian, wearing a black shirt and blue jeans. Slowly, he sipped his tea while eating a croissant. He was panning, studying the area. Something did not feel right. Disposing of his garbage, he turned the corner, departing down the ramp to Union Station.

I scrolled through our photo database—no hits.

"Come in, Private James."

"James here."

"Be alert for a white male, black shirt, blue jeans. Watch him."

"Roger that, Sir. I have a visual. Your suspect just cleared the overpass."

I kept scrolling the photos. "Private, I still show no hits, but watch him, report back."

"Parker here. Your suspect got on at T1 thirty-five minutes ago."

"James here. Captain, he has been sitting on the bench next to the piano for the last five minutes, looks like he is watching the commuters.

"Wait. He is on the move—taking the downstairs toward eastbound GO Trains. Might be nothing, but I am on his tail."

"Via Train 38 bound for Oshawa, Cornwall, Montreal, and all points east now boarding at Gate F," blared over the PA.

"Captain, false alarm. Suspect boarded the eastbound train toward Montreal."

Mohammad grasped the steel post, pulling himself erect. Six steps and he was out of the commuter car. Casually walking past the café, he descended the ramp into Union Station.

Everything looked normal; *no opportunities here* were his thoughts. Mohammad glanced past the entranceway toward the middle of the Great Hall. Poised in the middle of the hall, five feet in diameter, sat the large clock. The translucent face was trimmed in gold and glowed white. The large black hand clicked downward to 10:30 a.m.

Checking for security weaknesses, Mohammad silently muttered, "An hour to study the commuter traffic should be adequate, then I head to the streets."

From behind the service counter, Private James saw him coming. "Lieutenant, I have eyes on a Middle Eastern male, coming from your direction. Did you see him?"

"No," came the reply.

Stepping from behind the counter, Private James turned, heading toward the clock, casually preparing to intercept the lone male.

"Captain, I should be able to photograph him as he passes the clock."

Slipping his phone from his waist pouch, the private headed toward the Front Street entrance. Next to the door, he casually turned, gazing up at the clock. Slowly, he centred the photo, then snapped the shutter repeatedly. Seconds later, the photos reached Command.

"Suspect confirmed, Mohammad Hassan. Continue surveillance. I'm on my way."

Rushing across the ramp to the Great Hall, I saw Mohammad descend the stairway to the eastbound tracks, all the while scanning the congested room below.

I have not seen the lower level; where does it go? Plunking himself down onto a wooden bench, Mohammad began recording his new observations—washrooms to the right and left, low ceiling, lots of people. This room would work, though human destruction would be limited.

Low-decibel radio chatter heightened. "Your suspect is now sitting on a bench, writing in a black book."

"Private, pull back. He is not to be alerted. I repeat, pull back."

"Roger that, Sir. I should be able to watch him from the top of the stairs."

Ascending the stairs, the private flipped open a newspaper, positioning himself on a nearby bench. The location presented a clear view of Mohammad recording his observations of the crowd—habits, positions, movements.

Thirty minutes passed, then the silence in the captain's earbud ceased. "Suspect ascending the stairs."

Assuming the private's surveillance position, I watched as Mohammad rounded the corner, heading toward the Front Street entrance. Private James now repositioned, stood on the sidewalk just outside the door. Nodding a head gesture toward Mohammad, Private James identified him for the others as he exited the door.

The security station outside stood empty. Seizing the opportunity, I walked over and sat down. Casually glancing toward the doorway, I saw Mohammad as he walked outward toward the streetside vendors. Heavily, Mohammad sat down at an unoccupied picnic table. Opening the book, he started taking notes. By this time, many agents had descended on the open-air restaurant. A female agent walked past Mohammad; she turned and sat down at the table next to him.

As Mohammad wrote, he became uneasy, sensing he was being watched. Looking up, he noticed the agent gazing in his direction. She smiled then averted her gaze. I had to do something before our cover was compromised. Casually, I motioned for her to get up and approach the vendor booths. I needed to divert Mohammad's attention away from the agent. Walking over, I quickly placed my arm around her shoulder. His suspicions ceased; Mohammad went back to writing. Our bluff, successful.

Mohammad sat gazing, studying the surroundings. The old marble structure across the street was adorned with flags: the Canadian, the US, the Union Jack, all gently swaying with the breezes. The opulent trims, the mullioned windows—such a proud building, yet it paled in contrast to the towering, multi-coloured glass and steel structures only metres away. Copper, green, and silver glass super-structures surrounded the old hotel's majesty— old and modern architectural monuments, both unique in their own way. Mohammad scoffed, all the luxury—pompous capitalism. Capitalism… waste… sheer waste…

Mohammad completed his notes, pulled his phone from his jacket pocket, then snapped several photos.

Satisfied, he headed east, continually taking notes. Gradually, he headed back into Union Station. He mused joyfully to himself, "*Continual trains arriving, commuter mobs flooding the adjoining streets—this is perfect. Hundreds, maybe thousands of people... Glass... lots of glass... Praise be to Allah!*"

Mohammad's lips now moving ever so slightly, he mumbled, "Here I will use two vials. This location—perfect... Such destruction! Praise be to Allah!"

Mohammad continued through the station, eventually boarding a north-bound UP Express. What was his next destination?

"Cowalski, what is your position?"

"Heading north, currently coming into Weston Station, Sir."

"Good. Hop off there. Wait for the next train. Mohammad Hassan is in the second car, wearing blue jeans and a bright yellow shirt.

"Follow him. Gather all intel.

"We will have surveillance cars waiting at T1, T3, and the Viscount stations. You're to immediately identify Hassan's vehicle. Other agents will tail him as he leaves the parking garage."

"Roger that, Sir."

Mohammad sat staring out the window at the old wooden homes, all sandwiched together below the overhead track. Dirty, soiled buildings with little more than inches between them, each reminded him of the shanty towns back home.

Entering the last car of the train, Sergeant Cowalski could see Mohammad through the windowed door. Fitted out in a blue transit uniform, the sergeant seamlessly blended in with other transit personnel. A multitude of thoughts and processes ran through her head: *Hassan is very observant, unpredictable, intelligent. I will need to be vigilant in my cover. I will remain here and wait for him to move.* Momentarily, her mind flipped back to one of her father's favourite sayings: "Sometimes discretion is the better part of valour."

Settling in, the sergeant provided her status. "Captain, I have eyes on Hassan. I repeat, eyes on. Will report on any status change."

Sergeant Cowalski sat tucked in the corner, not wanting to attract attention. Reluctantly, she stood, motionless, resisting the urge to walk past Mohammad. All the weapons were stowed in the lead car. Hopefully, the need to access them would not arise—this was to be a surveillance detail only.

"Come in, Captain." Cowalski uttered.

Part Forty-Two

"Cook here. Status report, Sergeant,"

"Mohammad is now exiting Level 7, heading toward the ground-level T1 parking garage, driving a grey cargo van, Ontario plate 431-Xray-Bravo Kilo."

"Good work, Sergeant. The RCMP detail will take over."

Only minutes later, Mohammad turned the corner, pulling into the underground parking of a six-storey apartment building. The surveillance vehicle continued past the apartment building, turned, and came to a stop seventy yards west in a local strip mall. There the duo waited, watching.

Two, two-man teams in different vehicles had been arranged; Mohammad was now under surveillance; twenty-four seven. I could feel the tension building as the hours passed.

"Ok, we now have a location. I announced over my radio.

"Mohammad has been traced to an apartment building in the northwest part of Toronto.

"I want the names and background of every single person living in, entering, or even pissing on the bushes at that address. Now! We need to rip their lives apart—we may have just uncovered his Toronto cell."

PART FORTY-THREE

THE CHEMIST—IRELAND

Jimmy O'Brien rested his head in his hands, pondering. If he sent the coded message now, he may be exposed. Too many strangers were hanging around. Too many people were asking questions. MI6 informants were lurking. If MI6 suspected something, other agencies would also be looking. Somehow, word of this new DD90 had surfaced—all the big players wanted in on the action. It must have been the chemist. What had he done? For the moment, no one suspected his friend Ralph to be the chemist. But it would be only a matter of time. Jimmy needed to act fast.

Approaching the back door, Jimmy tapped three times, the signal they always used. Atop the door, he could see window curtains flutter. *Good, he's home.* Jimmy sighed as footsteps approached. The deadbolt moved, first squeakily, then ending with a clunk. The old wooden door opened. Ralph looked worried. Peering down the alley, Ralph stepped back as he ushered Jimmy through the half-open door.

Ralph stuttered, "We… we need to get this shipment out of here—too many people asking questions."

Jimmy waited before asking, "Who did yee tell?"

"Nay a one, but it seems someone heard about the Angola test. I overheard two blokes yakking at the local pub the other day; they are looking hard."

Jimmy thought for a second. "Ralph, yee be calm. We'll move it tonight; I be 'ere at 10:00 p.m. with a pickup. Now, let's get it ready. We load them crates now, worry about that delinquent chatter later."

Ralph again stammered. Jimmy could see he was worried. "No. No. No, I want them out now. Yee must!"

Jimmy watched Ralph as he became increasingly agitated. Ralph had never shown such emotion. Clearly, he was ready to crack. Not good. Operation Serpent was unravelling. Ralph, his long-time asset, was quickly becoming a liability.

Jimmy backed the truck through the overhead door into the warehouse. Hand over hand, Ralph yanked on the chain until the large wooden door rested firmly on the floor. Together they grabbed the five boxes, lifting them one by one onto the bed of Jimmy's truck. When loaded, Jimmy rushed up to the mezzanine office for the bank account number, the detonators, and battery packs. Ralph stood behind his old wooden desk as Jimmy placed the detonators and batteries into a small cardboard box.

"These will have to be repacked, no time now. Hurry.

"Ralph, I hate to be the materialistic one here, but when will you transfer my cut? I assume you have sent it?" Ralph rolled his eyes as he reached into his pocket and pulled out his small black notebook.

Jimmy peered over Ralph's shoulder as he read aloud the banking info. Ralph had complete trust in Jimmy, not thinking twice about sharing his information, sweat beads rolled down the sides of his balding brow—signs of obvious stress.

Cold steel now rested in Jimmy's hand. As the last detonator was stuffed into the box, he moved in close behind Ralph. Six inches of shiny steel sliced into Ralph's liver. Death came almost instantaneously. He would miss his old friend, but Jimmy knew it had to be done. Releasing his grip, Jimmy dropped the lifeless body to the floor. Reaching down, he promptly grabbed the black book; he would look through it later. For now, it rested inside his coat pocket.

Mounds of paper lay scattered about the office: files and loose papers covered with scribbled notes and formulas. All had to be destroyed. Gathering every piece, Jimmy piled it all in the middle of the room, ensuring all traces of the formula were destroyed, burned. The chemical sample could be analyzed in Canada and the formula derived. Here, now, no written record could exist.

The warehouse stood alone in a remote, rundown part of town. The building was old and windowless, built in a time when fire protection was not a consideration. It was a ripe place for crime. Piling the papers tightly around the body then sprinkling gas, Jimmy set the fire. With luck, the body and any sign of the fire would not be detected for weeks. By then, Jimmy would be long gone.

Before leaving, Jimmy stood back, away from the stench of the burning flesh, all the while watching, waiting, making sure all traces of Ralph and the formula were destroyed.

PART FORTY-FOUR

DD90 ARRIVAL—TORONTO, CANADA

I smiled as I read the email aloud: "'Venom secure. Will be shipped from Belfast Friday. Chemist has taken an extended vacation. Six wooden boxes in total will go out by air cargo. Five boxes will be under one manifest. The detonators will be shipped separately. I will forward copies of the shipping manifests tomorrow.'

"OK, let's get this show on the road." Director Sharpe commented loudly.

Reaching upward I turned on the monitor. The room buzzed with activity. Everyone knew why they had been summoned. The large presentation room was full. CSIS, CBSA, military advisors—all investigative teams were present for this crucial review.

"Tomorrow I will be receiving the manifest for the DD90; the shipment is heading here from Ireland.

"The chemist has been eliminated and all evidence of the DD90 formula, destroyed.

"Six wooden boxes have been secured and prepped for shipping.

"For CBSA agents, the manifest will list the shipment as hair shampoo.

"The detonators and power packs will be sent under a separate waybill."

Director Sharpe drew in a breath as he pulled up the second slide, showing contents of the smaller crate.

"At no time are the contents of the DD90 crates and the detonators to be together."

"Once the crates are received at the GTAA freight terminal, CBSA will place them into a quarantine area.

"The warehouse facilities operate twenty-four seven, so as an added precaution all warehouse staff will be called to a closed-door meeting.

"During this time, Alpha team will switch the DD90 for the incendiary chemical. Staff at the freight terminal will then inform the consignee that their shipment is ready for pickup."

Switching slides, the director drew attention to a street map of the area surrounding Mohammad Hassan's residence. "Thanks to diligent police work on September 11 of this year, we were able to identify and trail Mohammad Hassan to his residence. He has been under constant surveillance for the past two weeks.

"His habits and movements have been attentively studied.

"Thanks to him, and his lack of security, we now have taps on all phone lines coming into the apartment building.

"All the numbers he contacted in the last two weeks have been logged into our Incident Software, and all individuals frequenting the residences, photographed.

"Multiple threat levels have been heightened as the population of this cell has been growing exponentially in the last two weeks.

"Hassan's associates in Windsor, Vancouver, and Montreal have all been identified and logged in as well.

"Local RCMP detachments are currently setting up their operations. We expect they will be equally successful in identifying and apprehending key individuals in each of the other cities.

"In short course, a coordinated take-down in all cities will go into motion.

"Twenty-six different phone numbers have also been identified in the Toronto area.

"Unfortunately, we expect the number of involved individuals will grow considerably as our surveillance continues."

Director Sharpe stepped back from the podium. "Captain Cook will now take over and describe the upcoming operation."

"Good morning. Nationwide, we had expected September 11 to be the bombing date.

"9/11 had increased activity, but we now believe that it was merely a scouting day—preparation for what's to come.

"Recent chatter leads us to believe Canada's Remembrance Day, 11/11, is now the anticipated attack date, and since the delivery of the DD90 is imminent, we believe our intel is correct.

"Until RED ALERT is initiated, all teams will remain on their present work detail, reporting in as usual.

"Determination of who will attempt to explode the bombs has not been ascertained.

"Based on the number of individuals at each residence, our surveillance teams have also been increased. We have set up, two-men teams to cover each male at the twenty-six residences. This number will be increased if needed."

"As you know, most pedestrian traffic occurs during rush hours. We expect the explosive packages will either be picked up or in transit by at least seventeen-hundred hours on that day.

"Historically, the execution of major terrorism events has been around twenty-three-hundred hours—acts usually planned for high-traffic hours. Therefore, we will have to maintain tight surveillance until at least zero-one-hundred hours, November 12.

"To avoid leaks, local EMS forces have not been read in, except to say that they will be instructed as usual to stay alert to any suspicious activity.

"For optimum take-down of suspects, five main teams have been established.

"Director Sharpe and the CSIS team will continue to monitor operations from the Command Centre.

"Union Station, major events, and the UP Express will be covered by Alpha, Bravo, and Charlie teams. RCMP and local police services will continue to monitor the freight carrier depots and residential leads. GTAA security will cover all airport activity.

"As detailed earlier, the DD90 will be swapped for the incendiary chemical tomorrow."

At zero-nine-hundred, Alpha Team and airport security stood outside, awaiting approval to enter the terminal. The warehouse employee meeting would take only thirty minutes, so speed would be of the essence. Private James turned the key to the quarantine lockup as Private Dunsmoore lowered the skid from the back of the truck. Turning the cart toward the incline ramp, he manoeuvred the crates into the warehouse.

The boxes bounced around on the small wooden skid as he crested the top of the ramp. Ahead, Private James waited for him with the tracking devices in hand. Carefully drilling a small hole into the bottom of each crate, he slid a tiny nail head transmitter into each of the boxes. Command could now individually track the boxes within a twenty-mile radius. With a mere five minutes to spare, the dolly descended the ramp. Loaded up, the DD90 sat in the back of the security truck, ready for removal. Cautiously, Privates James and Dunsmoore set out for the security vault located fifty feet below the Infield Terminal. Underground, surrounded by six-foot thick walls of concrete, the DD90 would sit until they could figure out the composition and how it could be neutralized.

Stationed in the freight carrier lobby, Sergeant Cowalski sat behind the small folding table. Posing as a warehouse employee, she awaited the arrival of whoever would try to claim the shipment. Intel was needed; this was our best opportunity.

PART FORTY-FIVE

THE PICKUP—PEARSON INTERNATIONAL AIRPORT

Mohammad reached for his phone. He usually waited for three rings, but this day he was anxious; he expected a call, the call that would alert him to the arrival of his shipments.

"*Marhaban*," Mohammad uttered into the receiver.

"Can I speak to Saabira Hassan, please," came the voice from the other end.

Switching to English, Mohammad asked, "Who is calling?"

"This is the air freight terminal at Pearson International Airport. We have a shipment from Ireland ready for pick up."

Just in case something went wrong, Mohammad had arranged for Jimmy O'Brien to address the shipment to Saabira. Mohammad had chosen his wife to pick up the shipment. Subservient, she would do exactly as instructed, and, if need be, she was expendable.

"Do we come to your warehouse to get it?" Mohammad raised an eyebrow in surprise. He thought he knew what the answer would be.

"This is a personal shipment. You will have to pick up your documents here at the warehouse, then go to the Infield Customs Office to clear the goods.

"Once CBSA has cleared the shipment and taxes have been paid, you will then come back here for your packages."

"CBSA, is that the Canadian Border Security Agency?" Mohammad asked.

"Yes, that is correct." Came the reply.

This seemed like quite an ordeal. Mohammad worried—his wife might screw it up. After all, she was just a woman—a lesser being in the eyes of Allah. Although he did not want to, he knew he must accompany her.

Identification in hand, Saabira approached the small table. "I have a parcel to pick up—Saabira Hassan."

As Sergeant Cowalski flipped through the pile of manifest papers, she tried to study the individual. Only her brown eyes were visible, the burqa covering her from head to foot. Sergeant Cowalski pondered, *How the hell can I get any kind of ID when all I can see are her eyes?*

Extracting the paperwork, Cowalski instructed Mrs. Hassan, "First you must go to the desk to retrieve your paperwork, then go to the infield office to clear your shipment. Once this is completed, come back here to claim your packages."

Mohammad sat in the rear of the truck, concealed from the outside. A small curtain hung loosely behind the driver's seat. He could see out, but no one could see in. Behind the curtain, he watched as his woman approached the van.

Cowalski quickly discerned, her vehicle would be the only way to obtain the information needed. Sergeant Cowalski waited, exiting the warehouse in time to see the woman enter a grey van—431 Xray-Bravo-Kilo; that was all she needed. It was the same van she had noted at the parking garage. Sharply, she turned toward the loading docks, stopping to wave at an approaching male. Hopefully, if Mohammad was at all suspicious, this would help.

Mohammad screamed, "You stupid woman. You have been followed." He so wanted to hit her. She deserved it. It was his right.

Saabira, although visibly afraid, shakily voiced her objection as she drove toward the infield offices. "But Mohammad, the woman, she's only a terminal employee, the one who gave me the papers."

Mohammad muttered, "That woman looks familiar. Where? Where have I seen her?"

Alerted, CBSA supervisors prepared for the suspect's arrival. The Infield Customs Depot trained new agents each was taught to ask a lot of questions. Each question was an attempt to reveal truths and lies—whichever be the case. Often, it was the harder place to clear a shipment.

Today, a selected agent had been briefed. As directed, the agent would allow the shipment to clear with as little difficulty as possible. We needed Saabira to be at ease, to take the shipment quickly. We needed to find out where the shipment would be sent. As Saabira approached the wicket, the video surveillance cameras zoomed in on her from all directions. Many eyes watched as the paperwork was stamped. Successful, Saabira headed back to her vehicle.

"Miller here. Hassan is heading west on Britannia Road, turning north on Dixie."

Director Sharpe interjected, "Stay back. Maintain visual. Report back to me when she has the shipment."

Prior to returning to the warehouse terminal, Mohammad instructed Saabira to turn into a coffee shop along the strip. He exited the van. Across the street from the terminal, he had a direct view of all people entering and leaving the loading docks.

"I will remain here in the coffee shop until you return." If something went wrong at the terminal, Mohammad did not want to be present. He could deny everything.

Adjacent to the corner, tucked behind the bank, Private Miller watched the exchange—the pickup of the DD90.

"Miller here. Sergeant, the Hassan vehicle is approaching."

Patiently anticipating their movement, Director Sharpe sat watching the stationary blink of the tracers. He expected to see them follow the route to Mohammad's residence and was not surprised when the dots turned left.

"Captain Cook, come in."

"Cook here."

"Captain, you can pick up Saabira Hassan's vehicle at the 407. She is heading toward Airport Road and Derry. I expect she will head north, then across to Mohammad's residence. All three tracers are active, so you can stay back a bit. I will let you know if they deviate."

Nearing the end of the month, transport activity was staggering, bogging down every intersection. Today traffic was especially heavy.

"Miller here. Can someone confirm that the van is still on Airport Road? We have lost it."

I reported, "The van has turned off, now going east between two buildings. I can see them from here. Miller, go past to the intersection then wait in the plaza at the northwest corner."

Tucking my Ford Escort in beside a parked Escalade, I could see clear to the other end of the laneway. Red brake lights glowed bright as the van came to a stop. Halfway down the alley, two men approached the driver's window.

"OK, people, it looks like they intend to transfer one or all of the parcels. Director, are you still seeing the tracers?"

"Yes, all three are still active, stationary at your location."

"Cook here. They have moved two of the packages into a grey Ford Ranger and are on the move again. Are the tracers separating?"

"Affirmative," came back over the radio.

"Miller, drop back to cover the Ranger. I will stay with the van."

Ducking down in the front seat, I waited for the vehicles to pass. Inching into traffic, the surveillance teams paired up with the van and the Ford Ranger. Northbound, I watched as Private Miller shadowed the truck, now heading west on Steeles Avenue.

Briefly, I wondered where the Ranger was headed; *not my job* flashed through my mind. For now, I had to stay focused on the van. It came as no surprise when the grey van, as expected, headed directly northwest toward Mohammad's residence.

For thirty minutes, Director Sharpe watched the blinking dots as the tracers in the Ranger gradually moved toward the trucking warehouse at Dixie and Britannia Road.

"Director Sharpe here. They are slowing down, drop back a bit; let's see what they do."

The director's earlier certainties paid off. The tracers ceased moving. Several surveillance teams had previously reported following individuals to this same location. As suspected, the warehouse was being used by Mohammad and his group. Not wanting to risk exposure, Director Sharpe called in two additional teams.

"Team One, fall back. Relocate to the apartment. Wait with the wiretap team until I get back to you. Team Three, drop into place and follow the Ranger. Team Four, assume street surveillance on Mohammad's apartment building; stay alert for any known suspects. Whoever is delivering the bomb should arrive soon."

I suspected Mohammad may want to inspect the shipment. Possibly even repackage it.

Mohammad grasped the rechargeable drill, inserted the Phillips bit, then backed out the screws. Cutting the tape, he peered inside. He could not see through the sealed black container, but he could hear the contents slosh around as he removed it from the wooden crate. Everything looked fine, no spillage. Although curious, he resisted the urge to open the black container and peer in.

Muttering to himself for reassurance, Mohammad proclaimed, "No point in blowing myself up; I am so close. We will be ready soon, then the infidels will learn. Allah will be proud of me; Jannah awaits us all."

Closing his eyes, he envisioned the explosion and the ensuing destruction: tonnes of rubble cascading down, glass and stone collapsing onto the unsuspecting commuters. It would be a glorious moment.

Lights shone around the edges of the thin drapes in Mohammad's dimly lit apartment. Through the drapes, shadows of two males could be seen moving from room to room. Beside the large patio door, a single carry-on suitcase stood. Beside it, the shipping crate lay open; newspaper flyers lay strewn about the room. The contents had apparently been repacked.

Into the wee hours of the morning, Mohammad could be seen grasping the extended handle and walking the case around the room. He was preparing, practising his plan. As the video camera rolled on, small red beams of light could be seen flashing around the room. Mohammad had a new toy.

Twenty-four hours had passed with little activity—I sensed Mohammad would be getting impatient.

"Come in, Director." I prompted.

Director Sharpe answered quickly, "Sharpe here. Go ahead, Captain."

"Sir, we have movement. Mohammad Hassan and a single male are leaving the apartment with a small suitcase. Do we tail them?"

"Affirmative, Captain. Reports are building; numerous other suspects appear to be on the move as well. We may be seeing signs that a meeting is about to occur."

The grey van turned east onto Derry Road. I observed, following at a safe distance, suspecting that Mohammad was going to visit the warehouse.

He had not gone near the warehouse since the DD90 package had arrived, although three other suspects had been coming and going regularly.

Twenty-four seven surveillance confirmed the three crates of explosives were still there. Reports from all other teams confirmed the same. All suspects appeared to be moving in the same direction—toward the warehouse. A meeting was on.

Director Sharpe turned on the listening devices strategically placed throughout the warehouse—there were only so many locations where a meeting of this size could occur. With the tapes running, and the translators listening, the team waited to hear Mohammad lay out his final plans.

Doors opened and closed as the suspects arrived, each heading toward the rear meeting room. Six individuals were already present. The tracer beacons had not moved from this location since delivery, the crates appeared unaltered.

The final crate, the one that Mohammad possessed, had long since been discarded. I impatiently watched the blinking lights, hoping that Mohammad was still in possession of that vial of explosive. Idle chit-chat could be heard as the group sat waiting for the final two to arrive. All eyes turned to watch the door as Mohammad and his lone companion entered.

"Praise be to Allah," Mohammad uttered as he approached the head of the table. All present repeated the comment before descending into their chairs.

Mohammad spread his arms toward the centre of the table. "We have toiled long and hard. Now, we will finally be able to stab our daggers deep into the heart of the infidels. November 11 is our day! Excitement filled the room.

"I have personally picked the locations for our glorious display. We have five vials of explosives. Two vials will be detonated on Front Street outside Union Station, the other three will satisfy Allah outside Air Canada Centre.

"On November 11, we will do much damage. People of all nationalities will know our names.

"We will detonate all the explosives at the same time, 7:00 p.m. The first three explosions will be close to the entrances. We will deliver them in these rolling luggage bags."

Unzipping the suitcase, Mohammad proceeded to demonstrate. "We will place flyers at the bottom. We will then pack more flyers around the explosive, concealing it out of sight."

Mohammad could be heard extending the handle on his small suitcase while shuffling toward the farthest end of the room.

"You will attach extra flyers to the outside of your case. So that we do not attract attention from any security people, we will stay away from the doors. Once you arrive, you will only have a few minutes to set up. You will hand out the flyers on the top of the case and then open the side zipper."

Mohammad had only taken one of the lasers out, leaving the remainder of the crate intact. Grabbing the wooden box off the table, Mohammad pulled out the pen-like object.

"This, my friends is the detonator. This little device is about to change the world. The beam from these lasers *must* hit the explosives."

The assembly of the battery pack and detonator pen took only seconds. By pressing the small clip, a bright red light appeared on the ceiling. Instantly, the paint darkened as the beam burned the surface.

"As you can see, this is a very powerful beam. Do not activate it until you are ready."

Mohammad continued, "The explosive is light sensitive. The detonator must not be pointed at the bag until you are ready. Since we will need to detonate the bomb in crowded areas, we, ourselves, will become part of the blast. We are all prepared to die in his name. Allah will greet you each with your seventy virgins."

Selecting the four individuals that he would entrust with this sacred task, Mohammad called them by name and embraced each of them. "Your rewards await you in Jannah."

Sitting face in hands, I listened intently as the translators converted their conversation to English, all the time I wondered, *how could these extremists justify the carnage, the destroying of buildings, monuments, books, manuscripts, and other significant treasures worldwide without a single care as to their inherent value.* They reminded him so much of the Nazi regime in Germany.

I knew I must never allow Canada to be dragged down or inherit their radical beliefs.

Under my breath, I re-affirmed my soldier's oath to defend this country to the death, swearing that I would never allow our civilization to be destroyed by backward-thinking fanatics.

My mind drifted back to my dad. My blood started to boil. The longer I listened to this bigoted bastard, the more infuriated I became. With all the training and time, I had spent fighting these people, I still had not come to terms with what they had done to my father. I was not sure I ever would. I needed to stop them, no matter what the cost.

Mohammad clicked off the laser, stuffing it into the side pocket as he prepared to depart.

"Mohammad, I would wish to have word with you." Approaching, the young anxious male stared at Mohammad. "I have been a loyal soldier for Allah; I wish to be included in your efforts."

"Aaron, I am aware that you have served me well. But I have you in mind for another task, one that will reward you handsomely. Do you have your nail vest and explosives ready as I requested?"

Annoyed, Mohammad looked into Aaron's eyes, taking a step closer.

"But—"

Stroking softly along the back of his hand, he drew Aaron closer. "If you can come by at eleven tonight, I will show you how appreciative I am. Ah... for your sacrifice... you will have an additional virgin waiting when Allah greets you. Allah will make sure he is of your liking."

Walking away, the youth mumbled back, "I will not be silenced. I will show you."

Mohammad had given us enough information; we too would be ready.

PART FORTY-SIX

ASSIGNMENTS—CSIS, OTTAWA

Director Sharpe stood in front of his mission board at CSIS headquarters. Below each of the team names photographs of Mohammad and the four suicide bombers were pinned to the corkboard. His task now was to review their assignments and alert the appropriate forces. The commander expected minimal collateral damage, unless Mohammad discovered the liquid was not explosive. There was a possibility for spectators nearby to get burned; regretfully no additional first responders or medical teams had been requested. The potential for an information leak was too great. The local police forces had been advised that their status would remain "medium alert, maintaining their "see it—report it" status." This would be upgraded as required.

"Director, we have a special alert for you. Aaron Master was present at the warehouse. Since his peace bond has been lifted, we have no grounds to arrest him. Do you wish us to pick him up? Maybe put a little pressure on him?"

"No. For now, we will need to follow him. I will send out a bulletin to airport security and local police forces. We need them to be ready. Keep tracking Master and report back what you see. If he was in the meeting with Mohammad, he will surely be up to something.

"Surveillance at his residence is to be stepped up immediately."

"Roger that, sir."

Meanwhile, at CSIS Command, the teams listened intently as the director described the details of the operation. The sliding walls between the six meeting-sized rooms had been retracted, leaving one huge command centre. Multiple TV monitors displayed real-time activity from each of the locations. Under the Alpha Team banner sat seven individual monitors. Although each was marked, I easily identified their locations by the camera angles.

Waiting for the presentation to start, I watched as a commuter exited a UP Express car, heading toward the overpass. The next camera clearly showed him walking down the stairs toward the large clock in the middle of the main hall. The remaining four monitors covered the lower eastbound platforms and outside views at each end of the food court.

Below the monitors, communication receivers, radios, earbuds, and computer equipment lay scattered neatly across the tables. In the centre of the huge room was an elevated platform: a circular stage surrounded by a white wooden railing. The commander stood erect, sliding his hand lightly along the railing as he circled the room. It was easy to see that he was no stranger to this type of pressure; he was poised and confident within this operational environment.

Inside the lead-lined walls of this mini-amphitheatre, his voice carried clearly to all. The acoustics sounded excellent. It was evident no expense had been spared—state-of-the-art equipment only.

Pointing toward the surrounding wall, Director Sharpe adjusted his audio mouthpiece before commencing his presentation.

"Good morning, ladies and gentlemen. Please take a seat at your team stations. Before we get started, I would like to welcome our newest arrivals.

"Most of you already know each other and have been intimately involved with the operation. For those new on the scene, I have brought in three additional teams. Their call names: Bravo, Charlie, and Tango. They will work in conjunction with Alpha Team, providing operational field support. The new teams are already up to speed. They have spent the last week studying their locations, local traffic, and pedestrian movement.

"Six operational teams will be used, Alpha Team will cover Union Station, Bravo Team at Gate 5 on the east side of the Air Canada Centre, Charlie Team to cover Gate 9, and Tango Team to be stationed around at Gate 15.

"The RCMP will provide continuous surveillance of all the residences as well as Mohammad's storage facility."

Pausing momentarily, the pocket laser moved upward. "As well, the GTAA security team will be monitoring their facilities around the airport.

"Here at Central Command, I will oversee the complete OP.

"We have established video links at Union Station, all the UP Express stops, Pearson International, and all twenty gates at the Air Canada Centre.

"Our intel confirms Mohammad Hassan and his Toronto cell plan to attack and destroy both Union Station and the Air Canada Centre at nineteen-hundred hours, November 11. At each of your workstations, there is a translated copy of his recent warehouse meeting. Please study it; it will be his Bible. We do not expect that he will allow any of his people to deviate from the plan.

"We intend to let the bombers ignite themselves. Unless the public is directly threatened, we will not intervene.

"We believe the bombers will not wait to hear any other explosion. They will all trigger their packages at precisely nineteen-hundred hours. According to the voice recordings from the warehouse, Mohammad will remain remote from the blast areas. It is also our belief he has no intention of being near any of the bombers or risking his own life.

"The RCMP teams will continue to run separate around-the-clock surveillance teams on Mohammad. Man, woman, or child—it is our full intent to arrest and imprison anyone remotely associated with this cell. In front of you are the photos of the suspected bombers.

"Any suspicious activity is to be immediately reported to Command. We will direct immediate responses, or actions, as required.

"OK, let's break for lunch. We will resume at thirteen-hundred hours."

Lunch, as usual, seemed to be the fastest hour of the day. There was barely enough time for introductions of the newest members before everyone shuffled back into their chairs.

Adjusting his mouthpiece, Director Sharpe commenced pointing to the screens above his head. "Please observe the monitors. This is the live feed at Mohammad's residence."

From across the street, remote cameras showed Mohammad sitting in his small, dingy kitchen. During the last four days, he had been recorded staring at and fondling the box of detonators. He was fixated on the box. The voice recorder clicked on as Mohammad lifted the phone. The number on the display indicated one of the many 905 extensions that he had been regularly calling.

Across the monitor at the Command Centre scrolled the name, "Aaron Q. Master."

"Mohammad, am I to come now?"

"Yes, yes Aaron. Please do."

Moments later, the small Honda Civic pulled up to the three-storey building. Shadows from behind the opaque curtains disappeared as the overhead lights blinked off. Fast-forwarding on the tape to zero-seven-hundred hours, the camera showed Aaron sliding into the driver's seat. As the darkest hour of dawn gradually resigned to the rising sun, his Honda rounded the corner, out of sight.

"Mohammad is ready. Tomorrow, we will be ready as well. You all have your assignments. Dismissed." Before going blank, the date on the bottom of the monitor blinked November 10.

The translator program quickly converted Arabic into English. Mohammad stated, "The time has come. We will meet at the warehouse at noon tomorrow."

Three more times Mohammad dialled out, leaving the same message.

Director Sharpe picked up his receiver; the light for line five blinked on his phone. This could mean only one thing: the RCMP had new information.

"Commander, from our surveillance, the meeting has been set for twelve-hundred hours tomorrow at the warehouse. They are ready to proceed.

"Yes, confirmed, we have observed the transmission," reported Director Sharpe.

Continuing, the chief stated, "Mohammad made only four calls last night; he has five vials of DD90. Now that Aaron Master is involved, could something else be in the works?"

"Yes, Inspector, you may be right. Watch to see if Master goes to the rendezvous at the warehouse. If he is involved, a raid is to be conducted at his home. We must stave off any other plans for which we have no intel."

The director hesitated, analyzing this latest intel. "We must maintain our focus, but yes, all suspicions must be investigated. Tomorrow, you are to engage the local police. As quickly and quietly as possible, conduct a raid at his residence and apprehend him. If he goes out early in the day, follow him. Do not take him down until late in the afternoon. Just in case he is expected to show up at the meeting. Try to do it quietly. We cannot afford for the media to get the raid onto the evening news. We need to apprehend Master after Mohammad makes his move downtown.

"If at all possible, wait until seventeen-thirty hours. By that time, there will be little chance that the media will screw things up. Have SWAT report back to me once Master is in custody."

Immediate alerts went out to all teams. By twelve-hundred hours on November 11, they were to be on location awaiting further direction. Readied, everyone knew it was going to be a long day.

Director Sharpe sat watching the monitors as Mohammad's entourage arrived at the warehouse. By eleven-hundred hours, all the known suspects had arrived. Seated at the long table, they watched, waiting for their packages. The dingy meeting room was a beehive of activity as people packed the suitcases with the handout flyers. Eventually, Mohammad stepped forward with the vials. Carefully inserting one packet into the side pouch of each suitcase, he could be heard calling each of the bombers up to the front of the room. To each, he gave words of encouragement and a blessing from Allah.

Inserting the detonator and power pack into their overcoat pockets, Mohammad placed his right hand onto each of their heads, chanting, "May the mercy, peace, and blessing of Allah be upon you. May he guide you forward with steady hands."

PART FORTY-SEVEN

SHOW TIME—DOWNTOWN TORONTO

Intently, Director Sharpe watched the monitor. The tiny surveillance camera had been positioned perfectly. The ground-level door to the warehouse opened, exposing a shiny new van—this van had not been seen before.

The director shouted, "Get me information on that vehicle!"

As the vehicle emerged, the camera zoomed in. Stuck to the right bumper, a small piece of masking tape fluttered. Covered in paint, it revealed the truth.

"Look, there, on the bumper—they have painted the van." Now light green, it had almost fooled them. "Check the plates."

Panning back to the right, the blue and white lettering of the Ontario plate showed 431 Xray-Bravo-Kilo, confirming it was Mohammad's van. In the front driver's seat sat a female, though her face was not visible; Saabira Hassan was the suspected driver.

Everyone listened intently as the commander's voice broke the silence in their earbuds. "The packages are leaving the warehouse. Everyone, stay alert."

"Advise all agents, we are now following a light green van, plates 431 Xray-Bravo-Kilo,."

By seventeen-hundred hours, the van had travelled downtown and parked under the Gardiner Expressway. None of the occupants showed any signs of leaving. The parking lot was not yet full, but soon patrons would be arriving, and the streets would be crowded. Anticipation built as agents watched intently. No one had exited the van, but soon the bombers would need to leave to be ready for the stadium opening. Slowly, the rear door of the cargo van opened. To everyone's amazement, Mohammad stepped out.

"Director here. Alpha Team take note, Mohammad Hassan is on location. I repeat, Hassan is on location."

Today Mohammad intended to blend in. Clean-shaven, wearing a Toronto Maple Leaf jersey, he looked like any other sports fan. Concealed behind the darkened glass of their van, agents relayed descriptions of each bomber. Except for their black bushy beards, they looked just like everyone else. One by one, all five suitcases passed from the rear of the van to the asphalt below. The cases looked harmless.

Captivated by the conversation flowing from my earpiece, I could not believe what I was hearing. Mohammad Hassan was going to be involved in the action tonight. For a moment, it seemed Mohammad was not as cowardly as I had envisioned. I had always viewed him as a despicable creature, one who used others to do his dirty work—plain and simple, a coward. Maybe Mohammad just needed that extra rush of being in the middle of the carnage. Maybe he needed to see it firsthand. Either way, I could see—almost taste—that moment when I would throw him to the ground, feeling the cold of the metal handcuffs as I squeezed them painfully around his skinny wrists.

All the locked-up emotions started to flow back: the hurt, the tears of youth swirling around inside wanting to come out. My years of sacrifice seemed worth it now. The man who represented everything evil was right there—right within my reach. The airborne words seemed distant as the pictures in my mind became reality. Tonight, Mohammad would taste the pain, the anguish that he so often cast on others. Allah would not reward Mohammad tonight.

The words "they're on the move" jolted me back to reality.

Cameras zoomed in and out as the bombers strolled below the overpasses, continually panning back and forth, following their every move. As they disappeared from one camera, they were picked up by the next. With conviction each man headed toward his appointed location.

"Cook here. Alpha Team, meet me street-side on Bay, below the overpass at Union Station.

"Move people, they are just about in position. All other agents, stay alert."

Glancing down at my watch, I could see there was less than an hour to showtime and five minutes to get to our meeting spot. Hopping off the last step to the asphalt of the street below, I could see my team already waiting. Another update echoed through my earpiece.

"All bombers heading toward Bay Street."

Standing nose to nose, huddled in the corner, I delivered my final instructions. "Sergeant, I want you to take Miller, James, and Jones down to the end of Bay Street below the overpass. Wait there for Mohammad's group to arrive.

"Once you are there, each of you identify a target; then tail them to their assigned locations. Remember, we have other agents present at each entrance. Keep smart; let's not give the surveillance away. Go!

"Sergeant Cowalski, you will stay here with me at Union Station. Hustle."

Disappearing between the throngs of moving bodies, the four team members cautiously moved south. Glancing at Sergeant Cowalski, I could not help but wonder, was my choice purely a Command decision, or was it an attempt to keep her safe? Either way, she was with me.

Leaning against the temporary construction barricade, Sergeant Cowalski signalled. Mohammad was dragging his two small suitcases northward toward Front Street. Acknowledging the signal, I dropped back, sliding in behind Mohammad as he passed. Within arm's reach, I could easily have taken him down. However, our orders still stood. Allow the bombers to detonate the explosive packages—maximum legal penalties demanded capturing these extremists executing the act.

I could never remember being so excited. Jumping out of a plane at five thousand feet or dodging bullets in Afghanistan, my heart had never raced like this... "*Stay calm, Spencer, slow down.*"

Pacing myself just fast enough to keep up with the flow, I trailed Mohammad as he wound his way through the maze of people lined up to gain entrance, slowly we headed toward Union Station. I struggled to find sense, trying to find the logic—why would Mohammad have two bombs? Surely, he could not detonate both at the same time. This made no sense; Mohammad would not take his own life. This demon had something else up his sleeve!

Gradually, I fell into step just a few feet behind him. The incendiary has a ten-foot danger radius. First, he would have to stop and unzip the bag. That would give me plenty of time to tackle him and foil any attempt to reach for the detonator. Far enough back to avoid detection, I stared at the back of Mohamad's head. *If only I could read his mind; if only I knew what Mohammad would do...* Countless ifs, none of which I could ever expect to answer.

Across the street, Sergeant Cowalski kept pace as the duo approached Front Street. In the distance were cries of the street vendors and ticket scalpers; everyone rushing to find their gate, eager to see the evening show.

"Hey, boys, would you like to make a quick fifty bucks… each?"

Two young males approached Mohammad as he held out a handful of money. The eyes of the boys opened wide as they viewed the cache of bills. Sergeant Cowalski could see they were barely in their teens. The temptation of making that much money was exciting, clearly showing on their faces.

The older of the two, eager to grasp the opportunity, asked, "What do we have to do?"

"Well, all you have to do is hand out these flyers. When they are all gone, I pay you."

The boys nodded at each other. "We can do that."

"Well, all right then! One of you should stand over here by the doorway to the station. I will take your friend across the street. Once you have given away the flyers on the top, you may open this side pouch where you will find a ten-dollar bill. You may keep the ten-dollar bill, but you must leave the pouch open so I will know that you have completed giving away the first of the flyers. You can then open the top zipper and start handing out the flyers inside."

Pulling out a couple of flyers, Mohammad demonstrated how to pass them to the oncoming pedestrians.

"You need to be polite. If they do not want one, just pass it to someone else. Any questions?"

"Yes, sir. Where will you be, and when will you be back to pay us?"

"I must go and get two other boys set up. As soon as I am finished, I will be back to see you. I should be about thirty minutes; just enough time for you boys to hand out your flyers."

EIGHTEEN-THIRTY HOURS

Across the street, Inspector Thornton studied the small stone house. Toronto SWAT lay concealed. Through the partially open screen door, a rifle lay perched, pointed toward the rear door of Master's home. Local police forces had just finished blocking off street traffic and now hustled to remove the balance of residents from the adjacent homes. So far, all was continuing as planned.

Tailed from Mohammad's apartment to his residence, Aaron Master had yet to show any signs of leaving. West of the home, the sun dropped slowly below the trees, casting shadows across the short, paved driveway. Down the long dead-end street, the neighbourhood stood silent. No kids, no cars, not even a dog barking.

"Director, Inspector Thornton here."

"Go ahead, Inspector."

"We are in position and ready. Aaron Master called earlier for a cab; we are now ready to send it in. We will apprehend him as he leaves the house." Behind the tall wooden fence, officers waited for Master's to exit.

Two hours had passed since the police intercepted Aaron Master's call to the cab company. Around the corner, the cabbie stood next to the unmarked SWAT vehicle. Replaced by an officer, the cabby watched as his vehicle pulled away. Moments later, the yellow cab drove into the driveway. With the beep of the horn, curtains parted. Aaron glanced at the waiting vehicle. Seconds later he appeared, moving rapidly toward the waiting cab. Aaron apparently had been waiting fully dressed for a considerable amount of time; beads of sweat ran down his temples, and his forehead glistened .

Across the street, Inspector Thornton watched. Ready to rush the small two-storey building, the SWAT teams lay in wait. Given Master's latest tweets,

Inspector Thornton was surprised when Master stepped out wearing the three-quarter-length leather coat—peculiar, given the weather. A warm fall day with temperatures still in the mid-twenties. Too warm to be dressed like that.

Master walked briskly toward the waiting cab. The driver slowly opened the rear door. Master turned, bending his head down and dropping into the stained rear seat.

"Aaron Master, this is the Metropolitan Toronto Police, stay where you are."

By this time, the officer had dropped to the ground. Expecting the worst, he concealed himself, hoping the metal of the vehicle would protect him. Without delay, Master's closed the door.

"Aaron, we do not want this to escalate. Raise your hands."

Lying prone across the adjacent lawn, a lone SWAT officer pointed his Remington 700P at Master, the crosshairs steady, fixed on his forehead.

"Inspector, target acquired. Supply target status. Repeat, what is our status?"

Aaron Master sat motionless in the rear seat of the yellow cab. In his right hand, a black object—above it, his thumb pressed tightly on a tiny red button.

"Green light. You have a green light. Neutralize."

In unison, the rifle shell shattered the window as the vest bomb spread metal and glass throughout the taxi. Shattered glass and torn upholstery lay strewn all around. What remained of Aaron Q. Master slumped sideways onto the already bloody seat. The stench of burning flesh drifted down the street as officers rushed the scene—converging from all directions. There would be no need for their drawn weapons. Master lay in pieces, no longer a threat.

In unison, windows on all sides of the house shattered as tear-gas canisters tore through glass, exploding and filling the tiny building with eye-burning smoke. Crashing down the front door, armoured SWAT stood waiting for the robot to relay photos from inside.

"Commander, Inspector Thornton here.

"Aaron Master is neutralized. We are sweeping his premises now.

"No civilian casualties or injuries; minimal property damage to the adjacent houses.

"A final sweep of the house will start shortly; we should be wrapped up here in roughly two hours."

"Roger that, Inspector. Excellent work. I expect your report on my desk at zero-nine-hundred tomorrow."

In a rare display of emotion, Director Sharpe banged his fists onto the table, exclaiming, "Yes, it is about time that thudfuck bit a bullet."

From my post at Union Station, I watched. What was unfolding was beyond belief. Mohammad would do anything, even use innocent kids, to fulfill his bidding.

"Cowalski. I need you and Dunsmoore to stay with the boys. I will follow Mohammad.

"Roger that, sir."

"Nineteen-fifty hours, evac the area. And Cowalski, no civilian casualties—understand?"

"Yes, Sir. Roger that, Sir."

Mohammad turned, waiting for an opening in traffic, then ran back across the street. From the doorway, he could see each of the boys handing out flyers. He smiled; his plan was unfolding.

"Dunsmoore, come in." I knew we were close to running out of time.

"Dunsmoore here," resonated in the earpiece.

"Need you to Front Street ASAP."

"Roger that. ETA, thirty seconds."

"Good. Meet me street-side."

I had not yet figured out from where Mohammad planned to detonate the vials. If he was not nearby at street level, then where was he going? I tried to surmise his next move as I followed him through the doors opening onto the lobby.

"Command, I have Mohammad inside Union Station. Unclear of his next destination. Need assistance."

Director Sharpe leaned in toward the monitor. "Lieutenant, I have him on camera three, just passing the piano, now turning left into the small service corridor."

The building's blueprints lay open on the table. Director Sharpe stood leaning inward over the drawings; with his hands cupped on the edges of the table. Instantly it became apparent.

"Lieutenant, the only doors in that area are for the washrooms or a stair-well that leads to the roof."

"Director, that's it! He plans to detonate from the roof."

As the camera zoomed in on the small hallway, Mohammad reached into his jacket pocket and pulled out a small piece of paper. With all the security in this building, I was astounded Mohammad had the roof access code.

"Director, he must have insider help—only maintenance and security people have those codes."

"Roger that, Lieutenant. I will get the names. I will take care of them"

"Commander, give Mohammad a small lead, then override both the hallway and the roof door locks. Security has stairwell and roof cameras at all levels; I should be able to follow him. Allow him enough time to get onto the roof. Leave the door locks disengaged. I will be close behind him."

Mohammad feverishly punched the four digits into the keypad as though keying those numbers was a daily activity—numbers etched into memory. As soon as the lock clicked, he opened the heavy steel door, silently he slipped into the narrow stairwell.

Thirty seconds passed before I approached the door. "Cowalski, evac the area!" I commanded.

Director Sharpe watched the monitor, waiting for the roof door alarm to sound. Mohammad had stepped through the door onto the roof. All cameras showed the stairwell clear. The commander disengaged the main-level door lock.

"All clear. Captain, you have entry into the stairwell; the roof lock is also open. The roof camera shows Mohammad nearing the outer parapet."

Mohammad looked around. The noises of the street below increased in volume as he approached the wall. Across the street, the glass office windows looked black, empty. Everyone had gone home. He could work freely. No prying eyes. All his people would now be in place, Mohammad glanced down at his watch. He had only ten minutes before Allah would praise his name. Smiling, he reached into his coat pocket. Extracting the two laser power packs, he placed them on the parapet. Testing the first laser, he pointed it toward the adjacent stone wall.

Staring down at the street below, the lights cast their illumination onto his targets. The small suitcases stood out clearly against the dirty grey of the sidewalk. *Where!? Where are my people? Where are those snivelling brats? Where? Where is everyone? No traffic! No people! Why? Why?*

Off in the distance, sirens wailed.

"Director Sharpe to all agents. Situation at Pearson, Terminal 1, Departures Level—suicide bomber threat. Situation neutralized. Repeat, situation neutralized.

"GTAA security has neutralized the assailant.

"We have only three minutes to the planned detonation. Regardless of what you hear, remain focused—no distractions. I repeat, remain focused."

Grasping the knob, slowly I turned pushing open the roof door. I could see clear across the roof to Mohammad; exposed, frantically staring over the narrow wall. Only thirty feet of open roof stood between me and the man I reviled. More than anything, I wanted to see Mohammad blow himself up—his morbid soul laid at hell's gates.

Staring across the short distance, I awaited my opportunity—once Mohammad rose, I would charge out, tackle him. Like a sprinter at the starting line, I braced my foot against the door frame. Rising and out in one steady motion, I sprang forward, landing firmly onto the roof. Seconds later I closed the gap.

I heard the bang of the door as I readied myself to tackle. Startled, Mohammad turned as he felt himself being driven against the roof parapet. All my anger, resentment, frustration pouring out… With blow after blow, I was drawn further back in time, the flashbacks of that fateful day in South Africa fuelling my fury—my father's, my family's life forever changed.

Mohammad lay bewildered, rolling around trying to gain control, fear suddenly overtook him. He would not bring pleasure to Allah! He suddenly realized what was happening—his plan, failed!

He was not accepting... his mind roiled. "Where are my people? Why no explosions? Why? How could this be? The plan, it... it is perfect! My plan is perfect!"

My anger, my rage, continued pouring out—I kept striking. Blow after blow landing squarely on the face of the near motionless form. Mohammad's ability to protect himself faltered with each volley of punches. My hatred ignited me—each blow, the crunch of knuckles against bone. Nothing else mattered now. Not the other people, not even the other bombers.

Mohammad had been beaten many times before, many times worse than this. Looking squarely into my eyes he yelled, "Is that all you have? Hah... you hit like a girl. Just like those pussy Canadian soldiers you sent to Johannesburg! Hah! You pussy."

My eyes widened, rage surging again.

It had been him, Mohammad Hassan. All these years, no one had taken credit for that blast, the blast that forever changed my family's lives... All these years, there had been no face, no name to chase. I drew back my bloodied right fist, ready to strike what I thought would be my final blow, one more time—suddenly, violent, sharp burning pains ripped at my ribs. I grasped my side, falling to the roof. Hassan had struck.

Springing to his feet, Mohammad ran to the roof's edge, redirecting the laser down toward the street. Locating the first bag, he aimed the laser toward the small pocket of the suitcase, then pressed the button. Pushing, pushing—no explosion, only the flash as a ball of flames rose ten feet high. Why? Why was there no explosion? With his fervid angst growing, he swung around to locate the second youth. Again, he anxiously pushed on the button. Nothing! Again, only flames!

His hysteria and fury mounting, Mohammad turned back in my direction, screaming, "My plan must not fail! It must not fail! What have you done? You shall die at my pleasure!"

Raising the laser to eye level, he pointed the tip between my eyes. "Pray to your God now. We will see if he helps. Hah... he will not pity your worthless soul."

The last words my mother had said to me at basic training were rushing through my whole being: "You come back alive."

"This moment may well be the end." Flashing through my consciousness, the bitter awareness that I had failed to avenge my father exuded more pain than I could bear.

Closing my eyes, I prayed, aloud, from my soul… "The Lord is my shepherd, I shall not want."

"Louder, shout it louder! I shall prove to you that your God is useless. He does not listen!"

Suddenly, the roof door sprang open. Alerted by the noise, Mohammad turned to see Sergeant Cowalski rushing onto the roof. "You again. I knew I recognized you. No escaping now! Your end has come!"

Redirecting the laser toward her, Mohammad fumbled to find the button. Laying crouched against the cold brick of the roof wall, I screamed. "Mohammad!"

Distracted, Mohammad turned back toward the wall only to see a bright flash of light followed by a loud bang. The pain of lead hitting bone, the bullet rushed through Mohammad's shoulder, pushing him off balance, spinning him around.

Looking into the black emptiness of his eyes, I yelled my promise. "You will hurt no one else!"

I pulled the trigger, in unison from across the roof, two more loud bangs rang out. Mohammad Hassan fell, limp, lifeless. From beneath his coat, pools of red trickled.

Gasping as pain shot through me, I collapsed face-first. Struggling with consciousness, I saw Cowalski standing, pointing her pistol at the lifeless form of Hassan. Lowering the gun, Sally sprinted to my side.

The burning gash in my side throbbing, I yelled; "Sally, Quick, grab the lasers."

Securing the lasers, she swiftly turned her attention to my injuries. Shakily, I reached out my hand, attempting to caress her face as she dropped to one knee. Without a moment's delay she ripped open my jacket, exposing the wound. The night air stung as it drifted across my seared flesh.

Smiling, Sally exclaimed, "Well, look at this. Awww… you big baby, get up, you are not even bleeding." Briefly I smiled, understanding her attempt at humour.

It hurt to laugh, but it was either that or cry. Like a drug addict, I came crashing down—a lifetime of emotions erupting!

Cauterized by the heat of the laser, not a drop of blood dripped from the wound. The rooftop stank as the pungent smell of burned flesh and gun powder permeated the air. I grimaced as Sally held my shirt aside. The wound was clean, a straight line across my ribs. Seared brown from the heat, the opening extended a full half-inch deep, exposing the white of my ribs. Sergeant Black's basic training words echoed in my head: *"Pain is your friend—as long as you hurt, you know you are still alive."*

My hurt and tortured prayers began ebbing, toward joyous thoughts. "Maybe. Just maybe, I will live to see another day!"

"Captain, it seems my prayers were answered."

"How's that, Doc?"

"Well, Spencer, darling, looks like you will have a nice big scar to show our kids!"

With a humbled smile, I said, "Guess I owe you one, huh, Sarge?"

"You bet your ass you do. When this is all over, my intention is to collect in full."

The streets around Union Station erupted in sirens and flashing lights.

"Come in, Director. Sergeant Cowalski here."

"Go ahead, Sergeant."

"Sir, Captain Cook is down. Medics, gurney post-haste Union Station roof!"

"Roger that. Paramedics engaged. ETA rooftop, momentarily."

"Director, sir, confirmed kill by Captain Cook—Mohammad Hassan is down."

Pregnant silence filled the airwaves. "Sergeant, keep the lieutenant stable. Air EVAC is on route, ETA five minutes."

The following weeks became a flurry of activity as global media outlets scrambled to get the latest scoop on the story. Each passing day saw more people arrested. Collective global security forces were relieved. Operation Serpent, a skillful success—the threat was terminated.

Weeks of recovery and rehab found me lounging in Dad's favourite La-Z-Boy. Resting in his chair felt foreign. Only weeks before, I would not have even thought of sitting in it—watching Dad sit here was the norm. As if by some mysterious plan, he passed away only days after I gave him the news that Mohammad Hassan had been killed. Unfolding the old newspaper, I glanced again at the photo of Dad standing tall in his dress uniform.

The obituary read:

"Mr. William Spencer Cook, husband of Mary Cook, father to Spencer, and Randy Cook, passed away peacefully in his sleep on December 1st, 2011.

"A decorated military officer, William Cook served his country faithfully and fully for thirty years.

"He will be sorely missed by all."

Rumours echoed around Command—the director was retiring, and I was the expected successor.

Gazing out the window of our small family kitchen, I pondered, *What's in store for me now?* Sensing the tides about to change, I had something I needed to do... something I had put off doing for a long time...

Slowly, I started typing on the keys.

"Dearest Sally, would you join my mother and me for dinner at eighteen-hundred hours on Friday?

"P.S.: Dinner attire, black tie."

Clicking SEND, I waited...

Disclaimer

The story, and all names, characters, and incidents are fictitious. No identification with actual persons, places, buildings, or products is intended or should be inferred.

CPSIA information can be obtained
at www.ICGtesting.com
Printed in the USA
BVHW051934300622
641057BV00001B/3